"It's common knowledge that Adele and Mr. Langdon are lovers," Thelma said, and Brooke, who had been about to rise, abruptly sat again. It wasn't something she'd known.

"Hush, Thelma, not so loud! No one knows that for certain."

"I've suspected it, and so have you. They've often been seen together, you know."

"That doesn't have to mean anything," Celia scolded.

"Of course, who could blame her?" Thelma went on, as if Celia hadn't spoken. "Julius had his good points, I'm sure, but he was rather unrefined."

"I liked him."

"You like everyone, Celia. No, I'm not surprised Adele looked elsewhere. I'm only surprised it took her so long to do so. And I'd be very surprised if she's grieving."

That was too much for Brooke. If this was what married society ladies talked about, she almost wished she were still single. Rising, she tore her unfinished letter in two and strode across the room, thinking about the conversation she'd overheard.

She knew that many marriages were failures, and that wives, as well as husbands, often looked elsewhere for companionship. But to have an *affaire* with your husband's business partner was somehow more sordid; to travel with him on the same ship as your husband was worse. And yet, if it were true . . . Brooke shivered. If it were true, then Adele would have a reason for not wanting her husband around. For wanting to kill him. What appeared to be an accident might just be something more sinister . . .

Books by Mary Kruger

DEATH ON THE CLIFFWALK
NO HONEYMOON FOR DEATH
MASTERPIECE OF MURDER

Published by Zebra Books

MARY KRUGER

No Honeymoon for Death

A Gilded Age
Mystery

KENSINGTON BOOKS
KENSINGTON PUBLISHING CORP.

KENSINGTON BOOKS are published by

Kensington Publishing Corp.
850 Third Avenue
New York, NY 10022

First Kensington Hardcover Printing: December, 1995
First Kensington Paperback Printing: December, 1996

Printed in the United States of America
10 9 8 7 6 5 4 3 2 1

To my sister, Patricia Harrington, who was the first to see any writing potential in me and has always been a great source of encouragement.

Prologue

This damned voyage to Europe was going to ruin everything. Everything. It had taken a lot of work, and a lot of thought, to make plans, to work everything out to the last detail. How did one get rid of another person without becoming a suspect? There were so many problems involved, from the actual deed, to disposing of the body. And then there was the acting. It would be necessary to put up a certain front before others; not just the police, but friends and acquaintances. The police should never be underestimated, either. Corrupt they were, certainly, ignoring all sorts of crimes, as the recent Lexow commission investigations had shown, but smart, too. It meant being careful in every reaction, appearing bewildered, perhaps even a little guilty, as innocent people so often did, but not grief-stricken. Never that. Too much was known about the real state of affairs for that to be plausible.

And so the plans had proceeded, until this damnable voyage had been proposed. No way to get out of it, either, without looking suspicious, not when one had mentioned so often the desire to go to Europe. The plans would have to be postponed—but wait. There was one unanticipated piece of luck, and a circumstance that would actually make things easier. It should be possible to think of a way around the problems this voyage posed for its one major advantage. How much simpler it would be to dispose of a body at sea.

It would happen aboard the ship, then. The person who had plotted so long, so carefully, sat back, smiling. Yes. The enemy would meet his fate aboard the ship.

1

New York, April 15, 1896

Matt and Brooke Devlin had the first major quarrel of their married life as they were about to embark on their honeymoon.

It began, of all things, over Matt's clothes. Not that he looked shabby. In the months since his marriage he'd acquired a wardrobe that startled him, including a suit from Brooks Brothers and an honest-to-God dinner jacket. He was most proud, however, of the dress blue uniform of a detective sergeant in the New York police department that hung in his closet. Not bad for an Irish boy from Newport's fifth ward. However, when that Irish lad married a girl from the highest reaches of society, his life was bound to change, and that was part of the problem. Sometimes he didn't feel like himself. Sometimes the privileges of his new life made him uneasy.

Take this honeymoon, for example. Looking out the

window of the hansom cab as it drove along Fifth Avenue to the North River pier where they would board the Atlantic liner *New York*, Matt frowned. On the face of it, it seemed a reasonable idea: to take time for him and Brooke to be alone, just the two of them, and what more romantic setting than a ship at sea? However, when they were traveling not just first class but in a suite deluxe, and when the honeymoon was expected to last some three months, it was too much. He had been on the police force only a short time, and now he was taking an extended holiday. If that caused raised eyebrows at headquarters, it was nothing compared to his inner turmoil. He loved his work. He also loved his wife, and marrying her had meant making changes to his life. This change, however, made him feel guilty and uneasy.

And so, when Brooke had made the perfectly innocent remark that, since she intended to visit the Paris couturiers, Matt should look in at a Savile Row tailor, he'd exploded. He was a cop, by God, and an honest one, and that was something hard-come-by in these days, when everyone was routinely on the take. How did she think it looked for him to be away from the job for so long, and he only on the force for seven months? If he wasn't good enough for her, he concluded bitterly, maybe she shouldn't have married him.

Brooke's stunned silence at this unexpected attack lasted only a moment, and before long they had a proper row going. Now they were settled in opposite corners of the hansom cab, looking out the windows at the congestion caused by traffic at the intersection with Broadway, and fuming. It was a fine, warm day, if not so humid as the day before, and the signs of spring in New York were everywhere: nursery maids in the parks pushing prams; gaily striped awnings on shops; burgeoning flowers in window boxes. Neither noticed. The three months loomed before them like a prison sentence.

Matt recovered first, as always. His temper was quick to flare up, and just as quick to die down. "I'm sorry," he said into the strained silence, turning to look at her. "What I said—it was out of line."

Brooke stared fixedly out the window. He had learned, to his cost, that she could hold onto her anger as long as she wished. "I was a cop's daughter," she said, finally, without turning.

"I know." Of course he knew. Her father and his had been partners together on the Newport police force, and he and Brooke had grown up together.

"Have I ever put on airs with you, Matt? Have I?"

Matt relaxed as the hansom cab moved at last. Good, so they wouldn't be late. Traffic was bad this morning, the streets crowded with cabs and carts and wagons, and if they got held up any longer they'd miss the ship. "You don't mean to."

That made her turn. "What?" She leaned forward, her chin jutting out, and if she'd been standing her hands would have been on her hips. "When have I ever acted like that, Matt? When?"

"Well . . ." He let the silence spin out, interrupted only by the clamor of iron-covered wheels on pavement, clopping hooves, and the clanging of the Broadway cable cars. "Sometimes you do sound like your aunt."

It took a moment, but then the corners of her mouth twitched, as he'd hoped they would. Then she was smiling, if a trifle ruefully, for they both agreed that her Aunt

Winifred, while meaning well, tended to be too concerned with society and position. And, while Brooke and Matt were honeymooning, Winifred would be decorating their new apartment at the Dakota. The thought made Matt shudder. "Heaven forbid. If I become like her, Matt, I expect you to tell me."

"Oh, I will." He smiled back at her, and then the smile faded. "It's just a hard time to be leaving. Here I am, new on the force. Came in as a detective and not a patrolman, and that's enough to make them resent me."

"For heaven's sake, Matt, you've been a policeman long enough, and you've certainly proven yourself."

"Doesn't matter." He stretched out his hand, and, after a moment, she took it. "Plus, I'm married to a rich woman—no, I'm not saying that to upset you," he said, as she opened her mouth to protest. "You know, and I know, that that doesn't matter to me. But others don't see it that way. Especially," his face darkened, "when I take a three-month honeymoon."

"Aunt Winifred meant well," she said apologetically, for the honeymoon was a wedding gift from her aunt and uncle.

"I know." The truth was, he knew Brooke wanted it, too. In the old days, before her parents' death, before she'd gone to live with her wealthy relatives, had she longed after such things? Or had she been as down to earth as he remembered? "I'm leaving behind a lot of work. There's that body that turned up yesterday. Looks like a robbery gone wrong, and God knows that's a lot of work. And the fraud case I was working on, he comes up for trial next week, and—"

"Matt." She put her finger to his lips. "Someone will handle it all."

"I know," he said, sounding not the least convinced.

"It's not as if you're going to be away forever. If you give it a chance, you might even like it."

His smile was wry. "That's what I'm afraid of."

"And you're not the only cop in New York."

"True." Hard to admit, though. Maybe he did need to get away for a time, away from random violence and enforcing nonsensical laws, away from the crime-ridden world that sometimes felt like it was the only reality. "Maybe I'll even like a life of leisure," he said, with self-mockery that held just a hint of truth in it. Maybe he would, and that was part of the problem.

The cab came to a stop again. Washington Square, with the new white arch, and more traffic. But then they were turning, driving down Christopher Street through the heart of Greenwich Village. "We're nearly here."

Brooke leaned over to look out his window. "Oh, good." She straightened her hat, some silly affair of straw and feathers that somehow looked good on her. "Thank heaven we sent the trunks ahead. And the maid." She made a face. Like everything else, the maid was Aunt Winifred's idea, to help Brooke dress. Essential, considering the clothes she'd brought—and why women needed so much he didn't know—but something Brooke nevertheless disliked. So did he. "We're here in good time. Sailing day is always so confusing."

Matt held out his hand, a peace offering, accepting at last this part of his life. "I'm glad we're doing this."

Her smile lit her eyes. "So am I," she said, just as the

hansom jolted onto rough cobblestones, sending them swaying, and then coming to an abrupt stop.

The door opened, and the driver stuck his head in. "This's as far as I can go. Crowded here, this morning."

Matt nodded. "Thank you," he said. Handing the driver the fare, he rose and stepped out. In the act of turning to help Brooke down, he stopped, staring. "Holy—!"

Brooke glanced up as she emerged from the cab. "What is it—oh, the ship."

"That's our ship?"

She cast him a glance as she stepped to the ground. "Yes, Matt."

"Holy—it's big."

"Well, what did you expect?" Brooke took his arm as they joined the throngs of people, all straining to reach the ship. Matt continued to stare. From this far back on the pier he couldn't see much; just the sharp clipper bow of the liner, and three tall black smokestacks banded in white, all in a line. The stern of the ship was lost in the distance, seemingly halfway across the Hudson to New Jersey. A huge ship, a floating city, and for a man from a small, insular town, who hadn't yet become accustomed to New York's crowding and chaos, it was both daunting and exciting.

Beside Matt, her arm tucked through his as they made their way across the pier, Brooke smiled. It wasn't often she saw him flustered, but certain things seemed to stun him: Aunt Winifred's extravagances, for example, and now this ship. Not that she blamed him. Brooke had made the Atlantic crossing twice before, but she found the prospect thrilling, too. Especially on a ship as large and luxurious as the *New York*.

The pier was chaotic. Around them milled people and carriages and conveyances; cabin class passengers, like them, in their finery, the men's top hats glistening in the sun, the women sweltering in their furs on this unseasonably warm spring morning. Hansom cabs moved nimbly through the crowd, disgorging their passengers, while heavy drays filled with produce trundled across the cobblestones towards the sharply slanted ramp where their goods would be loaded aboard. There were well-wishers and curiosity seekers and passengers, all raising a cacophony of sound that almost overwhelmed the rumble of the ship's engines and the sharp cries of the gulls wheeling overhead. Almost, but not quite. The chaos of sailing day meant one thing. She would be at sea again, and after being pent up in the city for what felt like ages, Brooke found the prospect exciting.

"Is it always like this?" Matt shouted over the babble as they pushed their way towards the gangplank, his hand holding hers tightly so that they wouldn't get separated in the crowd.

"Yes," Brooke called back, hastily reaching up to straighten her hat, which was in danger of coming loose as she was jostled by someone in the crowd. It was a new hat, too, of Leghorn straw with ostrich feathers dyed a pale peach to match her walking suit of peach and amber, and one of her favorites.

"Watch it there!" Matt glared at the man who had jostled her, though he was already several feet away. "Do you have everything?"

"What?"

"Your purse, watch, jewelry. Did he take anything?"

"What?" Brooke glanced down at her purse, held securely by her side. "No one took anything from me."

"Prime crowd for pickpockets," he muttered, drawing her arm through his, his narrowed eyes scanning the people around them.

"For heaven's sake, Matt. There are no pickpockets here."

"How do you know?"

"I just do. Come, there's the gangplank at last. Heavens, what a queue!"

"If we'd left when I wanted to, we wouldn't have to wait," Matt grumbled as they joined the end of a long, long line.

"It's just past nine, Matt, and the ship doesn't sail for another hour. Besides," she added with serene self-confidence, "it won't sail without us."

"Huh," Matt said, but he subsided, looking again at the ship. From here it rose above him, a solid expanse of black steel pierced at intervals by round portholes. The white-painted superstructure, like a long, low building dropped onto the deck, was surrounded by masts and funnels and davits for lifeboats, and surmounted by those three huge smokestacks. From them smoke already belched, as the ship's engines heated the steam that would propel them across the Atlantic. It looked solid and steady, and yet Matt didn't trust it one bit. He'd grown up near the ocean, and he'd heard of too many disasters at sea to be entirely at ease.

They inched their way up the gangplank, while Brooke conversed with the people around them, many of whom she knew. Matt's uneasiness grew, until at last they were at the top of the gangplank, aboard the ship. A blue-

uniformed man took their tickets; another pointed out
the general direction of their cabin. With that behind
them the pressure of the crowd lessened, and Matt relaxed
a little. Once he got settled, knew where he was, he might
even enjoy himself.

"Let's explore a little bit," he said, as Brooke turned towards a doorway leading inside. "I'd like to know where
everything is."

"We can't. At least, not now."

Matt followed her as she turned into the first of a bewil-
dering succession of passages. "Why not?"

"We have guests coming to our suite to see us off, have
you forgotten?" They moved up a staircase, and out onto
a teak-floored deck. To one side was a railing, and beyond
that a warehouse-lined wharf; to the other the deckhouse,
dotted here and there by doors and windows and bisected
by corridors. The deck itself was wide, and divided into
two sections by an awning deck of canvas supported by
steel beams near the railing, above which hung lifeboats
on davits. Nearer to the deckhouse, some passengers were
already sitting in steamer chairs, while the passageway
formed by the awning deck was bustling with people preparing for departure. "I don't want Aunt Winifred to get
there before we do."

"Can't have that."

"No, of course not, since she's paying for it."

Matt stopped. "I thought that was Henry." He understood Henry and Winifred Olmstead's reasons for paying
for this trip. He did. But it was a sad day when a man
wasn't even allowed to pay for his own honeymoon.

Brooke turned. "Oh, Matt. I didn't mean—"

"I know you didn't," he said, and though his voice was

still clipped he reached for her arm. "Never mind. Is our suite around here?"

"It should be." Brooke stopped at one of the corridors. Glancing down it, Matt could see doors opening off it and the other side of the deck. "In fact, it should be here," Brooke said, and, as if by magic, a white-jacketed steward appeared.

"Mr. and Mrs. Devlin? This way," he said, opening one of the doors.

"Thank you." Brooke sailed into the room; Matt, a bit more bemused, followed, stepping into a sitting room furnished with velvet-upholstered sofas and chairs. Beyond was the bedroom, equally luxurious with its big brass bed, and to the side was a private bathroom, with a convex wall to follow the curve of the smokestack. The windows overlooked the promenade deck. God only knew what this cost, he thought, turning from checking that the blinds fitted tightly, letting in neither light nor curious eyes, to see Brooke bouncing on the bed. " 'Alone at last,' she said dramatically," Brooke said, smiling up at him, and all his irritation, all his uneasiness, dissolved. This was their honeymoon. Nothing else mattered.

He held out his hand to her, and she rose, coming into his arms. She had just raised her face to his when there was a knock on the outside door, followed by the sound of it opening. "Brooke? Matthew? Are you here?"

"Oh, heavens." Brooke and Matt sprang apart, he straightening his tie, she smoothing her hair. "Yes, Aunt Winifred. We just got here ourselves."

"Really, Brooke, that was cutting it close, wasn't it?" Winifred Olmstead gazed about the suite with narrowed eyes. "This will do, I suppose," she said, thus dismissing the overstuffed sofa and armchairs, the porcelain fixtures in the lavatory, the thick pile carpets. "If one must travel, and I suppose one must to be civilized, then one should do so in comfort. The *St. Paul* is an ugly ship," she went on, running a gloved finger across the top of a mahogany dresser and frowning, even though the glove remained spotless, "and *Campania* rattles, there is no other word for it. Cunard always was more concerned with speed than with their passengers' comfort. No, I did well in choosing this ship for you. I dare say you'll enjoy yourselves."

Matt glanced at Brooke and then as quickly looked away, at the laughter he saw bubbling in her eyes. "It was very good of you, ma'am," he said, in a voice that was only a bit strangled, and held out his hand. "Henry. Good to see you."

"And you, too, my boy." Henry's hands went back in his trouser pockets after he'd shaken Matt's hand, as was his habit. It was easy to ignore Henry Olmstead in the presence of his forceful wife, but in the past months he and Matt had grown to like each other. Even if Matt had once arrested him for murder, falsely, as it turned out. "Sure you'll survive all of this?" he added, his voice lowered.

Matt shrugged. "God knows. And then Europe, afterwards." He paused. "It's a generous gift, Henry."

Henry waved that off. "Brooke means a lot to us." He looked up at Matt, his eyes unexpectedly keen. "We want her to be happy."

"I know that." Something in Matt's tone must have been reassuring, for Henry nodded, and the intent look left his eyes. Matt knew the truth, though. Henry was a more complex man than he appeared. "I think," he began, and at that moment there was another knock on the door. Nodding at Henry, he crossed the sitting room to open the door.

"Matt, my boy," boomed the man who stood there. He sauntered in, his shoulders thrown back and chest thrust out, as if he owned the world. "Came to see you off. Done well for yourself, my boy, that you have."

"Thank you." Matt shot another glance at Brooke and saw that she was suppressing laughter again. "I don't believe you've met my wife's relatives. Mr. and Mrs. Olmstead, Thomas Nevesey."

"Delighted to meet you," Nevesey boomed, holding out his hand. He was a small man, and yet his presence filled the room. His sandy mustache bristled with vitality, and his tan herringbone suit, while of impeccable cut, seemed on him to be almost garish. "Let me guess. Republicans, are you?"

"Tom," Matt muttered.

"Indeed." Winifred's voice was glacial. "I've heard of you, Mr. Nevesey."

"Don't doubt you have. Your niece married a good man, Mr. Olmstead. I hope you know that."

"I'm aware of that." Henry's eyes held the same twinkle as Brooke's. "You are Matt's, ah, ward boss, I believe it's called?"

"That I am." Nevesey stood with his legs braced, as if the ship were already at sea, his thumbs tucked into his vest pockets. "Helped Matt get his job, I did. Can always use a man like him on the force."

"Er, yes," Matt put in, fidgeting, hating the appearance of impropriety. Nevesey hadn't really gotten Matt his job, but he might just help him keep it. Last year the dauntless

Theodore Roosevelt had been named to the board of police commissioners; he had since waged a one-man campaign to clean up the corruption uncovered by the Lexow commission. Among other things, he had forced the resignation of patrolmen and detectives alike and brought in new people, Matt among them. Yet among all this reform, politics still lurked, and ward bosses still held power. A wise police officer kept on their good side. There was no need to advertise that, however. "Would you like to see the cabin, Tom?"

"That I would, my boy." Nevesey's voice lowered as he followed Matt into the bedroom. "Looks like you've landed yourself in clover."

"It won't affect how I do my job."

"Never thought it would, my boy, never thought that." Nevesey glanced quickly around the bedroom, and his voice lowered still more. "Though when you came to me to tell me you wanted to go on this honeymoon—you know you'll have some trouble when you get back?"

Matt nodded. He'd already faced resentment from his fellow officers over his good fortune. "I expect it."

"Good. Just so you know. Of course, with Mrs. Devlin and all, can't say I blame you."

"No, sir."

"Not many men have a rich wife. Enjoy it, my boy."

"Yes," Matt said, his voice stiff.

"Bothers you, does it?" Nevesey's gaze was sharp, belying his genial, jovial manner. "Well, don't let it, my boy. Not many get the chance. Now, before I go, there's someone I'd like you to meet."

Matt followed him out into the sitting room. Winifred drew back as they passed, ostentatiously pulling back her skirts from Nevesey, but Matt made himself ignore it. Soon enough all the guests would be gone, and he and Brooke would be alone. Maybe then it wouldn't matter that their backgrounds were so different. "Who?"

"Ambrose Smith, ship's detective. He's just outside, here. Helped him get this job, you know. He was a sergeant here in New York until all those commission hearings," Nevesey said, opening the door.

Which meant that he was less than honest, Matt thought, looking at Brooke, whose own look was curious. Nevesey was an irresistible force, however, and so, shrugging, Matt stepped out, closing the door behind him.

"A most distasteful man," Winifred declaimed into the sudden silence, ringing with the absence of Nevesey's voice. "I wonder you can tolerate him, Brooke."

Henry turned away from the window looking onto the promenade deck, where he'd stood since Nevesey's arrival. "Not a man to underestimate, I'd think," he said.

"No. Matt owes him rather a lot," Brooke said. "And I like him."

Winifred stared at her. "How can you, possibly?"

"Well, I do. Aunt, what do you think I should buy in Paris?" she asked, and the conversation immediately turned to the more pressing matters of Paris couturiers and style. Poor Matt, she thought, listening to her aunt with only half her attention. He was feeling much the same as she had when first she had come to live with her aunt and uncle, very much out of his element, with the added pressures of his job. She'd never ask him to give up his work; it meant too much to him. She only hoped that by the time they returned to New York he'd be more reconciled to the changes in his life.

The ship's horn blew two short blasts, drowning out all conversation and startling everyone. "That's the signal for going ashore, my love," Henry said, coming forward and taking Winifred's arm.

"Oh, dear." Winifred fumbled in her purse and brought out a lace-edged handkerchief, touching it to dry eyes. "I do hate goodbyes. Are you certain you'll be all right, Brooke?"

"On this ship? Of course. After all, I have Matt. And," she went on quickly to forestall whatever Winifred was about to say next, "Mr. Nevesey will not be sailing with us."

"I should hope not!" Indignation replaced Winifred's sadness. "A man like that on the *New York*—well! I know standards are sadly lowered these days, but we must fight against them when we can."

"Yes, aunt," Brooke murmured, shepherding them out onto the promenade deck. The pier was thronged with people to see the big ship start her voyage, and from a few feet away Matt strode towards her. "Mr. Nevesey is gone, Matt?"

"Yes." He leaned forward to kiss Winifred on the cheek, a salute she suffered in silence, and shook Henry's hand. And then Henry was leading Winifred away, though she continued to call back admonitions and advice, until they reached the stairs and were gone. An absurd lump rose in Brooke's throat, and she swallowed it. No need for sadness, not when she was on her honeymoon.

The ship gave another blast on its horn, and there were shouts from lower decks and the pier as the thick cables that held the *New York* to the land were let go. Matt joined

Brooke at the railing, both of them waving at the people below as the *New York* edged out of her berth. The buildings of Manhattan began to recede; ahead was open water and Europe. As if at a signal, Matt and Brooke glanced at each other, and grinned, silently agreeing in that moment to leave their conflicts back on land. Their honeymoon had begun.

At precisely seven that evening the gong rang for dinner. "This thing is choking me," Matt grumbled, tugging at the wing collar of his starched white shirt as he and Brooke turned in from the promenade deck to the mahogany stairs leading to the grand saloon for dinner. Sandy Hook Lightship, the official beginning of an Atlantic passage, had already been passed, and land was long behind them. The ship was alone, a majestic, lonely city, and the sea had taken over. The sway from side to side made footing on the stairs, now rising, now falling, uncertain at best.

"Don't," Brooke reached up a wifely hand to straighten his tie. "You look good in a dinner jacket, Matt."

"I feel like a monkey. Will I have to dress up every night?"

"Yes," she said firmly, biting back a smile. Of all the trials of his new life, she suspected Matt found his new wardrobe the worst. Certainly he complained about it enough, but in this company it wouldn't do for him to wear his old tweed suits that had come off the peg from Sherman's store in Newport. Snobbish, perhaps, but there it was. She was proud of Matt. She didn't want anyone disdaining him for such a foolish reason as his attire.

Her hand resting lightly on his arm, she was pulled up

short when he stopped dead just inside the doorway to the grand saloon. "Holy . . ." he began, and stopped, staring. This afternoon they had explored the ship, looking in at the oak-paneled library with its hundreds of volumes; the comfortable, clubby smoking rooms, where women were not allowed; and the ladies' drawing room, with its plushly upholstered sofas and ottomans. Nothing, however, matched the grandeur of this room. It stretched far, far away from them, twice as long as it was wide, with long tables covered by snowy white linen cloths marching away, converging in the distance like railroad tracks. Domed chandeliers shed brilliant light over the scene, while the softer glow from hundreds of candles in silver holders glanced upon arrangements of spring flowers: daffodils, jonquils, hyacinths; and glittered off the sparkling crystal, fine porcelain dishes, and polished silver. Upon the wall frolicked creatures of the sea, mermaids and dolphins and tritons, while high overhead arched a ceiling of glass, dark now with night. White-jacketed waiters, towels folded in precise creases over their arms, flitted among the tables, filling with sumptuously garbed passengers, nearly three hundred of them. Only first cabin passengers here; second and third class had their own quarters, and were kept strictly separate. Matt wondered now if he'd feel more comfortable there.

"I don't believe this," he said, flatly, moving forward at last as someone jostled them from behind. "It's as grand as anything in Newport."

"And you dislike it just as much, don't you?" Brooke said, slanting him a look.

"I didn't say that. It just—takes getting used to."

Her hand tightened on his arm, as if in reassurance.

"We'll be spending a lot of time here," she said, as they followed a waiter to their table. "There's an organ, up there," she pointed to an oriel window set high in the wall far across the saloon, "and a pulpit there, for Sunday services." Another oriel window, in the opposite wall, behind them. "Any entertainments they have planned will be here. All the information will be listed in the ship's newspaper."

Matt hesitated as the waiter turned a swivel chair, bolted to the floor, toward him, and then sat. Beside him Brooke was already seated, smoothing down the skirt of her pale green satin gown. He liked her in green, though he wasn't certain he liked the low cut of this gown, or the fact that the man across the table was winking at her. "The ship has a newspaper?"

"The ship has everything. Mr. Hoffman." She was smiling at the man who had just winked at her again. "What a pleasure to see you here."

"Miss Cassidy." The man beamed at her, and Matt's temper rose. No matter if Brooke knew him; she was *his* wife, and nobody was allowed to treat her in such a way. "Sorry, it's Devlin now, isn't it? Julius Hoffman," he said, holding out his hand to Matt. "You're Detective Sergeant Devlin."

"Yes," Matt said, slightly taken aback, and looked to Brooke for guidance. Hoffman was vaguely familiar, but Matt had met so many people in the last few months that even his trained eye couldn't recognize everyone. He was a middle-aged man, balding, and not above medium height. His dinner jacket, though well cut, sagged upon his sloping shoulders. His black mustache bristled with vitality, however, and the eyes that met Matt's were dark and bright and shrewd. Not a man to underestimate. "Have we met?"

"Mr. Hoffman is a broker," Brooke explained, lightly touching Matt's hand; only the little line that had appeared between her eyes showed that she was annoyed. "He was at Aunt Winifred's New Year's Eve party."

Now Matt remembered. That awful evening, when he and Brooke were so newly married, and the society of New York had stared at him as if he were an oddity. Hoffman, at least, had been friendly. "I remember, sir," he said.

"Call me Julius," Hoffman said, and winked again, this time at Matt, who blinked. "You remember my family. My wife, Adele." Julius indicated the woman sitting next to him, a tall, regal beauty, her fair hair pulled back into a top knot that emphasized the clean, pure lines of her face. She nodded as she sipped from her crystal water glass, barely acknowledging the introduction. "My daughter, Julia." Another fair-haired beauty, seated next to her mother, who also afforded Matt a scant nod. "And my son, Chauncey." A sullen youth, next to his father.

"You're traveling to Europe for pleasure, then," Brooke said, laying aside the menu the waiter had handed her. Matt was still studying his, frowning a little. The menu was in French, and though in the last few months Matt had attended many society dinners, he still wasn't sure what he would be eating. *Consommé printanier* to start with, some kind of soup apparently, followed by trout done up in a fancy sauce. With the soup would be served an Amontillado sherry; to drink with the fish, a German riesling. For the entrees there were veal marengo, whatever that was, and *ris de veau suprêmes*. It took him a mo-

ment to figure out that the latter dish consisted of sweet-
breads; queasily he wondered if Brooke would be embar-
rassed if he asked for good old American steak, or *bifsteak*,
as it was likely to be called aboard the ship. With the en-
tree there would be a rich red Bordeau; with the dessert, a
chocolate souffle, Dom Perignon. By the time this voyage
was over, Matt thought, at last laying the menu onto his
dinner plate, he would likely be both dyspeptic and a dip-
somaniac.

"Business and pleasure," Julius was saying, in answer to
Brooke's question. "Hoffman, Langdon and Company is
looking to expand into Europe in the future. We're thinking of opening a London office. You've met Richard Langdon, haven't you? He's at that table over there. The young
man with him is my secretary, Gregory Tate."

Beside him, Brooke turned to look at the man Julius indicated with a wave of his fork. "Who's watching the
business, then?" she said, smiling.

"It's in good hands, Brooke. We've trained good people to run the firm while we're gone. Actually, Richard
was going to come by himself, but we have our own reasons for traveling. My daughter's getting married. To the
Earl of Lynton."

"Yes, I saw the announcement." Brooke picked up her
own fork as the fish course was set before her, and smiled
at Julia. "My best wishes for your happiness, Miss Hoffman."

"Thank you," Julia mumbled, her head bent, and Julius
beamed at her past his wife.

"Only the best for my daughter, eh, puss?"

"Father, I've asked you not to call me by that terrible

name." Julia shot him a severe look. "And marrying Lynton isn't my idea."

"It is the best thing for you," Adele proclaimed, apparently agreeing with her husband in this instance. "And to have the wedding at the earl's estate is definitely a *coup*. You were married at your uncle's house, were you not, Mrs. Devlin?"

Brooke looked at Matt, and smiled. "Yes, we were."

"A small wedding, as I recall."

Brooke kept her smile firmly in place, even as Adele's eyes flicked over her, as if looking for some hidden secret. "Yes, very intimate and warm." She laid her hand on Matt's arm. "We're on our honeymoon now."

"Are you."

"The police don't mind letting you go, Devlin?" Julius said.

"They'll manage without me," Matt said, taking a sip of water to cover his feelings. Julius might be friendly, but he was sharp, and Adele, for some reason, was hostile. Against them, he and Brooke had banded together. He could feel it.

"Not what I hear," Julius said, chuckling slightly. "I hear you're expected to go places."

"Oh?"

"Especially after the way you handled that mess in Newport last summer."

Matt glanced at Brooke before answering. "That was a different situation."

"Your father was a policeman, was he not?" Adele put in, looking straight at Brooke.

"He was," Brooke answered quietly.

Under the table Matt squeezed her hand. "I think

Brooke would have made a good cop herself," he said, earning a startled glance from her and another blank look from Adele. What, he wondered, would it take to bring any emotion into those ice-blue eyes? And what must it be like to live with her?

"If more police looked like Mrs. Devlin, maybe I wouldn't mind getting arrested," Julius said, winking.

"Father," Julia protested, leaning forward. "That's a terrible thing to say. And you're winking again."

"Am I?" Hoffman looked blank, and then smiled, sheepishly. "Sorry. A habit of mine when I'm tense."

"Oh, I'm not offended," Brooke said quickly, still looking at Matt. "Do you really think I'd be a good policeman?"

"You're stubborn enough," he said, smiling to show it was a compliment.

"It's a difficult job, Brooke, as you no doubt know," Julius said. "I have nothing but respect for the police."

"You've spoken out on corruption, haven't you?" Matt asked quietly, suddenly remembering where else he'd heard Hoffman's name, in discussions with other policemen, and with Nevesey.

"Yes, and I'm proud of it. A man must do his civic duty, and if that means exposing corruption among the police, then so be it." He stabbed at the air with his fork. "But just because there are a few bad apples doesn't mean the force isn't solid. The police have a difficult job, always dealing with deceivers and crooks."

"Mm-hm." Matt nodded, unconvinced, noting with only half his attention the startled look Adele gave her husband. The last thing he wanted to discuss just now was corruption among the police, or to defend the indefensible.

"A man like yourself, for example," Julius was saying, and Matt looked up, his face polite. "I followed the Newport thing from the beginning. When I read about the first maid getting killed on the Cliff Walk, and then the others, I knew there was something wrong. How many did he kill, altogether?"

"Five," Matt said, his estimation of Hoffman rising. In Newport, few in society had cared about maids getting killed, until one of the victims turned out to be one of their own.

"A distasteful subject," Adele said, her lips pursed. "Especially when someone from society was arrested. I find it hard to believe that he could do such things."

"He confessed." Brooke's voice was quiet, her face serious, and Matt touched her hand. Neither of them would ever forget the day when Brooke had so nearly become a victim of the Cliff Walk killer herself. "Tell me, Miss Hoffman. Are you really getting married on the earl's estate?" she asked, and the conversation at last went onto other channels.

Somewhat to Matt's surprise, the dinner was pleasant. The food was superb, the wine excellent, and if the ship rolled a bit too much, causing china and crystal to shift on the fine linen tablecloths, that was one of the hazards of going to sea. Even the conversation was enjoyable, about the unseasonably warm weather, Julia Hoffman's upcoming wedding, and the entertainments they could expect during the voyage, including tomorrow night's play to be put on by some of the passengers, with Julius Hoffman in a leading role. Matt was greatly relieved, though, when it was at last over. For six days he would be obliged to be polite to polite society, but not, he hoped, every moment. This was, after all, his honeymoon, and his first holiday from work for years. Smiling at their dinner companions, he and Brooke left the grand saloon, where already the tables were being cleared and the oriel window had been opened for an organ recital. There'd be time enough to sample the ship's entertainments another night.

The April night was brisk. At their suite Brooke threw a shawl about her shoulders, and they went out to the promenade deck, leaning on the railing and looking at the reflected lights of the ship in the sea, far below. The ship rolled in the swells, making Matt feel just a bit queasy after consuming such a big meal, but he ignored his stomach to concentrate on other things. The moon, for example, a sliver of pale light in the sky, and the stars, so much brighter here than ever they were on land. And the woman next to him, not caring if the wind ruffled her hair or gown. It was one of the things he liked about Brooke, that such things didn't bother her. He put his arm about her shoulders, as if to keep her warm, and she smiled up at him.

The promenade deck was nearly deserted, few wishing to brave the cool night air when the delights of the grand saloon beckoned, but even so he led her across to the deck house and a sheltered alcove where they could have privacy. They were, after all, a couple on their honeymoon. They spent some pleasurable moments together, until sounds from farther along the deck intruded into their private world. A loud splash, a cry, the sound of running footsteps, and then the words that everyone at sea dreads to hear: "Man overboard!"

2

"Matt!" Brooke gasped, startled, pulling away from him as the ship's bell chimed six times. Eleven o'clock. "Did you hear—?"

"Yes." Already Matt was rushing out of their quiet, secluded alcove onto the deck. Evidently they weren't the only ones who had heard the splash; other passengers were running over to the railing and looking down. "Who is it?" Matt called, pulling Brooke along behind him by the hand.

A man in evening dress turned towards him. "Don't know. I was taking a turn on deck for a smoke," he gestured with the cigar in his hand, "when I heard it. Didn't see anything, though."

"Then who yelled?" Matt asked, and as he did so heard in his memory footsteps running away, and what he now realized had been the sound of a door slamming. "Stay here." He abruptly released Brooke's hand and plunged into a door in the deck housing, ignoring her protest.

Something was wrong here. He had to find out what it was.

He found himself in a stairwell obviously not intended for passenger use; it was bare and utilitarian, with steel railings and rubber treads that carried, faintly, the echo of footsteps. Again he acted without thought, grabbing the railing and swinging himself onto the stairs, running down, and down again. At each landing he paused for less than a second, listening for the footsteps, still running, still distant, mocking him. Another flight, and another, and the sound of a door slamming shut somewhere in the distance. Matt didn't bother stopping now; he continued on, a little out of breath, but more determined than ever, his cop's instincts on full alert. People didn't run away like this without reason.

He came to the bottom of the stairwell at last, and confronted another steel door. There had been doors at every level, but, even allowing for the echoing in the stairwell, he guessed that this was the one he'd heard close. It boomed shut behind him as he stepped through, leaving him in a narrow corridor that stretched far to either side; not the full length of the ship, but far enough. It was dimly illuminated by bare incandescent bulbs set into the ceiling at intervals, enough to show him that the corridor, pierced by doors on either side, was empty. He stopped, cocking his head, listening. Nothing. Not a footfall, not a creaking hinge, nothing. Only the sounds of the ship's engines whining in protest as they were put into reverse, louder here than they would be above. Nothing, and no one. Whoever he was chasing had gotten away.

His mouth set in a grim line, he pushed through the door back into the stairwell, aware as he hadn't been before of the ship's sway and his own increasing queasiness. Impeded by that, he climbed the stairs at a more moderate pace than he had descended them, though within him something clamored, urging him on. Something was very wrong.

Brooke turned from the railing as he came back onto the promenade deck, her face white. "Oh, Matt, it's awful. I think someone really did go over."

Matt put his arm around her shoulders, as much to steady himself as to comfort her. "Is there any sign?"

"No." She glanced up as the ship's powerful searchlight swept over them, illuminating gray, treacherous waves. "There's nothing floating. But wouldn't a body . . . ?"

"Not right away," he answered, when she didn't go on. "Once someone drowns, it can be days before he comes back up to the surface." Brooke shivered, and he tightened his hold on her. "The only way we're going to know is if someone turns up missing.

Brooke nestled closer. "Where did you go just now?"

"I heard someone running away."

She stared up at him. "Running! But, who?"

"I don't know." He stared grimly out over the railing. "Whoever it was got away."

"But, Matt, that could mean—"

"I don't know what it means," he interrupted, "and neither do you. And until we do it's better not to get any rumors going."

"Yes, of course." She shivered again, but not from the cold. In the past year she'd seen more than her share of violent death. "Are you going to look into it?" she asked, abruptly.

Matt shook his head. "No. I'll report what I heard, but

this isn't my responsibility, Brooke. There are probably procedures set up for this kind of thing, and if anything does look wrong, there's a ship's detective to investigate. The only way I'll get involved is if I'm asked."

"Oh." She rested her head against his shoulder, only partly comforted. This was wrong. Something terrible had happened, and she doubted this was the end of it.

It took a long time for the ship's speed to slow; even longer for her to turn and retrace her course, the search-light constantly stabbing through the darkness and light-ing up the sea. Neither the watchers on the decks, for most of the passengers had crowded outside now, nor the crew in the bridge or on the masts, saw anything, not a body, no evidence of debris that might indicate where someone had gone down. Only the cold, gray sea, ever restless, ever moving. And though the ship continued to retrace her course through the night, nothing ever showed up on the dark, shifting waters.

Eventually the passengers began to drift back to their staterooms, a person here, a couple there, until the deck suddenly was less crowded. Brooke and Matt stayed by the railing longer than most, but at last Matt turned away, taking her arm, and they returned to their suite. It was not, Brooke thought, as she got ready for bed, the most auspi-cious beginning for a honeymoon. But then Matt came into the bedroom, and they both forgot, for a time, the events of the evening.

Thursday, April 16

The sun rose with a brilliance that made a mockery of the night's dark happenings. Cruising along on a sun-washed sea of azure and emerald, it was hard to believe anything had happened. Even the passengers and crew seemed largely unaffected, Matt thought as he and Brooke emerged onto the promenade deck the following morning, after having breakfasted in their suite. The sausage and eggs he had so unwisely consumed sat uneasily on his stomach; though he hadn't actually developed seasickness yet, he very much feared he would. Not much of a honeymoon, he thought, unconsciously echoing Brooke's thoughts of the evening before.

"Brooke, my dear." A tall, matronly woman with a bosom like the prow of the ship had stopped in front of them and was holding her hands out to Brooke. On this brisk spring morning she was swathed in furs, and a fur toque sat upon her head. "I'd heard you were aboard. Such a terrible thing last night, wasn't it? You must feel as if disaster is following you around. First finding Rosalind's body, and now this."

"Good morning, Mrs. Standish," Brooke said, in the polite voice that Matt had learned meant she didn't particularly care for the other woman. "You remember my husband, I'm sure? Mr. Devlin."

"Oh, yes, of course, the policeman." Mrs. Standish waved her hand, as if in dismissal. "I hope you're not offended, but I do believe in plain speaking. Do I not, Emily?"

The girl who trailed behind Mrs. Standish, a pale shadow of her mother in a merino coat trimmed with fur at the collar, stepped forward. "Yes, Mama," she said, and though her eyes were demurely lowered, Matt saw something flash in them. Resentment, perhaps? "Hello, Brooke."

Brooke's smile was still polite as she nodded. "Emily."

"You must know about what happened last night," Mrs. Standish said, her eyes avid as she looked at Matt. "With your work, and all."

"I'm on my honeymoon, ma'am." The ship's bell chimed twice, signaling the time: nine o'clock. Matt looked up from adjusting his watch, allowing for the forty-five minutes lost each day on an eastward voyage, and forced himself to smile. "I don't know anything more than anyone else."

"No? You surprise me. You too, Brooke, after all the questions you asked last summer."

"That was different," Brooke said, quietly. "If you'll excuse us, we were about to take a turn on the deck."

"Oh, I wouldn't dream of detaining you. Emily? Come, we shall walk with the Devlins."

Matt and Brooke looked at each other, and this time he saw her lips twitch, as if she held back a smile. Thank God for her sense of humor, he thought, tucking her hand more securely through his arm. He wasn't certain he'd survive life in society without it. "Have you heard any word of who went over? If anyone did."

"If no one did, it was a dreadful prank to play, was it not? No, I believe someone did go over. Likely someone from second class."

"Why do you say that?" Matt asked, goaded both by the look of distaste upon her face and the way Brooke's lips twitched again.

"Well, Mr. Devlin, one of us would hardly do such a thing. So undignified, to kill oneself."

"Is that what you think it was?"

"It must be. Everyone says so."

"Oh. Of course," he said, and beside him, Brooke made a strangled noise that sounded like a cough. He gave her a look, and she glanced away, making that noise again.

"Seriously," Brooke said, her voice sounding tight and breathless, but otherwise normal, "if someone did go over, what else could it be? It was too calm last night for there to be an accident, unless whoever it was was on the railing for some reason."

Matt's amusement fled. It had been too calm last night for an accident. That left only two possibilities: suicide, and something else. Something darker. The unease he'd felt last night in the stairwell returned, stronger now.

Still holding Brooke's arm, he wandered over to the railing and looked down, as if he could find the answer in the churning waves. The ship's wake was slight today, her cruising speed slow as her crew continued to search for signs of a body. Who on board this ship was a murderer? It could, he realized, be anyone, but until he knew who had gone over, he'd have no place to start. *Huh.* As if he'd be doing any investigating. At home this was the kind of case he relished attacking, but here, on this ship, he was on alien ground. He was both glad, and regretful, that if there had been foul play he wouldn't be involved in investigating.

Brooke touched him lightly on the arm. "Matt?"

"Yoo hoo! Mr. Langdon, good morning!" Mrs. Standish called at that moment, her penetrating voice carrying the length of the deck. Turning his head, Matt saw a man in tweeds and bowler hat come to a stop, his shoulders stiffening, and then turn. Matt searched his memory for the man's name and came up with it: Richard Langdon, Julius Hoffman's business partner. It wasn't that which put him on alert, though, but the white, strained look on Langdon's face. Again his unease returned, very strong, and he stepped away from the railing.

"You look unwell, Mr. Langdon," Mrs. Standish continued, her voice still braying out. "I do hope you're not suffering from *mal de mêr.*"

"No. No." He stood still wiping his brow with jerky movements, as Mrs. Standish advanced upon him; though the day was cool, sweat beaded on his brow. "Good morning. If you'll excuse me, there are things I have to do."

"Something's wrong," Matt muttered to Brooke, and moved away from the railing, her hand in his.

"Do you think he knows something?" she asked, in an equally quiet voice.

"I don't know, but I don't like the way he looks."

"Such a fine morning as it is, surely you can spare a few moments?" Mrs. Standish was saying, looking up at Langdon with what could only be called a simper.

"I'm sorry, I must go to Adele—" Langdon broke off. "You don't know," he said, looking at them keenly.

"Know what, Mr. Langdon? Pray, tell us. I can see it's something important, and I am positively dying to know."

"Yes, well." He mopped at his brow again. "They know—they think they know—who went overboard last night."

"Everyone's been accounted for, then?" Matt said.

"Yes." Langdon fastened his gaze on Matt's face, seeming just a bit relieved to talk to someone besides Mrs. Standish. "They've counted and everyone's here. Everyone but one. Ju—"He choked again, and then squared his shoulders. "Julius Hoffman is missing."

3

The *New York* steamed on. If there were people who thought that heartless, their protests went unheeded. The ship had a schedule to meet, and, with no sign of Hoffman's body, there was no reason to continue searching. It might be days before the body came to the surface, especially in the cold North Atlantic; and then, with currents to account for, it might be found miles from where it had gone into the water. The best thing to do, Captain Wood had concluded, was to continue on and conduct some kind of inquiry into the mishap.

And that was where he came in, Ambrose Smith thought with great satisfaction as he tramped along the promenade deck towards the Hoffman suite. It was a cushy job, being detective on a ship like this. Usually the worst he had to deal with were the occasional con men or card sharpers who traveled the seas, looking for likely victims. He should be content, but he wasn't.

Truth to tell, Smith missed New York and his old pre-

cinct near Broadway, missed knowing the best places for a
free drink or meal, or something even more lucrative. His
face darkened as he pounded a fist into his open palm,
making an elderly couple passing by eye him in alarm. A
cop's job was hard to do without its little perks and privileges. So if a tavern keeper or a shop owner paid him a
little extra for protection, what was that to anyone? No
one's business, it was, until that damned Reverend Park-
hurst and his band of like-minded, self-righteous citizens
had begun stirring things up. Good cops like himself had
lost their jobs as a result. One of those honest citizens had
just met a fitting end, though, he thought, and smiled.

His good humor restored, he raised a meaty fist and
pounded on the door of the suite. It was opened a moment
later by a sharp-faced maid, who demurely lowered her
eyes when she saw him. No good blustering or bullying his
way in here; dealing with first cabin passengers took tact,
something Smith had never before thought he had. These
passengers would have to be handled even more carefully,
especially in light of what had been found in the purser's
safe.

"Good morning," he said mildly, removing his hat. "I
would like to speak with Mrs. Hoffman."

The maid cast a glance into the suite and then looked
back at him, shaking her head. "Madame is resting," she
began.

"It's all right, Claudette." A man's voice, from inside
the suite. "Let Mr. Smith in."

Claudette glanced back into the room, and then, shrugging, opened the door. Smith kept his face impassive as he
walked in, though what he saw was startling enough. Mrs.
Hoffman, in some sort of fluffy pink lounging gown, of

the type he associated only with the wealthy, sat on the sofa with Richard Langdon standing at her side. So. Langdon was already comforting the widow, Smith thought. Interesting.

"Good morning," he said again, nodding at them each in turn. "I'm sorry to bother you, but there are some things I need to know—"

"At a time like this?" Langdon interrupted. "Mrs. Hoffman has just lost her husband. Have you no sense of decency—"

"Richard." Adele Hoffman's voice was quiet, but sharp. "Of course Mr. Smith has questions. The sooner they're asked, the sooner we'll find out what really happened."

"Adele, are you sure you're up for this—?"

"Now, Richard, enough! If you really wish to be useful, please light me a cigarette. Yes, Mr. Smith," she said, at what must have been his look of surprise, "I do smoke from time to time. I find it relaxes me." She took a long drag on the cigarette Langdon handed her, sitting at her ease. "Please ask whatever you wish."

Interesting, Smith thought again, quickly revising his estimate of Adele. Tougher than she appeared, that was for certain. Not a hair was out of place; not a tear marred either her complexion or her self-control. Of the two people facing him, she was the one to watch. "I'm sorry to bother you at a time like this, ma'am," he said, standing with his hat held before him. "And may I also say how sorry I am for your loss."

"Thank you." Adele tapped off ash into a crystal ashtray. "What happened, Mr. Smith?"

"Well, ma'am." He shifted his feet, as if uncomfortable. "I was hoping you could tell me that."

"Me? I know nothing about it."

That he doubted, more and more. "Yes, ma'am. But as Mr. Hoffman was your husband—"

"It's just like Julius to do something like this, you know," she interrupted, stubbing out the cigarette with unnecessary force. "But my poor children." Her face briefly softened. "They're taking this very hard."

"Yes, ma'am. Are you saying Mr. Hoffman killed himself?"

"For God's sake," Langdon protested.

"I am saying no such thing, sir!" Adele said at the same time. "If there is one thing I know, it is that Julius liked himself too much to commit suicide."

"It was an accident," Langdon said, his lips tight. "It had to be."

"Maybe. But the railings are high, you see?" Smith said, softly. "Hard to understand how he could have fallen over."

"Well, it wasn't suicide." Adele sat back with the air of one preparing to do battle. "Julius wouldn't kill himself, if only to vex me."

"Adele," Langdon put in. "You shouldn't say such things."

"It's true." She looked up at him, reaching up to lay her hand on his, which was resting on her shoulder. "I swear that was the man's purpose in life. Not that his dying isn't vexing, of course, and in such a way, but he knows— knew—his presence would annoy me more."

Interesting, Smith thought again. Apparently all had

not been well in the Hoffman marriage. "Then you saw no signs he might commit suicide?"

"None. He left no note, and he certainly didn't act as if he were thinking of such a thing. Did he, Richard?"

"No." Richard shook his head. "He'd have no reason, as far as I can see. The business has been running well." His eyes shifted briefly away, and a frown line appeared between them. "I won't deny we've hit some rough patches, but lately things have been fine. We wouldn't be thinking of opening a London office otherwise. Now that will have to wait."

And that was another thing, Smith thought. Why were both partners in the business away from it at the same time? "Who is running things in New York while you're gone?"

"We have a young man we're thinking of making a partner." Langdon frowned. "We were thinking of it. Now I don't know."

"This puts you in difficulties, then, does it, Mr. Langdon?"

Langdon stiffened. "I'm not sure I take your meaning."

Oh, he took it well enough, Smith thought. "Will Mr. Hoffman's death cause problems with your firm?"

"It shouldn't."

"Good. Then you won't mind if I take a look at any ledgers you might have along.

"I beg your pardon?"

"Ledgers, Mr. Langdon. The company's books. Surely you must have some with you, if you're planning on doing business in London."

Adele and Langdon glanced at each other. "What do

you need them for?" she asked, her tone noticeably cooler.

"Just routine, ma'am. Part of the investigation."

"If it's routine, then I don't see why you need to see them at all," Langdon put in. "What good would they be to you—if you can read them?"

"Oh, I know how to read a ledger, Mr. Langdon, have no doubts about that," Smith said, pleasantly, though his jaw was clenched. "I cannot go to the courts about this, you see? Not at sea. But I can go to the captain. His word is law."

For a moment there was silence, as the two looked at each other again. Then Adele sighed. "You may as well give them to him, Richard."

"But, Adele—"

"Give them to him, or we'll have no peace."

"Thank you, ma'am," Smith said, as Langdon, face tight, went into the bedroom and came out carrying several leather-bound books. "I won't keep these any longer than I have to."

Adele nodded. "Is that all, Mr. Smith? Because I am rather tired—"

"Just a few more questions, ma'am. Nothing serious." His voice was soothing. "Where were you last night at eleven o'clock?"

"I was here, in bed." Her chin was raised. "My daughter can vouch for me, and so can my maid."

Smith nodded. "And you, Mr. Langdon?"

Langdon frowned. "Do you suspect us of having something to do with Julius's death?"

"Just routine questions, sir. Trying to find out who last saw Mr. Hoffman before he went over."

"Well, it wasn't me," Adele said. "Julius liked to take a brandy before retiring. I suggest you ask in the smoking room if he was there."

"Yes, ma'am. Mr. Langdon? Where were you last night?"

"In my stateroom, of course," Langdon said, glaring at him.

"Of course. Do you have anyone to vouch for you?"

"Do I need to?"

"Now, sir, no need taking that tone. I'm just trying to do my job. Can anyone say they saw you there?"

"No," Langdon said after a moment. "I don't believe so."

"It shouldn't be a problem, sir." Smith hefted the ledgers. "I'll just be going now. Sorry to disturb you, but these are things that have to be done."

"Of course," Adele said. "We want to know what happened as much as you do."

"Of course you do, ma'am." Smith reached for the doorknob, and then turned. "There's just one more thing."

Adele had relaxed; now she stiffened again. "Yes?"

"Do you know Edward McCabe?"

Adele and Langdon glanced swiftly at each other. "Yes."

"And did you also know that he's on this ship?"

"Yes, Mr. Smith. I was aware of that."

"Were you? Good." Smith tucked the ledgers under his arm. "I'll leave you to rest, now. Good day," he said, and went out.

For a moment Smith stood in the corridor, head bent towards the suite; but the door was solid, and he could hear nothing of what was being discussed within. He could guess, though. Grinning, he set off, turning onto the outer part of the promenade deck. Got them thinking and worrying, and that was good. Worried people made mistakes. If either of those two had anything to do with Hoffman's death, he'd soon know about it. And McCabe. Yes, he thought he'd look at Mr. McCabe a little more closely.

His grin stretching wider, Smith tramped on. This case was going to restore his reputation, see if it didn't! And no one was going to take it from him.

"What a shame about Mr. Hoffman," a woman's voice said, breaking into Brooke's reverie, some hours after the news of Hoffman's death had spread throughout the ship. Brooke had come into the ladies' drawing room, ostensibly to write letters, but in reality for something to do while Matt had a cigarette in the smoking room. Ladies weren't allowed in the smoking room, something that annoyed her no end. Not that she particularly wanted to go into such a smoky atmosphere, but it made her feel rather left out. The men would be discussing Mr. Hoffman's death, of course, and she was intensely curious as to what they had to say. "Poor Adele, I understand she's quite prostrated."

"Well, of course she would be," another voice answered, accompanied by the rustle of starched petticoats and taffeta skirts. Brooke, relieved that she wasn't the one being addressed, turned her head and recognized the two ladies crossing the room as Thelma Osgood and Celia Vaughn, two stylish matrons from New York who were far more interested in society than she was. Relieved that they hadn't seemed to notice her, but were instead crossing to one of the overstuffed mauve brocade sofas placed in a curtained alcove looking out onto the promenade deck, she bent her head again, sighing. She did so dislike ladies' gossip.

"Even if she and Julius weren't close," Mrs. Osgood went on, sitting down, her back very straight as she carefully pulled off her beige kid gloves. "Yes, we would like tea." This to the stewardess who was standing obsequiously before them. "And some poppyseed cakes, if there are any."

"Really, Thelma, I don't know how you keep your figure," Celia complained. "I must confess I was rather hoping to be seasick, so I would lose some weight. It is so trying to be plump when being fitted for gowns."

"One cake won't hurt. Of course, suicide is a shock," Thelma went on, as if the topic had never been changed.

"Terrible," Thelma agreed. "I never saw a sign of it, did you?"

"No, and of course Adele would never let on that anything was amiss. I do wish we could have seen her." There was a brief pause as the stewardess served the tea and cakes. Brooke, no longer bored, bent over her letter, waiting. Maybe she would learn something, after all.

"She needs to know her friends are here for her," Celia said, finally.

Thelma snorted; there was no other word for it. "You're as curious about it as I am, Celia Vaughn, and don't deny it! You want to know what happened, too."

"Well, of course I do," Celia said in a matter of fact tone, pouring out the tea. "But Adele and I have known each other since we were girls. I'm one of her oldest friends."

"I'd forgotten that." There was another pause, during which Brooke glanced discreetly around, to see the two ladies drinking their tea. She wondered if they realized she was here; tucked away in a corner as she was, she wasn't immediately noticeable. To get up now, though, would only draw attention to herself, even though she hadn't meant to eavesdrop.

"I really thought Richard was beastly about our visiting her. Imagine, turning us away like that!" Thelma went on. "Though I can understand it, of course."

"Thelma, you're not talking about those old rumors, are you?" Celia said, gently reproving.

"Oh, my dear, don't be such a prude. It's common knowledge that Adele and Mr. Langdon are lovers," Thelma said, and Brooke, who had been about to rise, abruptly sat again. It wasn't something she'd known.

"Hush, Thelma, not so loud! No one knows that for certain."

"I've suspected it, and so have you. They've often been seen together, you know."

"That doesn't have to mean anything."

"Of course, who could blame her?" Thelma went on, as if Celia hadn't spoken. "Julius had his good points, I'm sure, but he was rather unrefined."

"I liked him."

"You like everyone, Celia. No, I'm not surprised Adele looked elsewhere. I'm only surprised it took her so long to do so. And I'd be very surprised if she's grieving."

That was too much for Brooke. If this was what married society ladies talked about, she almost wished she were

still single. Rising, she tore her unfinished letter in two,
and then turned, smiling at the other ladies, who stared at
her over their teacups. "Good day," she said, nodding,
and strode across the room, glad to reach the deck and the
clean, fresh air, which blew away her lingering unease. She
was certain that Celia and Thelma would now gossip
about her, and while that was disturbing, she shrugged it
off. More disturbing was what they had discussed. Not
that she was naive. She knew that many marriages were
failures, and that wives, as well as husbands, often looked
elsewhere for companionship. But to have an *affaire* with
your husband's business partner was somehow more sordid; to travel with him on the same ship as your husband
was worse. And yet, if it were true . . . Brooke shivered. If
it were true, then Adele would have a reason for not wanting her husband around. For wanting to kill him. What
appeared to be an accident might just be something more
sinister.

Lips set, Brooke set off towards her suite. She had to
talk to Matt about this. If Mr. Hoffman had been murdered, they couldn't let it go. There was no honeymoon
for death.

Matt knocked on a door deep in the ship. No trappings
of saloon class here, no fine carpets or gilding or expensive
mahogany paneling. Instead the narrow corridor was gray
painted steel, while the floor was of ordinary rubber tile.
This was part of the working section of the ship, and as
such was without frills.

"Come in," a voice called from the other side of the
door, and Matt stepped into the office of the ship's detec-

tive. It was furnished only with a scarred desk, two chairs bolted to the floor, and a plain oak cabinet against the wall. "Detective Devlin," Smith said, rising, his voice surprisingly jovial, considering the events of the day. "And what is it I can be doing for you? Some whiskey, by the way?"

"No, thank you." Matt shook his head as he sat down in the chair near Smith's desk. Maybe the whiskey would help settle his stomach, but he doubted it. After more than a day at sea, he probably wasn't going to succumb to seasickness, but this continual queasiness was annoying. He would not want Smith's job. "How do you like working on a ship?"

Smith shrugged. He was a big man, broad of shoulder, thick in the neck, with muscle that was slowly, but steadily, turning to fat. "It's easy work. Not much to do, keep an eye on steerage, and that's what it is, even if the company calls it third class. Of course, that's worse coming back than going out, what with all the immigrants and all. Oh, we have some thievin' and card sharpers, too, but petty stuff, you see? It's not often we get a jumper."

Matt sat forward, alert. "Is that what you think? That Hoffman jumped over himself?"

Smith shrugged again, a little smile on his face. "Maybe. You were on deck. You hear any kind of a scuffle?"

"No," Matt said, reluctantly, but then, he had been otherwise engaged. "I find it hard to believe Hoffman killed himself, though. I saw him at dinner last night, and he didn't seem like a man planning suicide. Was there a note?"

"No, no note, but then, they don't always leave one, you see? It's suicide, right enough. The only other thing it could be is an accident, and how would that have happened? You tell me that, detective.''

Matt got up, pacing across the unsteady floor. "He didn't seem to be drinking much at dinner. Was he drunk?" he asked, turning suddenly.

"Not so's anyone noticed. Maybe he climbed up on the railing, but why? Maybe he leaned so far over he fell, but again, why? No, detective. It was no accident.''

Matt rubbed at his mustache and sat down again. "What about the footsteps I heard running away?"

"Funny thing about them." Smith smirked at him. "No one else seems to have heard them. Not even your wife."

"They were real. I heard someone running away from the deck. Running down the stairwell, and a door closing.''

Smith shrugged. "Probably you heard someone running to see what the 'man overboard' was about. And that's another thing, detective." There was no mistaking the slight mocking note in his voice. "Say someone did push Hoffman over. Why would he call attention to it, and then run away?"

"I don't know. Yet."

"Oh. You don't know. Don't have any evidence, then, do you, detective? But then, it wouldn't be the first time."

Matt bit back an angry retort. He could almost understand Smith's hostility, a little. After losing one job he wouldn't want this one threatened, and Matt's questions could do that. Hoffman's death bothered him. Because of it he'd been unable to settle into any of the usual shipboard activities, of strolling or playing deck games or simply sitting in a steamer chair, watching the other passengers. Because of it, he was here. "I know damn well people kill themselves without giving any reasons," he said. "But Hoffman didn't strike me that way."

"You knew him well, detective?"

"No." No, he hadn't known Hoffman, but he was good at sizing up people; he had to be. Hoffman hadn't struck him as being depressed. Apart from anything else, he'd had too many plans for the future. Possible business expansion aside, a man would have to be a monster to so disrupt his daughter's wedding plans. Hoffman had seemed to be a fond, if not doting, parent. No, he didn't think the broker's death was a suicide, and he was inclined to agree with Smith that it wasn't an accident, either. That left only one other possibility.

"Maybe there's evidence you're overlooking," he said, crisply, and rose. "I can't help that. But if I were you, I'd do a little more checking before I reached any conclusions."

"Well, you're not me, you see?" Smith rose, bracing his hands on the desk and leaning forward, a technique Matt had himself used to intimidate people. "And I'll thank you not to meddle in my affairs."

Matt shrugged. "It's not my problem. I'm on my honeymoon," he said, and went out, closing the door behind him. It wasn't his problem, he told himself as he walked down the corridor, nor was this ship his jurisdiction. Questionable though he found Hoffman's death, he had no authority to investigate it. The sooner he accepted that, the better.

The ship rolled, and his hand shot out, bracing himself against the corridor wall, the soup that had been all he could consume at luncheon sloshing back and forth within him. If this kept up, he'd be considerably thinner by the time they reached England. He'd be better off up on deck, in the air, concentrating on something else; he'd be better off forgetting about mysterious deaths and murder, difficult though that might be. Taking a deep breath, he pushed himself away from the wall and carefully walked along the tilting corridor to find Brooke.

Brooke was just opening the door to their suite when he reached it. "I thought you'd be here already," he said, reaching past her to open the door.

"I don't plan to spend my days inside," she said, a trifle waspishly. "Where have you been?"

"Around," he said defensively, and then shook his head. "Does it matter?"

"Yes. I was looking for you. You said you'd be in the smoking room."

"I was. Look, I don't want to argue, Brooke. Not unless there's something to fight about."

Brooke stared at him for a moment, and then blew out her breath, lifting a strand of hair away from her face. "I don't, either," she said, dropping down onto the sofa. "But it's been a disagreeable afternoon, Matt. Not at all what I expected."

"No one expected this. I was with the ship's detective," he went on, before she could ask again where he had been.

"Oh?" She straightened. "Did he have anything to say?"

"Not much. Except that it's his case, and he doesn't want me interfering."

"Oh." She frowned. "But, Matt . . ."

"What?" he said, when she didn't go on.

"It can't have been an accident." Still frowning, she pulled off her gloves, one finger at a time. "The railings are too high. And Mr. Hoffman really didn't seem as if he planned to kill himself. So . . ."

"You know what you're suggesting, don't you?"

"Yes. Someone killed him."

It was out in the open. "Maybe."

"Don't tell me you haven't thought so yourself, Matt! What about that person you chased last night? And if it were suicide, why didn't he leave a note?"

"Suicides don't always do that, Brooke."

"I still don't believe it," she said, stubbornly.

"I don't want to get involved in this, Brooke."

"No? Aren't you curious?"

"Curious, yes. But it's not my job."

"I heard something today." Her voice was abrupt. "I heard that Mrs. Hoffman and Mr. Langdon are, well, close."

Matt rubbed his finger across his mustache. "Any indication that's all it is?"

"What do you mean?"

"I mean that if there's more to it, if, say, Mrs. Hoffman wanted a divorce and her husband wouldn't give it to her, that would give either of them a motive."

Brooke glanced away. "I thought the same thing."

"Look." He leaned towards her. "I don't know that anyone killed Hoffman, and neither do you. For all we know, it really was suicide. Though I doubt it," he added, softly.

Brooke's eyes were troubled. "Matt, what can we do?"

"Us? Nothing. This isn't my jurisdiction, Brooke." He leaned forward. "And the last time you tangled with a murderer, you almost became one of his victims."

"Don't remind me," she said, shuddering, as a knock sounded at the door. Matt answered it, giving her a look.

A white-jacketed steward stood in the open doorway. "Mr. Devlin?"

"Yes?"

"Captain Wood would like a word with you, sir."

"About what? Did he say?"

"No, sir. He's asked me to bring you to his stateroom."

Matt turned back to Brooke, eyebrows raised in surprise, and then nodded. "All right. I'll be out in a moment." He shut the door.

"What do you think he wants?" Brooke asked.

"I don't know." He picked up his suit coat from the chair where he'd left it and shrugged into it. "Probably wants to know what we heard last night."

"But we've already told that." She paused. "You're not wearing that suit, are you?"

Matt stopped at the door. "Why? What's wrong with it?"

Brooke opened her mouth, and then closed it again. "Nothing."

He gave her another look. "This probably won't take long. When I get back, why don't we take a walk out on the deck?"

"I'd like that."

"And don't go asking anyone anything while I'm gone."

"Who would I ask? And what?" she said, surprised.

"I don't know, but I know you, Brooke. I'd rather you didn't get involved in this."

"I don't particularly want to get involved, either."

"Good," he said, and at last went out, following the steward along the promenade deck, hoping that Brooke would keep to her word. Curious though he was about the circumstances concerning Hoffman's death, he really didn't want to get involved in any investigating. Of course Brooke would talk about it with other people; it was all anyone was talking about. It would be better, though, if that was all she did. And what, he wondered, as the steward led him downstairs and along corridors, was wrong with his suit?

The steward stopped at a paneled door far back in the stern of the ship, the traditional location for the captain's stateroom. Here the movement of the sea was far more pronounced than in the suite amidships, making Matt swallow against nausea. He stood back as the steward knocked, and, after hearing a voice within answer, went in to a spacious room, furnished, like Smith's office, more for use than comfort. True, the walls were panelled oak, hung with paintings of ships: clippers, early steamers, and the *New York* itself; and the thick rug underneath was Persian. There was a telephone on the wall, so that the captain could communicate with the rest of the ship, and sofas and chairs grouped near one wall. At a table, simple but of the best mahogany, sat three men, all looking grave. To the side, at yet another, smaller mahogany table, another man sat, dealing out a hand of solitare, as if distancing himself from the others. "Mr. Devlin." The captain, as evidenced by his navy blue uniform, walked towards him, hand outstretched. He was a neat, precise-looking man, with a sharply trimmed Vandyke beard, white, like his hair; and keen blue eyes set in skin weathered and wrinkled by the sea. "Thank you for coming so quickly. Have you met the others?"

"No, not everyone."

"Let me introduce you, then. You must be wondering why I asked you here."

"Yes, I was," Matt said, though he knew. It was about Hoffman's death, of course. The sight of Ambrose Smith, standing now and glowering at him, confirmed that. The other two men were strangers to him. One was a smallish man, with thinning hair and pince-nez glasses he touched nervously, while the other, who still played cards . . . Matt's lips pursed in a silent whistle. He'd seen that face before, with its bulbous nose and bristling eyebrows, if only in the newspapers. John Pierpont Morgan, eminent financier and owner of the American Line, so powerful that just last year he'd rescued the United States government from bankruptcy. Until now, Matt hadn't known he was aboard.

Captain Wood made the introductions, waved Matt to a seat, offered him brandy and a cigar. On alert now, Matt refused, wanting to keep a clear head and a calm stomach. The smaller man, Mr. Tuttle, was the agent for the American Line, but, seeing his nervous mannerisms and constant glances at Morgan, Matt dismissed him from serious consideration. Morgan was another story. A man didn't gain a reputation such as his for nothing. Matt would have to watch himself.

"I called this meeting because of last night's events," Captain Wood said, after everyone was settled.

"I'd guessed that," Matt said after a moment, since no one else seemed inclined to say anything. To his side Morgan threw down his cards, scowling, but his eyes beneath his shaggy brows were piercing, and his nose flashed a fiery red. Even quiet, he was a force to be reckoned with.

"Dear, dear, such an unfortunate happening," Tuttle

said, smoothing down his hair. "Of course whenever there's such an accident it's unfortunate, but—"

"We need to deal with the consequences," Morgan's voice rumbled, speaking at last.

"I can handle them, sir," Smith said, more deferential than Matt would ever have expected. Morgan glanced at him, grunted noncommitally, and sipped from his glass.

"Under normal circumstances, I'd agree," the captain said, "but this is hardly normal. Of course, you don't know what's happened, Mr. Devlin. There's been a new development."

"Oh, dear, yes." Tuttle cleared his throat as he reached for a paper lying on the table next to the sofa. "After Mr. Hoffman's unfortunate accident the purser looked in the ship's safe for his belongings. He found this." He handed the paper across to Matt. "It was addressed to the captain."

" 'Captain Wood,' " Matt read aloud, and then fell silent, his eyes registering the words but his mind refusing, at first, to take them in. The person writing had, so he said, been aware that his life was in danger for quite some time. Without going into details, he wanted the captain to be aware of his situation, should anything untoward occur. In the case of his incapacitation, or worse, death, there were some people he would ask the captain to look at very closely: his wife and his business partner. The letter was signed, in an upright, formal hand, "Julius Hoffman." "Holy God," Matt said. "Is this for real?"

"The purser found it in the safe," the captain repeated.

Matt looked up. "Has the writing been checked against other things written by Hoffman?"

"Oh, it's his, all right," Smith said. "We got some of his papers here, and I compared the writing, you see?"

"Yes," Matt said, looking at the letter again. "I take it no one's approached Mr. Langdon or Mrs. Hoffman yet."

The captain shifted in his seat. "As we just found this, no, nothing's been done yet."

"It's a delicate matter," Tuttle put in. "Among other things, we have to think of the company's reputation."

Matt stared at him. Tuttle was serious. His concern was less for solving the murder, if such it was, and more for the company. For once, though, Matt could see his point. Who would handle the questioning that would need to be done? Smith might have been able enough as a sergeant in New York, but he was out of his depth with this. *Holy God.* Matt suddenly knew why he'd been summoned. "How are you going to handle this?" he asked, turning and speaking directly to J.P. Morgan.

"I'm not going to handle it," Morgan said, and though his gaze was still sharp, Matt thought he detected a hint of something else there. Respect, perhaps? "I'm giving it to someone who knows what he's doing. Someone who's handled this kind of thing before. In short, Mr. Devlin," he looked directly at Matt, his eyes piercing, "you will handle it."

4

"He can't!" Smith shot up from his seat, automatically bracing his feet against the sway of the ship. "This is my case, and I'll handle it."

"Sit down, Mr. Smith." Morgan's voice was sharp.

"But—"

"Sit down, I said." Morgan glared at Smith, his nose seeming to flash, now bright red, now dark. It was a startling sight. Matt wasn't surprised when Smith sat down again, muttering under his breath. Morgan spared him no more glances, but instead looked directly at Matt. "Well, Mr. Devlin?"

Matt rubbed a finger across his mustache. Morgan wasn't a man to cross, but—this was his honeymoon. It wasn't the time to get involved in a case, no matter how much it called to him. In New York the type of crime he encountered was relatively simple. Already he knew the most likely places where trouble might flare, and the most likely troublemakers. The occasional homicide was simple, too, a drunken brawl at a saloon, a robbery gone wrong. Nothing like this, where he didn't have a body to start with. Nothing so complicated. Maybe that was why he wanted to take this case so badly.

"No," he said, crisply, before he could change his mind. "I can't do it."

"Can't, or won't, sir?" Captain Wood put in, in a deceptively genial voice.

"Won't." Tired of feeling confined, Matt rose and paced the room, stumbling only once or twice when the ship rolled. "I'm on my honeymoon."

Morgan frowned. "I realize that, sir, but—"

"No, you don't realize." Matt swung around, slamming his hands down on the back of a chair. "This isn't something simple where I can make an arrest and then forget about it. My God, the last time I got involved in something like this, back in Newport, I lost my job and I nearly lost my wife. Look." He took a deep breath, trying to calm himself. Because he didn't know which would be harder: refusing the case, or taking it on. "Do you have any idea what's involved in an investigation like this? It's not just talking to the victim's family or friends. It's checking times, places, who was where and when, who just happened to be at the wrong place at the wrong time, who did have a reason to commit murder. It takes manpower. I couldn't do it alone."

"You'd have Smith," Captain Wood said.

"No!" Smith bolted up from his seat again. "I won't help him, captain, so help me God! This is my case." He glared at Matt. "It's not as hard as he makes out. We have what we need to make an arrest, you see? We have the letter."

"You'd make an arrest on that basis?" Matt said, quietly.

"That, and the fact that Langdon wasn't in his stateroom last night, when he says he was."

Both Captain Wood and Matt turned to look at him. "How do you know that?" the captain asked.

"I have my sources." Smith sounded smug. "I can handle this, captain. You don't need anyone else."

The captain gazed at him for a few moments, and then turned back to Matt. Morgan watched in silence, as if he were no longer interested, and yet everyone in the room was aware of him. "Are you comfortable knowing that innocent people might be arrested?"

Matt's lips thinned. "No sir, I am not. Are you so sure that's what will happen?"

"But how it will look!" Mr. Tuttle exclaimed. "To arrest someone from cabin class! It's unheard of."

"Not quite," Matt muttered.

Smith let out a snort. "You think first class's any better'n you and me?" he demanded, chin thrust forward, and Tuttle's pale blue eyes blinked behind his spectacles. "Just 'cause they have money? No, sir. They're as bad as everyone else when it comes to certain things. Sex and money, you see? Sex and money."

Tuttle winced. "Mr. Smith, that's no way to talk—"

"Tuttle, don't be an old woman," Morgan said, and this time Matt thought the gleam in his eyes might be amusement. "The guilty party will have to be brought to justice, whoever he is. Do I make myself clear?"

"But, sir, the reputation of the ship—"

"Hang the reputation of the ship. I'm more concerned

about what will happen if the killer's not caught. And then what will you do, Tuttle?"

"We'll do everything we have to, sir," Captain Wood said.

"You had better. Well, sir?" Morgan stared hard at Matt from under beetling brows, his eyes dark and piercing. "Will you take the case, or won't you?"

"No," Matt said, shortly.

"You are certain?" Morgan's voice was soft. "Things could go very hard for you in New York."

Matt stiffened. "I don't like threats, Mr. Morgan."

"It is not a threat, sir." Morgan heaved his great bulk out of his chair. "I want the killer caught, captain. Before we reach Southampton," he said, and stalked out of the room.

"Five days," the captain said, into the heavy silence left by Morgan's departure. "Could you do it, Mr. Devlin?"

"It's not my case," Matt said, holding onto his temper by force of will. Morgan might deny it, but he had just made a threat, with the power to back it up. Commissioner Roosevelt in New York bowed to no man, but of necessity Morgan would be familiar with the old police guard. Should they ever return to power, Morgan could indeed make life difficult for Matt. Yet Morgan was right about one thing. If the killer weren't found before they reached England, he never would be.

"Our passage will be slower than normal, because of retracing our course to search for the body, but, still, we must reach Southampton on Tuesday. It's not much time. I need someone experienced to handle the investigation."

"Captain, I can do it," Smith put in.

The captain cut him off with a wave of his hand. "All

the resources of the ship will be put at your disposal," he said, watching Matt. "You have my word that the crew will cooperate with you. Now, sir." He stared hard at Matt, as formidable in his own way as Morgan. "Mr. Morgan may own the ship, but while I'm in command I'm responsible for it, and I agree with him. If there is a killer on my ship, he must be found. Will you do it, or won't you?"

Matt hesitated. He wanted to. Oh, he wanted to, difficult though it would be. There was no link between the ship and land, no way he could get information he might need from New York, no one to back him up. Only Smith, and that was a dubious prospect. It was a challenge. But . . . But he was on his honeymoon, and if he got involved in another case that concerned Brooke's friends, he wasn't certain how she'd react. "No," he said, and, like Morgan, stalked out of the room.

The suite seemed empty with Matt gone. Strange, because Brooke was used to being on her own; she had been for the past six years. Oh, her aunt and uncle were dears, taking her in as they had, but she'd never been as close to them as she had her own parents. It was nice, having someone to rely on again. It was also annoying that she was ignoring her inner resources.

Squaring her chin, she took a hat from her wardrobe and put it on, eyeing her reflection critically. Hats were her weakness. Evening gowns with their tightly laced bodices she found constricting, and daywear, with layers of petticoats and the ridiculously huge leg o'mutton sleeves still in fashion, was worse, but she loved hats. The one now perched on her head was a confection of netting and flowers and a silly little veil, meant to keep the sun off her skin. Matt, of course, probably wouldn't notice it. Not when he thought a suit from Sherman's in Newport was appropriate for an Atlantic cruise.

That made her shake her head and turn sharply away from the mirror. Heavens, quite the snob she was turning into, she reproved herself as she stepped out of the stateroom onto the promenade deck. What Matt wore didn't matter. She'd married the man, not his clothes, and she'd known what she was getting. She wasn't sorry.

The air was brisk, with clouds massing on the horizon. From the promenade deck, Brooke eyed them with the seasoned gaze of an ocean traveler. They might be in for a storm. She hoped not. She was a good sailor, but once or twice today Matt's face had gone pale. A storm would do him no good at all, especially since he seemed to think she didn't know he wasn't feeling well. For a policeman, at times he could be remarkably unobservant.

In spite of the cool air people were sitting on wooden steamer chairs, heavy plaid rugs across their laps, or strolling along the deck under the awning. Geraldine Standish hailed her, but Brooke only smiled and nodded, walking purposely on, not wanting to get into any conversations with her. At last she reached her destination, the ship's library. The smoking room, a male preserve, was forbidden to her, and the drawing room would be filled with gossiping women, but this was neutral ground. If all else failed, she could always find a book to keep her company.

She paused just inside the door, getting her bearings. For all that she pretended to Matt that she was at ease in her surroundings, the decor of the *New York* still stunned

her. The library was unique. Because of its location between two of the ship's stacks, it was hourglass-shaped,
lined with bookcases and paneled in oak wainscoting.
Upon the recessed shelves were carved the names of fa-
mous literary figures: Tennyson, Keats, Longfellow. She
had the odd sensation of swimming through a sunlit sea as
she crossed the room, the result of the light streaming
through the stained glass skyglass and windows, which
were inscribed with poems about the sea. It was a magical
place, and for the first time since Matt had left for his
meeting with Captain Wood, her spirits rose. She was glad
they'd chosen this ship for their honeymoon.

The shelves were crammed with books of all sorts,
nearly a thousand of them, from poetry to biographies to
the latest novels by Frances Hodgson Burnett and Paul
Leicester Ford. Brooke was reaching for one when a voice
behind her spoke, startling her. "The hat is acceptable," it
said, with just a touch of a Southern drawl in its depths.
"A little light for the rest of the ensemble, but you're
doing better, Brooke."

Brooke spun around, hand to her heart in surprise, to
see a tall, lanky form unfolding himself from one of the
comfortable brocade chairs that were scattered about the
room. "Jack!" she said, forgetting the book in her delight.
"I didn't know you were aboard."

"Hello, Brooke." Jack Everett's eyes crinkled at the corners as he smiled down at her. "But I knew you were.
Read the passenger list, you know. But then, you probably have better things to do than to read a lot of names."

To her credit, Brooke kept her gaze steady. "What are
you doing here? Oh, let me guess. It's spring. That means
you're going to England?"

"But of course. My wardrobe is sadly depleted, you know. High time I visited my tailor."

"High time," Brooke agreed. Not many men she knew patronized British tailors exclusively, avoiding their American counterparts, but then, Jack Everett wasn't quite like most men she knew. He lived for style, or so he claimed. He could support that style with money from the family's tobacco company, enough so that he never had to lift a finger to work if he didn't want to. That he sometimes did was something he kept quiet, and Brooke admired him for it. "How have you been?"

"Just fine, darlin', since I saw you—where was it last? At Mrs. Vanderbilt's, or Mrs. Van Renssselaer's?"

"Neither." She smiled. "Matt and I aren't terribly social."

He shook his head in mock dismay. "You'll never get along that way, Brooke. Don't you know that style is everything?" He looked her over again, brows lowered in what she knew wasn't a real frown. "The walking dress isn't quite right, darlin'. Good enough quality, but it lacks that certain cachet."

"Stop joshing me, Jack," Brooke said, settling into a chair near his. "Now. Tell me what you've been up to lately."

"All of it?" he asked, sitting again and stretching out his long legs.

"Yes. All of it."

"I'd rather hear about you." He fixed her with eyes unexpectedly keen. "Heard you and your husband are inseperable. Not done, you know."

"I know, but it suits us."

"So where is he now?"

Brooke's smile faded. "Captain Wood asked to see him."

"Oh?" Again Jack gave her that sharp, blue look. "About the Hoffman business, I gather?"

Brooke bit her lip. "I don't know."

"What else would it be, darlin'?" Crossing his feet at the ankles, Jack studied the shine on his shoes, the very picture of relaxed, elegant indolence. "Bad business, that. Been wondering if someone was going to get Hoffman."

"Going to get—you don't mean you think he was killed!"

"What other explanation is there?" He looked up at her, his eyes sober. "You were with him at dinner. Did he seem like a man contemplating suicide?"

"No," Brooke said, troubled. "He seemed, oh, full of plans and happy about his daughter's wedding. Why would he want to disrupt that?"

Jack tilted his head in the mannerism that passed, for him, as a shrug; a real shrug would spoil the set of his jacket shoulders. "Common knowledge the match is Adele's idea."

"But he seemed happy about it." She frowned. "He didn't seem to be contemplating suicide, true. But who know what goes on in someone else's mind, Jack?" She raised troubled eyes to him. "I found that out last summer."

"So I heard. You know that anyone is capable of murder as well as I do." He returned to contemplating his feet. "Especially after what I heard in New York."

Brooke sat up straight. For all his air of languor, or perhaps because of it, Jack was a man who heard things.

People tended to forget there was a sharp mind under that seemingly indolent exterior. "What did you hear?"

"I heard he'd received some death threats."

"No!" she gasped. "From whom? And how—"

"Don't know that, darlin'." He looked at her then. "But anyone who got through the panic with their fortunes intact made enemies."

"Even you, Jack?"

"No, not me." He waved a languid hand in the air. "I don't have enough energy to make enemies."

Brooke smiled mechanically. The Panic of 1893 had barely touched her or her family, but the country had suffered, with high unemployment and dropping wages. Some people had lost everything. Not Julius Hoffman, however. She suddenly remembered her uncle remarking that Hoffman, and most of his clients, had actually prospered. It made her feel vaguely guilty. "But it's been three years, Jack. Isn't that a long time to wait to take revenge?"

"Depends on who it is. People were angry in the beginning, true. But some people hold their anger. They cherish it." Jack spoke almost as if to himself. "Someone like that—he might well have waited, planning things very carefully."

Brooke shuddered at the image his words conjured up, of someone planning, so cold-bloodedly, to commit murder. The thought that it could be someone she knew made matters worse. "Who else knows about this?"

Jack tilted his head again. "Adele, I imagine. Richard, too. Hoffman didn't seem to take the threats too seriously, but who knows? And who knows if whoever made them actually followed him here?"

Brooke shuddered again, and rose. "Matt should be

back anytime," she said, looking down at the watch pinned on her bodice. "I should get back to the suite."

Jack unfolded himself from the chair again. "Let me escort you there, darlin'. Pretty girl like you shouldn't be roamin' around alone."

Brooke tucked her hand through his arm and let him lead her back onto the promenade deck, though she didn't take his compliment at all seriously. She and Jack had never been more than friends, though there had been times in the last few years when she'd been glad of that friendship. After the death of her parents, adjusting to life with her aunt and uncle had been difficult. Because her father had been a policeman, she'd been snubbed more than once. Never by Jack, however. She and Jack had liked each other from first acquaintance, arbiter of style though he claimed to be, and so it remained. She was glad he was aboard the ship. Her honeymoon was not shaping up to be at all what she had expected.

Matt was just opening the door to their suite when Brooke and Jack arrived. He turned at their approach, and instantly his face lost all expression. Something was making him wary. "Matt," she said, surprised that she sounded breathless. "I didn't think you'd be back so soon."

"So I see." He slouched back, hands in trouser pockets. "You managed to entertain yourself while I was away."

Brooke stared at him in surprise. "I went to the library and I met Jack there. Oh, that's right, I don't think you know each other. Matt, this is Jack Everett—"

"We've met." Matt's gaze was curt.

"Good to see you again," Jack said, sounding amused.

"Well. I see you're in good hands, Brooke, so I'll leave you."

"Thank you for walking me back, Jack."

"My pleasure." With two fingers, he saluted, and then ambled off.

Matt muttered something under his breath, and Brooke turned back to him. "Excuse me?"

"Nothing," he said, and walked into the suite, leaving her to follow.

"Well." She frowned at his back as she walked into the suite, and went into the bedroom to remove her hat. "You weren't with the captain as long as I'd thought."

"No." His voice was remote. "Who is that fellow?"

"Jack?" She leaned sideways, so that she could see him through the bedroom door. "You said you've met."

"A time or two." His back was still turned. "Who is he?"

Brooke stopped in the act of placing her hat on the dresser, startled. "Just a friend." She crossed the room to him. "Matt. Don't tell me you're jealous."

Matt stayed still for a moment, and then ran his hand over his face, turning. "No. Of course not. Sorry. It was that damned meeting."

Brooke curled up on the sofa, legs tucked under her. "Tell me about it."

He grimaced as he sat beside her. "Apparently Hoffman left a letter."

Brooke sucked in her breath as Matt briefly described the letter. "Then it was murder."

That made Matt look at her. "Why do you say that?"

"Jack told me he'd heard that Hoffman had received death threats in New York."

"Holy—!" Matt stopped, finger to his mustache. "Dammit, it does sound suspicious." He rounded on her, frowning. "I don't want you getting involved in this."

"I'm not involved in anything," she protested. Pausing, she gave him a pointed look. "Is there something to be involved in?"

"Possibly." He rose and paced to the window again. "It was the damndest thing. J.P. Morgan asked me to investigate."

"J.P.—I didn't know he was aboard!" Good heavens. This was serious. "You're going to, aren't you?"

"I told him no."

"Matt! You didn't!" She stared at him. "A man has died. How can you let that go?"

He made a slashing motion with his hand. "This isn't my jurisdiction. And, in case you haven't noticed, we're on our honeymoon."

"We'll be on our honeymoon for three months. Matt, think of—"

"You *want* me to investigate?" he interrupted, turning towards her.

"I think you should, don't you?"

"No, I don't think I should. God." He sank into a chair. "I'm tired of crime, tired of running into it every time I turn around. On the job it's one thing, but here." He rubbed his hand over his face again. "Smith can handle it."

"What if he doesn't?" She leaned forward. "Matt, once we reach Europe, everyone will go their separate ways. The murderer will escape."

"If there was a murder."

"You know there was!" She stared at him, finally getting angry. "Julius Hoffman was killed. How you can just sit there—well." She sat back, rearranging the folds of her skirt, though they hung neatly enough. "I guess I'll just have to ask some questions myself."

"No!" Matt sat bolt upright. "Dammit, Brooke—"

"I don't like it when you say that."

"—the last time you did that you nearly got killed."

"Someone has to do something! We can't just ignore this."

Matt stared at her, some of his own anger draining away. "Why do you care so much?"

She looked away. "I don't know," she said, finally, her voice muffled. "I only know—maybe it's because of all the stories I heard my father tell. It matters to me, Matt."

"Your father wouldn't have wanted you involved."

Brooke's chin jutted out. "Only because I'm female."

"Well, of course."

"Matt!"

"If you'd been a boy you probably would have gone on the force, like me." He grinned suddenly. "I'm glad you didn't."

"Matt." This time she sounded more exasperated than angry. "You're really not going to investigate?"

"No, I'm really not."

"But you want to."

He stood by the window again. "I don't."

"No?"

"No." He turned to look at her. "And I don't want you to, either."

"Matt—"

"Please, Brooke. I'm asking you."

Brooke lowered her eyes. "All right," she said, after a moment, fingers pleating her skirt.

"You mean that?"

"Yes."

"You won't ask any questions?"

"No."

"Good." Matt came towards her, smiling, his hand outstretched, and she placed her hand in his. "It's better this way, Brooke," he said, drawing her to her feet. "Think about it, and you'll agree."

"Mm-hm." She smiled up at him abstractedly. She wouldn't ask questions. People gossiped, though, and in that gossip could sometimes be found the truth. She was going to look for that truth, no matter what Matt thought. She had to.

Darkness had fallen as the passengers assembled in the grand saloon that evening after dinner. The stained-glass roof overhead was a vast, black expanse, broken by the brilliant lights of the domed chandeliers. The amateur theatrical that had been planned for this evening's entertainment had been canceled; in its place was a memorial service for Julius Hoffman.

Matt and Brooke took their seats at the table, swiveling to face the oriel window set high in the wall at the end of the room. Chatter was subdued and brief. Most of the cabin class passengers had known Julius, if not well. Brooke looked down at her linked hands resting in her lap, aware of Matt sitting behind her. Her earlier anger with him had faded. What she felt now was more disconcerting: disappointment. Her father never gave up on a case. Never. He'd worked as long as it took to solve whatever crimes he was investigating, and his integrity was beyond question. If she'd been born a boy, she would have become that kind of a cop, the kind that Matt was. Or that she'd thought he was. Now she wasn't so sure.

From the organ loft, music began to play, properly subdued and funereal. Brooke could only guess how difficult this was for the Hoffmans. It was bad enough losing a loved one, but without a body to bury it must be even worse. At least she'd had that when her parents' carriage had gone off the road in Newport, onto the rocks, into the treacherous surf off Brenton Point. Even now the thought of it made her shudder.

Matt leaned forward, placing his hand on her shoulder. "You okay?" he asked in a low voice.

"Fine." She flashed him a quick smile, noticing for the first time the strain in his eyes. "This isn't easy for you, either," she said.

He grimaced, his grip tightening on her shoulder. "I don't like funerals," he said, and sat back.

"Neither do I," Brooke said, facing forward. There was more to it than that. Perhaps he really did want to investigate, and had refused only because he'd thought she would mind. After all, it was their honeymoon. The rest of Brooke's anger dissolved. He'd done it for her. Even though she knew quite well what life with a policeman was like, he'd given up this opportunity to solve a murder because of her. The thought touched her, warmed her, and at the same time gave her new resolve. Someone had to find Hoffman's murderer, and the best person to do so was Matt.

The volume of the music increased, and, looking up,

Brooke saw that Adele, supported by Richard Langdon, had come down the stairs into the grand saloon and was taking a seat in the front. At the same time the Reverend Horton, who would be conducting the service, stepped behind the pulpit in the oriel window. Brooke straightened. The question of how to persuade Matt to investigate would have to be put aside for now.

The memorial service was long and tedious, the minister preaching generalities about a man he had never known. Matt was glad when the final hymn was sung. Though he no longer attended Mass regularly, he had been brought up to regard other religions with suspicion, and their services as a danger to his immortal soul. Maybe he was more skeptical now, but he did know that a good Catholic didn't sing "Rock of Ages" or "Amazing Grace"; those were Protestant hymns. "Ave Maria" might be sung at a funeral, but that was about it.

A babble of voices replaced the earlier hush as everyone in the grand saloon rose. "Thank God that's over," he said in Brooke's ear.

She turned. "We have to pay our condolences to Mrs. Hoffman, Matt."

He frowned. "She won't notice if we don't, in all this crowd."

"Matt. We have to. It's the polite thing to do," she said, when he hesitated.

"Oh, all right," he grumbled, and followed behind her as she inched her way past the long tables to where Adele stood, directly under the pulpit. To one side of Adele were her children, and to the other was Langdon, still supporting her. Hoffman's business partner, Matt thought, his interest in the man suddenly keen. What could he have been up to that Hoffman would have suspected him of murder? Or his wife, for that matter. There was an obvious answer to that question, one that he should look into further—if he were investigating the case, which he wasn't. He still thought he was well out of it. Working on the Cliff Walk murders last summer and dealing with society people in an official capacity had been enough for him.

As he and Brooke slowly moved forward, a man across the table from him shifted from one foot to the other. Matt caught his eye. "I didn't think it would be so crowded tonight."

"Free entertainment," the man answered, making both Matt and Brooke look at him again. He looked like any other young society man, dressed in black dinner jacket and tie, and he had the short-haired, clean-shaven look of the men in drawings by Charles Dana Gibson. Matt vaguely remembered seeing him in the smoking room that afternoon, playing cards. "Did you know Hoffman?"

"Not well, no." Matt reached his hand across the table, not caring whether it was polite or not. "Matt Devlin."

"Randall Snow. You were lucky," he said, shaking Matt's hand and releasing it. "He was a mean bastard."

Brooke's head whipped around. "I beg your pardon?"

"Excuse my language—Mrs. Devlin, is it?" Snow's smile was winning, but it didn't reach his eyes, which sharpened as he looked at Brooke. "No. Brooke Cassidy, aren't you?"

"Why, yes. Or I was." Brooke looked at him a little more closely. "Have we met?"

"We have, though I'm not surprised you don't remember. Of course, I've been out of town for a few years."

"Oh." Brooke turned away, inching forward. If her

shoulders rose any higher, they'd be up about her ears, Matt thought. Somehow he gathered she didn't like Mr. Snow.

"Of course, no one here will admit what he was really like," Snow went on. "But you should know, shouldn't you, Mrs. Devlin? Your uncle had dealings with him. But then," his voice grew bitter, "maybe Hoffman was honest with him."

Brooke continued to stare ahead. "What do you mean?" Matt asked.

The man in front of Snow turned to look at him, and then, face set, turned away. Snow made a face at his back. "Oh, nothing, nothing. But, you know, he had a lot of money."

"So?"

"So how do you think he got it? On the backs of others who he ruined."

"Sir." The man in front of Snow had turned again. "You are speaking of someone I knew as a fine gentleman."

"Then you are either a fool, or lucky."

"I beg your pardon!"

"Granted." Snow edged out of line, into the aisle formed between the ends of the tables. "You won't catch me paying my condolences. I'm not sorry he's dead," he said, and pushed through the crowd away from them.

"And good riddance," the man muttered, his gaze catching Matt's. "Never know who you're going to meet traveling nowadays. Used to be only the best people."

"Er, yes." Matt glanced towards the doorway, where Snow had just disappeared. "Who is he?"

"A thoroughly unpleasant fellow. Lost some money in the Panic of '93—well, we all did, didn't we?—and he blamed Julius for it. Caused quite a stir, coming to the Union League Club and just about attacking Julius. As if anyone could have predicted what happened." The man shook his head. "Obviously Snow made out all right, or he wouldn't be on this ship." Shaking his head again, the man turned away.

Matt glanced down at Brooke. "Did you know him?"

"Who? Mr. Snow? Yes, I vaguely remember meeting him." She paused. "He's very bitter, isn't he?"

Matt shrugged. "I suppose I would be, too, if I'd lost all my money."

"I wonder . . ."

"What?" he prompted, when she didn't go on.

"Well . . . if you were investigating Mr. Hoffman's murder, wouldn't you think Mr. Snow has a motive?"

"What, revenge? I don't know, Brooke. Three years is a long time to wait."

" 'Revenge is a dish best served cold.' "

"Showing off your fancy education."

"I mean it, Matt." Her brow was furrowed. "He's happy that Mr. Hoffman is dead."

"True. Which is why I doubt he's the murderer."

"All right," Brooke said, after a moment. "I agree. I wouldn't expect a murderer to gloat about his victim. But still, Matt, he has a motive." The line inched forward again. "So far he's the only person who does."

"Not quite," he muttered, and at that moment there was a commotion at the front of the room, as voices were raised in surprise and anger.

Brooke craned her head. "I can't see. Who is that with Mrs. Hoffman?"

Matt looked past her, and bit back a curse. "Smith," he said, shortly.

"Smith?" Brooke turned. "The ship's detective?"

"Yes, dammit." He should have known Smith would do something like this, approach a possible suspect in such a way. Didn't the man know that to get cooperation from someone like Adele, it was necessary to approach her carefully? Now, with the entire roster of cabin class passengers thronging the saloon, was not the time to ask her what her late husband's last letter had meant.

"Come on," he said, catching Brooke's arm and pulling her past the end of the table, into another row. And another, and another, until they'd reached the relatively uncrowded edge of the room. If he could get there in time, he'd have a chance of stopping Smith. Dammit, why hadn't Captain Wood stayed a little longer to prevent this from happening?

"Matt," Brooke said behind him, sounding breathless, "where are we going?"

"To talk to Mrs. Hoffman. Excuse me." This to people as he plunged into the crowd, Brooke behind him. "I need to stop Smith," he said over his shoulder.

"From doing what?"

"From mentioning that damned letter. Mr. Smith." He tapped the other man on the shoulder.

Smith turned to him, looking at first startled, and then angry. "What do you want?"

"I need to talk to you."

"Not now. I'm busy. Yes, Mrs. Hoffman, I'm sorry to be the one to tell you this." He turned back to Adele. "But it looks as if your husband was murdered."

"Dammit, Smith, this isn't the place for this," Matt said under his breath.

"But who would do such a thing?" Adele's face was pale, but composed. "And why?"

"That's what I was hoping you could tell me, ma'am."

"For God's sake, man." Langdon pushed forward, between Smith and Adele. "Can't you do this some other time? Mrs. Hoffman has just lost her husband."

"No, it's all right, Richard." Adele laid her hand on Langdon's arm, and a look passed between them. "We need to find out about this. What do you want to know, Mr. Smith?"

Matt leaned forward again. "Don't do this here," he said, urgently. "Go to her suite, go to the captain's stateroom, but don't do it here."

"Matt?" Brooke said, and at the same time Smith spoke.

"There's nothing for you to concern yourself with, Devlin. I'm sorry to be the one to tell you about your husband," he went on to Adele, with patent insincerity, "but you'll be glad to know his murderer has been caught."

A gasp made up equally of surprise and fascination went up from the surrounding crowd. "Who?" Adele asked, faintly, her hand at her throat.

Smith grinned. "Edward McCabe."

"Who?" Matt said.

"Edward?" Adele stared at Smith. "Are you sure?"

"Yes, ma'am. So you see, there's nothing for you to worry about."

"Nothing—oh, you don't know! Richard." She turned to Langdon, grasping his arm. "Please. Take me away from here."

"That's right, ma'am." You go and rest now. Everything'll be taken care of, you see?" Smith beamed at Adele as she turned away, looking suddenly older, supported by Langdon. "Everything's settled."

"Who is McCabe?" Matt asked.

Smith's grin broadened as he turned. "Told you I could handle it, didn't I? The case has been solved, and by me, Devlin. No one else."

"Fine," Matt said through gritted teeth. "But who the hell is McCabe?"

"Don't you know?" Smith pretended surprise. "A fine detective like you? Well, I'll tell you." He leaned forward. "Edward McCabe is Julius Hoffman's half-brother."

5

"His brother," Matt said, stunned. "What is he doing on the ship?"

"Don't know everything, do you, detective?" Smith stood with his legs straddled wide and his chest puffed out. "McCabe is a steward in second cabin. Happens I know that he's Hoffman's half-brother. Illegitimate, you see? I make it my business," his smile grew wider, "to know all I can about the crew and the staff."

"What was his motive?"

"I don't think that's your problem, Devlin. Now. I'm a busy man, you see? Don't have time for these questions." He turned, and then stopped, grinning back at Matt. "Enjoy your cruise, detective," he said, with just the slightest bit of stress on the last word, and bounded up the grand staircase, out of the saloon.

The chatter that had been hushed during Smith's confrontation with Adele had broken out again, loud with speculation. Brooke slipped her hand through Matt's elbow, unsurprised to find his arm as hard as a rock. He was furious. "It doesn't matter, Matt," she said, softly.

"Dammit, it does matter. To be shown up by someone like Smith—"

"How could you have known about McCabe? Though, now that I think of it," she frowned, "I do remember hearing rumors about him. Always hushed up, of course. Ladies aren't supposed to know about such things."

"Why didn't you tell me?" Matt said, sharply

"You didn't want to investigate." Brooke's tone was equally sharp. "Or isn't that what you keep insisting?"

Matt looked as if he were about to answer, but at that moment Jack Everett came up beside them. "Bad business, that," he said. As always he was impeccably dressed, in tails and black tie. Hanging on his arm was a very pretty young woman, her hair an improbable construction of golden curls, with the color in her cheeks owing more to art than to nature. What really caught Brooke's attention, though, was the adoring way she looked at Jack. "So it was McCabe."

"You knew about him, too?" Matt said, glaring at him.

"An open secret. Knew he was a steward on a liner, but not this one. Excuse my manners," he went on, as the girl beside him tugged on his arm. "This is Miss Shirley Willis. Miss Willis, Mr. and Mrs. Devlin."

"Pleased to meet ya." Shirley smiled, displaying slightly crooked, but very white, teeth, as she held out her hand. "Golly, this is grand." Her awestruck gaze traveled around the room, taking in the domed chandeliers and the glass ceiling. "Nothing like this in second class."

Brooke sent a startled look towards Jack. "You're traveling in second cabin?"

"Yeah. Jack here said it would be all right for me to come tonight, seeing as how it's a memorial service." An anxious frown puckered her brow. "It is, isn't it?"

"Of course it is," Brooke said, smiling. Though her aunt's connections insured that she was accepted in society, still she knew what it was like to be outside that charmed circle. Who was she to disapprove of anyone else? "Are you enjoying the cruise?"

"Miss Willis is," Jack said, "but I fear her traveling companions weren't so lucky. Good evening," he added to Thelma Osgood and Celia Vaughn as they passed by, the one holding her skirts back and sniffing, the other looking on with curiosity.

"No, they're downright sick," Shirley agreed, apparently unaware of the two women. "Me, I've always had a cast iron stomach. I wouldn't get sick, not on my first chance to see Europe." Her smile broadened. "Only chance, probably. I'm on a Cook's tour. What about you?"

"Oh, no," Brooke said, and again felt that disorienting sense of being from a completely different world. Tours organized by the Thomas Cook company were very definitely for the middle class. "We're on our honeymoon."

"Ooh. That's romantic, isn't it, Jack?"

Jack smiled down at her. "Very romantic, so I think we should leave them alone."

"I suppose so. Gee, what an awful thing to have happen on your honeymoon," Shirley went on. "With the murder, and all. Though I wouldn't have thought," her face puckered, "that Mr. McCabe could have done it."

"Looks like he did." Jack took her arm. "Let's take a turn about the deck, shall we?"

"Ooh, yes, that sounds nice. Nice to meet ya, Mrs. Devlin, Mr. Devlin." Smiling at them, Shirley let Jack lead her away, trailing behind her a cloud of scent that made Brooke's nose wrinkle.

Matt frowned after them. "I'll bet Everett knows more than he's saying."

Brooke looked up at him, startled. "What's that supposed to mean?"

"Nothing. Just that he'd be a good source of information."

"Matt. Are you thinking of investigating, then?"

Matt took her arm, leading her towards the broad staircase that led out of the grand saloon. "What is there to investigate? Smith probably knows what he's doing."

Brooke frowned, both at Matt's tone and at something that had been bothering her. "How did Smith lose his job?"

"In New York?"

"Yes, in New York," she said impatiently, as they reached the top of the stairs and walked out onto the promenade deck. Instantly the wind struck them, making Brooke shiver.

Matt let out a deep, gusty sigh. "There've been a lot of problems with the police and those investigating commissions, Brooke, you know that."

"I do. You know, my father used to do this to my mother."

He turned his head. "What?"

"Not really answer the questions she asked."

"I'm not doing that, Brooke."

"Yes, you are."

He let out his breath again. "It's the job," he said, finally. "No cop wants it to touch his family."

"But you're not on the job, Matt."

"I might as well be," he muttered.

"Don't shut me out. You can talk to me."

Matt ambled over to the railing, resting his forearms on it before answering. "I know I can."

Brooke regarded him for a moment. "What did Smith do?"

"He was a sergeant in charge of two patrols of roundsmen out of a precinct house on the East Side," Matt said, finally. "Powerful position, you know. Almost as powerful as the captain who runs the precinct. Anyway, Smith had a nice scheme going, where he told shop and saloon keepers and others he'd protect them. For a fee, of course."

Brooke was silent for a moment. "That's wrong, Matt."

"Of course it's wrong." He turned away from the railing. "That's why he was fired."

"And now you believe he's really solved Hoffman's death?"

"He's made an arrest."

"Which you don't seem too happy about."

He didn't answer right away. "Smith could be right. When someone's killed, it's usually by someone close. But this doesn't fit with that letter Hoffman left."

"Then investigate it, Matt."

He rubbed his mustache. "We've been over this, Brooke."

"Yes, and I still don't understand."

"I know."

"Do you know what I think?" she said, stopping by the railing. Below them light glittered faintly on the waves.

"What?"

"I think you're just being stubborn. I think that because you said a certain thing, you've decided to stick with it."

"There's more to it than that."

"I don't think so. You're as bullheaded as my father."

"The last time you accused me of that, you called me 'pigheaded'."

"That, too."

"I can't do it, Brooke," he said, after a moment. "Let's let it go at that."

Brooke sighed. "Oh, very well," she said, letting him take her arm again. She was troubled, though, as they strolled towards their suite. She wasn't anymore satisfied with Smith's solution to Hoffman's death than Matt was. They hadn't heard the end of this, she thought, and shivered again.

Friday, April 17

Ambrose Smith was a happy man. Leaning back in the chair in his office, he lit a fat cigar and took a long, luxuriant drag of the fragrant smoke. Ah, now that was good. Only the finest Havana for this, solving the mystery of Hoffman's death. And not such a mystery was it, really, not once he'd remembered the relationship between McCabe and Hoffman. There was motive, too. Here was McCabe, toiling as a second-cabin steward on the same ship where his brother sailed in luxury. Who wouldn't resent that? And since McCabe had no alibi for the time in question, everything was clear. McCabe had done it. A nice, neat solution. No messin' around with cabin class. No cruisin' with an unsolved crime hanging over his head. No, he'd proven himself. Smith took another long puff. In a murder case, look always to those closest to the victim, and that was what he'd done. Him, not Devlin. The thought made him grin.

There was a knock on his door. Smith straightened. "Come in," he called, and a moment later Matt strode in. "Good mornin', detective." Smith leaned back again and took up his cigar. "And what can I do for you?"

"Good morning." Matt sat down, carefully hitching up the legs of his trousers so that they wouldn't wrinkle. He'd thought long and hard about this interview, and he was playing it carefully, wearing the Brooks Brothers suit that effectively distanced him from Smith. Let Smith think he was no threat, that this was a friendly visit only. What its real purpose was, though, not even Matt knew, except that he found McCabe's arrest unsatisfactory. "Congratulations on such a quick arrest," he said, shaking his head when Smith offered him a cigar.

"Thank you." Smith leaned back, blowing out smoke, any suspicions apparently allayed. "As I said, detective. Good police work."

"Huh." Matt reached inside his suit coat and brought out his engraved silver cigarette case, a Christmas present from Brooke, making Smith's eyes narrow just a bit. "What made you think of McCabe?"

"Told you." Smith leaned back again, but his eyes were wary. "I know everything about who is on my ship, you see? And it didn't take me long to remember who McCabe is. In a case like this," he pontificated, waving his cigar for emphasis, "always look to those close to the victim."

Matt nodded. "Sound police work. Tell me. What was his motive?"

"Now that should be obvious to a fancy detective like you, see? McCabe's been complainin' about Hoffman keeping him from getting any money from their father. Ask the other stewards, they'll tell you," he said, as if Matt had protested. "Resentment, revenge, all buildin' up over the years—and then Hoffman comes aboard and McCabe has his chance. He was supposed to be on duty, but no one saw him. Very simple, detective."

"Huh," Matt said again, leaning over to tap the ash off his cigarette into a tin ashtray. "What about the letter Hoffman left?"

"What about it?"

"What does McCabe have to do with that?"

"Nothing. You ask me, detective, that letter doesn't have a thing to do with anything. Fine lady like Mrs. Hoffman wouldn't have anything to do with murder, you see?"

That wasn't what Smith had said yesterday to the captain, but Matt decided to let it pass. "Very likely not," he said, mildly. "But what of the death threats Hoffman received in New York?"

"Death threats?"

"Yes. Threatening letters."

Smith frowned, and then waved his cigar about again. "Probably from McCabe himself. You'll see, detective. After I get through with McCabe, he'll admit to writing them."

Matt's eyes narrowed. "The third degree, you mean," he said, softly.

"Sure, and why not? It works." Smith rose. "If you don't mind, detective, I'm a busy man. And you, I'm sure, have things to do. There's shuffleboard on the promenade deck this mornin'. Or so I understand."

"So there is." Matt rose, not a bit ruffled by Smith's animosity. "I'll be talking with you later. You see?" he said, and ambled out.

His face hardened, though, as he climbed the stairs to the upper decks. He didn't like this arrest, and not just because he hadn't had a hand in it. Too many things had been overlooked: Hoffman's letter; Langdon's whereabouts at the time in question; the alleged death threats. Quite possibly McCabe was the culprit, but Matt doubted it. If he were right, an innocent man would be made to suffer for a crime he didn't commit. Honeymoon or not, Matt couldn't stand by and let that happen.

Matt emerged into bright daylight on the promenade deck, and stood still for a moment to let his eyes adjust. The air was brisk, fresh; at the outer edges of the deck stylishly garbed people promenaded, while others sat farther in on steamer chairs, enjoying the view. At loose ends, Matt wandered over to the railing, reaching inside his coat for another cigarette. With the case officially solved, there was nothing for him to do, except to find Brooke and continue with their honeymoon. The thought should have been appealing, but it wasn't. For here, away from Brooke, away from the captain and any outside pressures, he could admit that he would have liked to solve the case. Why he hadn't agreed to do so was a puzzle, even to him, except for his reluctance to become involved in such a way with society people. The last time he had, both he and Brooke had paid for it.

Glancing briefly to the side, he saw another passenger, solitary like him, leaning his arms on the railing and gazing sightlessly at the restless waves below. It took him a moment to recognize the man, but once he did his reactions were swift and ingrained. "Good morning, Mr. Langdon," he said, quietly moving to the man's side.

Langdon started. "What? Oh, good morning—Mr. Devlin, is it?"

"Yes. I'm not sure we were ever introduced," Matt went on smoothly, thankful for the first time that in his new life he had learned, not only the niceties of behavior, but how to circumvent them, "but considering the circumstances . . ."

"Yes," Langdon said, after a moment. "The circumstances have been—difficult."

"Huh." Matt contemplated the sea. "How is Mrs. Hoffman this morning?"

"Holding up quite well, all things considered."

"It must be difficult for her, knowing who killed her husband, but a relief, too."

Langdon shot him a look. "Is this an interrogation, sir?"

"I'm not on the case." Matt took out his cigarette case. "Cigarette, sir?"

Langdon hesitated for the barest moment, and then nodded. "Thank you. My apologies, but I'm not quite myself just yet."

"Understandable." For a moment the two men stood in silence, smoking. "You're satisfied with the arrest?"

Langdon's shoulders twitched. "Of course. McCabe had reason, and he certainly could have pushed Julius—could have done it."

Matt glanced at him. "You know McCabe, then?"

"I've met him. He came into the office in New York a few times."

"Oh?" Matt took a drag on his cigarette. "Then he was friendly with his brother?"

"I wouldn't say friendly, no—why are you asking these questions if you're not on the case?"

Matt shook his head. "Sorry. Professional curiosity."

"Well, I don't think there's anything to be curious about. McCabe's been arrested, and that's that." Langdon tossed his cigarette into the sea. "If you'll excuse me, sir, I think I'll see how Mrs. Hoffman is doing."

"Of course." Matt turned away from the railing with him. "Since there's been an arrest, then, it doesn't really matter that no one knows where you were when Hoffman went overboard."

Langdon stopped. "I was in my room," he said, but his eyes had narrowed.

"Of course," Matt said again. "I won't keep you, sir. Good day."

Langdon stared at him a moment, and then nodded. "Good day," he said, and, turning, stalked away.

Left alone, Matt turned back to the railing. Interesting, the way Langdon had reacted to the question of where he had been the night of Hoffman's death. Maybe he had been in his stateroom, as he claimed; maybe not. And maybe he didn't have anything to do with Hoffman's death, but he was hiding something. Matt would stake his professional reputation on it.

And that meant that this wasn't finished, he thought, throwing his cigarette into the sea and at last turning from the railing. It meant that there was more to the case than had yet been discovered, with only four days left of the voyage. It meant, God help him, that he might have to get involved. Because if McCabe hadn't killed Hoffman, then somewhere on this ship a killer was running loose.

There was shuffleboard on the promenade deck, as Smith had mockingly pointed out. After luncheon had been served in the grand saloon, the sunlight streaming in through the high glass ceiling making it a far cheerier place than it had been the night before, Matt and Brooke took part in a game, laughing and trying to outmaneuver each other to win. Yet Matt's heart hadn't been in it, Brooke thought later that afternoon, when the game was over and he had gone to the gentleman's smoking room, ostensibly to get some cigarettes. More likely he'd gone to discuss Hoffman's death, a topic that had yet to pall on anyone. It was something she rather resented. Among the women, all she heard was gossip. But in the men's sanctorum, who knew what kind of information was available?

Frowning, Brooke strode along, wishing not for the first time that things were different, that a woman could be allowed to have as much say in the world's affairs as a man. Wishing she, too, could detect crimes, as Matt did. Yet it wasn't his fault that things were as they were. True, he didn't approve of her desire to solve this case; yet he'd shared any and all information with her, which was more than her father had ever done with her mother. She supposed she would have to be content with that.

"Mrs. Devlin," a voice said as Brooke neared her suite. "May I talk with you?"

Brooke turned. There, just inside a passageway leading to several suites, as if she were hiding, was Julia Hoffman. She wore a gray dress trimmed with mauve piping at the collar and cuffs, apparently the closest thing she had to mourning. "Of course, Miss Hoffman. Will you walk with me to my suite?" she added, aware that people nearby were watching them.

"All right." Julia's shoulders hunched as she left the shelter of the deck housing, as if to ward off the stares that must, Brooke thought, feel to her like blows. Poor girl. She was very young, and she'd just lost her father. Brooke remembered too well how that felt.

"I'm terribly sorry about your father," Brooke said, gently. "I didn't know him well, but he seemed to be a good man."

"Oh, he was." Julia's face brightened. "And a good father, especially when I was little. Of course, later—"

"Yes?" Brooke prompted.

"Well, one grows up, doesn't one?" Julia hunched her shoulders again. "At least, that's what Mother tells me."

Brooke frowned. "I don't understand."

"No, you were left in peace to marry someone on your own."

"Almost." Brooke smiled. "My aunt would really have preferred someone else."

"But you chose who you wanted. I admire you for that, Mrs. Devlin," she said, earnestly. "I know there's been a lot of talk about your marriage, but you chose the man you wanted and you didn't let anyone stop you."

Brooke glanced at her. "But you're about to make a wonderful match, Julia. Aren't you?"

"I suppose." Her shoulders hunched again. "He lives in an actual castle and he's very handsome and the title goes back generations. There's no money, of course. That's why he agreed to marry me. After all, I'm only an American."

"Do you love him?" Brooke asked, wondering what this was all about.

"I don't know. I only met him three times."

"Three times!" Brooke stopped short. "But that's terrible. How could your parents allow such a thing?"

"They like him. That is, Mother does."

"And your father seemed proud of you," she mused, walking again.

"He didn't know how I felt. How could he? He was old." Julia's voice was filled with youthful scorn. "Besides, it's not as if he and Mother married for love."

Brooke stopped again. It was one thing being a confidante to a troubled girl, but this was too much. "Why are you telling me this?"

Julia had the grace to look ashamed. "I don't know. I—forget what I said, please? I shouldn't have said anything like that about my parents."

"No." Even if it were true. And remembering how Adele had treated her husband, Brooke suspected that it was. That led her back to what Matt had learned from the captain, about the letter Hoffman had left. "Julia, what did you want to see me about?"

"I wanted . . ." Julia stopped, gripping the polished teak railing, suddenly looking very young. "You helped solve the Cliff Walk killings last summer, didn't you?"

"Not really," Brooke said, startled. Few people knew how much of a role she had played in solving the killings. How had this girl found out? "I was concerned, so I asked questions, but it was Matt—my husband—who really solved them."

"But you helped. Please, Mrs. Devlin." Julia grasped her hands. "Will you help now?"

Brooke gently freed her hands. "The case is over, Julia. Mr. Smith has—"

"But he's awful!" Julia wailed. "He's coarse and rude and I know that Uncle Edward didn't do it, I just know it!"

"You know Mr. McCabe?" Brooke said, startled.

"I—" Julia glanced quickly around the deck, though no one was close enough to overhear. "Please don't tell my mother, but, yes, I do know him. Father saw to that."

"He did?"

"Oh, yes. They were quite close. And Uncle Edward really is a very nice man. I tried to get in to visit him, but Mr. Smith wouldn't let me."

"Jail is an unpleasant place, Julia," Brooke said, gently.

"I don't care! He's my uncle, and no one else seems to care about him. I know he didn't do it, Mrs. Devlin, I just know it. Can't you tell your husband that?"

"What do you think happened, then?"

"I don't know! Please, Mrs. Devlin." She caught at Brooke's arm. "I'm terribly worried. I know my father didn't kill himself, he couldn't have, but I also know my mother didn't kill him."

It was Brooke's turn to stop, looking out to sea, and feeling old beyond her years. Of course Julia would think that; to believe anything else of one's parents would be impossible. But Brooke knew that too often in such a situation a murder victim's nearest and dearest were the best suspects. Brooke seriously doubted that Adele had killed her husband; she looked too cool for the kind of passions that might inspire murder. Since Julia didn't believe

McCabe to be the murderer, however, she might always wonder about Adele's role in her father's death. "I can't help you, Julia." She made her voice as gentle as possible. "This is different from last summer. My husband has no official standing here."

"But he could figure it out, I know he could! And you could help him! Oh, please, Mrs. Devlin." Julia grabbed her hands again. "If you don't help, I don't know who will."

"I'm sorry, Julia." Feeling absolutely wretched, she freed herself from Julia's grasp. "I wish I could do something, but I can't."

"But—"

"I can't," Brooke said, and turned away, walking as quickly as she could. She couldn't help, she told herself again. Not only did Matt have no official standing, because of his stubbornness, but the case had been solved, no matter how unsatisfactorily. Julia would have to learn to live with that. No matter how much Brooke might wish to help, she couldn't.

Or, could she? Hand on her door handle, she stopped, frowning. Something she had heard about McCabe, something someone had said—now, what was it? Something that at the time had caught her attention, but that had been superseded by other things. Had it been said this morning, or last night, by Smith or by Jack, or—oh! She remembered. Shirley Willis, Jack's companion, had expressed surprise at McCabe's arrest, in a way that implied she knew the man. If that were so, there might very well be other things she knew, as well.

Squaring her shoulders, Brooke turned away from the door and set off aft, to the stern of the ship. There was

more to McCabe's arrest than met the eye. She needed to
know what.

The promenade deck in the stern of the ship was reserved exclusively for the use of second cabin passengers.
There was no dividing line, nothing other than a sign to
indicate this, and yet as soon as Brooke reached this part
of the ship she felt a difference. It had to do with appearances, with the fact that her walking ensemble of sky blue
twill had come from one of New York's best dressmakers,
while all about her people wore clothing that was definitely off the rack. It had to do with voices that were less
than cultured and spoke with the distinctive accents of
Brooklyn or New Jersey. Mostly, though, it had to do
with how she herself felt. A few years ago, before her parents' deaths, she might very well have traveled among
these people, and felt perfectly at home. Now she was well
aware that she didn't belong here. Her life was different;
she didn't have to toil for a living, and she could afford to
cross the Atlantic in luxury. Though not so very long ago
she had felt equally ill at ease among society, she now realized how much she had changed.

I have become a snob, she thought, eyes searching past the
people playing shuttlecock or standing about in groups,
talking, for a particular person. She had been noticed;
more than one person was eyeing her frankly, apprais-
ingly, making her even more uncomfortable. Still, she
walked across the deck with purpose, head held high, as
she had when first she entered society, pretending not to
notice those around her. She'd come here for a reason,
and she wasn't about to leave. Not yet. But her quarry
wasn't among the laughing group of people in the shuttlecock court, or those leaning on shuffleboard paddles.

Nor was she sitting on a steamer chair, or leaning on the railing, studying the ship's wake. It meant, Brooke thought, holding her head even higher, that she'd have to go below, to brave the second cabin staterooms.

"Mrs. Devlin," a voice said behind her, and Brooke turned to see Shirley Willis approaching her, smiling broadly. "What are you doing here?"

"Hello, Miss Willis." Brooke returned the smile with one that was made up of equal parts relief and pleasure. "I wonder if I might have a word with you?"

The buzz of conversation in the grand saloon was loud and unintelligible, as people discussed the sighting of dolphins that afternoon, and the dramatic reading planned for the evening's entertainment. The main topic, though, was still Julius Hoffman's murder. Everyone was relieved that the culprit had been caught, and that there was not, apparently, any danger to themselves. Most also were thrilled at the scandal behind the arrest.

Brooke's face was serene as she glided to her seat at the dining room table, Matt behind her, but inside her thoughts were racing. Matt had returned to their suite barely in time to dress for dinner, and if he'd learned anything beyond what everyone already knew he hadn't told her. Because of that, she had decided not to tell him about her afternoon's activities. Childish, she knew, but she was tired of being treated as a lesser partner by him. She also didn't think he'd be too happy when he found out what she'd learned.

She was reaching for her menu when a strange thing happened. As if a switch had been thrown, all conversa-

tion ceased, leaving only the clanking of cutlery and china.
Startled, Brooke turned to see what had caused this state
of affairs, and saw a woman descending the grand staircase. It was Adele Hoffman, entering the saloon on Richard Langdon's arm.

"Good heavens," she murmured. The buzz of conversation began again and crescendoed as Adele, dressed in
black, swept down the remaining stairs and into the saloon, followed by her children. Her head was high, her
bearing regal, and if she realized that every eye in the room
was on her, she gave no sign. "She has courage."

"Or nerve." Matt watched Adele as she made her way
across the room to their table. Like the other men, he rose
as she reached her seat, and he spoke politely to her children. There was still a chair empty, however, a continuing
reminder of just what had happened two nights ago.

"Good evening, Adele." Brooke reached her fingers
across the table. "How nice to see you here again."

"Thank you," Adele said coolly, and looked to the side
as Richard Langdon slipped into the chair that had once
been occupied by Julius Hoffman. Brooke and Matt
glanced at each other, stunned. "I decided that it was time
we returned to normal. Julius is gone, and we must accept
the fact. And his murderer has been caught."

Julia, sitting beside Adele, muttered something, making
Adele glance at her sharply. "You are feeling well?"
Brooke asked after a moment. This was extraordinary behavior for someone like Adele, who usually observed all
the proprieties. She had been widowed so very recently.

"Quite well, thank you. Chauncey, do not slouch."

"Oh, Ma," her son protested, but he straightened,
slanting a resentful glance at Richard.

"Well, I don't think we should be here," Julia said, drawing Adele's attention. "It's disrespectful to Father."

"He would want us to go on."

"You mean you want us to go on."

"Julia, I will not countenance such a tone from you."

"You know it's not right, Mother. Everyone is staring at us and talking. And—"

"Julia." Richard's deep voice broke in as he leaned past Adele. "Your mother deserves respect. Apologize to her."

"Why? You're not my father, Richard."

"Julia! If everyone is looking at us it is because of you," Adele hissed.

"I don't care!" Julia's voice rose. "I know you didn't care about Daddy, but I do! And just because they think they've arrested someone doesn't mean this is over."

"Think?" Brooke put in, before either Adele or Richard could react. Julia's behavior was appalling, and everyone was indeed staring, and yet Brooke suspected that perhaps they were hearing some truth from the Hoffman family. "Why do you say that, Julia?"

Julia looked directly at her. "Because my uncle didn't do it, Mrs. Devlin. I told you that."

"That man is not your uncle," Adele snapped.

"I think this probably wasn't a good idea, Adele," Richard said, beginning to rise,

Adele's hand shot out to catch his arm, her knuckles white with strain. "Sit down."

"Listen, Adele, be reasonable—"

"Don't talk like that to me!" The ice queen was blazing; two spots of color warmed her cheeks, and her voice was hot with anger. "You aren't part of this family, Richard, and neither is that dreadful McCabe. And I, for one, would like to clear that up." Her eyes flicked over the table, and the passengers who had been listening with fascination quickly turned back to their menus. "Right here, so people will hear it right."

"Good heavens," Brooke murmured to Matt.

"She's got guts," he answered, in an equally quiet voice. "I'll give her that."

"Yes. Matt, there's something I should tell you—"

"That man is not part of our family," Adele repeated, glaring at Julia. "He may be your father's brother—and I am not even certain of that!—but your father in no way acknowledged him. Nor do I, and nor will you. And that is all I have to say on the matter."

"But, Mother," Julia protested.

"Enough, Julia! I have said all I am going to. We will have no contact with that man."

"I already have." Julia tossed her head and glared back at Adele. "And I will, again, if I'm allowed to visit him."

Adele's eyes blazed, revealing the volcanic passions that hid beneath her layer of ice. "When did you see that man?" she demanded.

"Adele." Richard's voice was urgent as he clasped his hand about her arm. "This isn't the time or the place—"

"You're not my husband yet, Richard," she snapped, thus making several of her unwilling spectators turn to each other in surprise. "I'll deal with my children as I please. When did you see that—that man?"

Julia tossed her head again. "I've seen him several times, Mother, with Father, and you didn't know it, did you?"

"You know, I'd like to see him, too," Chauncey piped up.

"Be quiet, Chauncey!" Julia and Adele both said, at almost the same time.

Chauncey's face grew red. "I will not. He's my family, too."

"That's right." Julia nodded. "And he didn't do it, Mother. He didn't kill Daddy."

"Why do you say that, Miss Hoffman?" Matt put in. His voice was mild, but there was a sharpness in his eyes that alerted Brooke.

Julia thrust her chin out. "Because I know him. He wouldn't do it. And when I visit him I'll tell him so."

"Matt," Brooke tugged on his sleeve. "There's something I have to tell you. She's right, he didn't do it—"

"I forbid you to do any such thing," Adele declared, pounding her fist on the table in a most unladylike manner. "I will lock you in your room if I have to. To think of you consorting with your father's murderer—"

"But he didn't do it," Brooke said, effectively stopping all conversation. All eyes at the table turned to her.

Matt was the first to recover. "How do you know?" he asked, the question of one investigator to another.

"I asked some questions. In second cabin."

He frowned. "When?"

"This afternoon." She took a deep breath. "Mr. McCabe couldn't have murdered Mr. Hoffman." She gave Matt a quick, apologetic smile, knowing he would not be pleased at what she was about to say. "I found the woman he was with that night."

6

Matt stalked back and forth in the sitting room of their suite. "Why didn't you tell me?" he demanded, yet again.

"Why wouldn't you talk to me?" Brooke retorted. "You know I can help with this case."

"We are not involved in this. Dammit, Brooke." He rounded on her. "You made me look like a fool."

"That wasn't my intention, Matt."

"Well, that was how I felt." He ran a hand over his hair, his anger apparently fading. "I don't seem to be able to stop you asking questions—"

"Are you going to tell me you haven't been doing the same?"

"—But I'd like you to promise me, no more surprises like tonight's."

Brooke's eyes lit up, in spite of her annoyance at his high-handedness. "It was worth it, though, wasn't it? Did you see everyone's face?"

"It's not funny," Matt said, but he grinned as he slipped

his arm about her waist, leading her across to the sofa. "Now whatever made me believe that society people know how to behave in public?"

"That was amazing." Brooke settled next to him on the sofa, her knees drawn up under her, her finger twirling the strand of hair that had, as usual, come loose from her chignon. "Adele Hoffman, of all people, to act in such a way! It must be all the strain."

"Probably." He turned to her. "You know what it means, don't you? If McCabe is innocent, we're back where we started."

"Mm. Adele is a suspect again." She rested her head against his shoulder. "And after tonight I certainly think she's capable of it. Matt."

"Yes?"

"You do know Mr. Smith won't be able to solve this?"

Matt leaned forward, his face stony. "It's not my problem, Brooke."

"Not your problem!"

"It's not. But, tell me. How did you find this woman? The one that McCabe was with."

"Well." She took a deep breath. "It occurred to me that if anyone could say where McCabe was, they'd be in second cabin."

"I imagine that even Smith thought of that."

"Ah, but I had a secret weapon. Shirley Willis."

Matt stared at her for a moment, and then put back his head and laughed. "Do you mean Everett's friend?"

"Yes. She really is very nice, Matt."

"I don't doubt it."

"Lord, I sound like such a snob, don't I?" she said, ruefully. "Do you know, she chews gum? And cracks it."

Brooke made a face. "But she's very warmhearted, and more than that."

"What?"

"She's one of those people who seem to know everything that's going on."

Comprehension dawned on Matt's face. "So she knows things others might not."

"Yes. Such as a stewardess having a romance with a steward."

"For God's sake." He stared at her. "Smith must be incompetent if he didn't find that out."

"Maybe not. Maybe it's because he's a man, Matt," she said, gently, for she suspected that he was thinking he would have had better results. But he, too, was male, and very obviously police. He would have to realize on his own, however, that women could be valuable in detective work. "Shirley was thrilled that I asked for her help. I didn't even need to ask her anything specific. She told me right away that she'd seen her stewardess with McCabe."

"When?"

"At the beginning of the voyage. Shirley was exploring since her friends were sick—really, she's quite resourceful—and she saw McCabe and the stewardess—her name is Ellen Reilly, by the way—in a service corridor. They jumped apart when they saw her, and so of course that made her suspicious.

Matt stared at Brooke. "Of course."

"Shirley rang for Ellen," Brooke went on, as if unaware of Matt's astonishment. "She didn't want to talk right away—apparently the company has rules about employees and this kind of thing. She was afraid of losing her job, but when I pointed out to her what could happen to

McCabe, she broke down. Poor girl." Brooke's face sobered. "They've been seeing each other for some time, even talked about marriage. She's been very upset." Brooke turned to him. "I hope you won't be too hard on her when you question her."

"I'm not questioning her, Brooke."

"No?"

"No."

"Then, poor girl. I can't think what Smith will ask her."

"Huh." Matt rubbed a finger across his mustache. "Did she definitely say she was with McCabe at the important times?"

"Yes, Matt. You see, Shirley rang for Ellen, and Ellen didn't answer."

"McCabe wasn't anywhere around, either," he muttered. "At least, so Smith says. This explains that, if she's telling the truth."

"Oh, I think she is, Matt. Why would she lie?"

"You'd be surprised," he said, rising. Brooke made a face at his back, but decided to let the remark pass. "All right." He shrugged into his dinner jacket, crumpled from having been tossed over a chair. "I'll do what I can about this."

"Where are you going?"

"To talk to the captain. And Smith." His grin was wicked. "I'm going to enjoy seeing his face when I tell him he's arrested the wrong man." Miming a kiss, he went out, closing the door behind him.

"You're welcome," Brooke muttered, leaning back against the sofa, but she smiled. A wry smile, but still, a smile. Eventually Matt would acknowledge her help. She couldn't expect him to change overnight; couldn't expect him immediately to see her as a partner, a helpmeet, rather than a helpless female to be cosseted and sheltered. But he'd come around. Her smile changed, grew as wicked as his had been. Matt had some surprises in store for him. She wasn't going to let him keep her out of this.

This time it was Matt who called the meeting in the captain's stateroom, after finding Ellen Reilly and persuading her to speak the truth at last. Smith roared with indignation at the news of McCabe's alibi. This was his arrest, he yelled, storming about the captain's stateroom, and he wasn't going to let some hick detective take it away from him, you see? Captain Wood looked stunned, but, after listening to Ellen Reilly's tearful testimony, even he had to admit that the case was not solved, after all. Reluctantly he gave orders for McCabe to be released, and for the investigation to be reopened. Matt left the stateroom with a wicked grin on his face. Maybe he wasn't in charge, but he had just prevented an innocent man being blamed for a crime he hadn't committed. But now what did he do? Brooke was more correct than she knew. He couldn't let this pass.

Ahead of him a man ambled along the deck, his clothing impeccable and his posture just short of a slouch. Jack Everett, not as detached as he liked to appear. With the evening's entertainment apparently over, he had a woman on either side. It took Matt a moment to realize that Brooke was one of them, and that, unaccountably, made his temper rise.

"Brooke," he said, and she turned. "Evening, Everett. Miss Willis."

"Matt." Brooke freed herself from Everett's arm and came to him. "Did things work out?"

"Yes. McCabe will be freed immediately."

"And Miss Reilly won't lose her position?"

"I don't imagine so," Matt said, surprised. "At least, nothing was said.

"Good," Shirley put in. "She was scared, I don't mind telling you that, even though she knew she was doing the right thing. Be a shame if she got punished for it."

"Well, I don't know what will happen. Do you have time for a cigarette, Everett?"

Surprise showed on Jack's face. "Certainly. Of course, we can't leave the ladies alone."

"Brooke and Miss Willis will be all right. Won't you?"

Brooke returned his look, her gaze annoyed. "Of course we will. If Miss Willis doesn't mind."

"Oh, do call me Shirley," she said, breezily. "You boys run along. We'll keep each other company. Now. I just know we're going to be good friends. . . ."

Jack's shoulders were shaking with mirth as he and Matt turned away, walking back towards the smoking room. "Think Brooke will forgive you?"

"Brooke's a good sort," Matt said, opening the door to the smoking room, though he knew he'd have to face her anger when he returned to the suite. Still, he couldn't let this opportunity pass by. Everett possibly had valuable information about the people involved in this case.

The smoking room, on the saloon deck in the aft section of the ship, was a clubby, smoky room, with scarlet leather chairs and booths, a long, polished bar, and brass spittoons placed strategically about the floor. Several men in evening dress stood at the bar, while others lounged about, talking. Still others, Randall Snow included, had got up a card game, sitting at a table under a green-shaded lamp. Matt's gaze sharpened on him and he hesitated, but then, shrugging, led Jack to a table in the back corner, for privacy. He wasn't supposed to be doing any investigating. "Brooke might be mad, but she won't hold it against me."

"Especially not when you're at work."

Matt's eyebrows rose slightly as he extended his silver cigarette case to the other man. He felt a sudden, sharp pang of nostalgia for the battered packets he used to carry, with their colorful trade cards advertising patent nostrums or baseball players. "What makes you think that?"

"Hard not to, after that scene with Adele." Jack lit his cigarette from his own lighter and then leaned back, stretching out his legs and blowing out a cloud of bluish-gray smoke. "So. What is it you want to discuss? Surely not the voyage." He grinned. "You don't look as if you're enjoying crossing the ditch too much."

"The ditch." Matt lit his cigarette, his tone wry. "Trust the wealthy to reduce the Atlantic to something small."

"Sounds like prejudice, detective."

"No. Observation."

Both men were silent as a waiter came over with their drinks of whiskey and soda. "And what have you observed lately? That something strange is going on," he added, when Matt didn't answer right away. "I don't know what happened to Hoffman, by the way."

"I didn't think you did." Matt eyed him with wary respect. This was not a man to underestimate. "How long have you known Brooke?" he asked, surprising himself.

"Years." Jack took a long drag on the cigarette. "Since she came to live with her uncle. But don't worry." He looked directly at Matt. "She wouldn't have me." One corner of his mouth turned up in a half smile. "Says I'm too lazy. She's right, of course. But then, I can afford to be."

"That's not what I hear." Matt leaned back, too, concentrating on his own cigarette as if it were all that mattered. "That you're lazy, I mean."

"But I am, old man. My father left me disgustingly well off. Stinking rich, as a matter of fact. Couldn't spend it all if I tried." He reached for a crystal ashtray. "Now. What did you want to ask me?"

Matt eyed him for a moment. In his months on the job he'd heard of Jack Everett. Quietly and without publicity, he worked in the settlement houses in New York's slums, helping people who lived in the most wretched of conditions better their lot. His special skill was building; Matt had heard that Jack had built more than one house in his time, and then given it away. Not the indolent socialite he appeared, not by a long shot. And not stupid. To Matt's surprise, he was a likeable man. "How well did you know the Hoffmans?" he asked, deciding to be blunt. He needed information, of the sort neither Smith nor Brooke, for all her resources, could find. Information that would be common knowledge among the gentlemen gathered in the smoking room, but that no one would tell him.

Jack studied the tip of his cigarette. "Looking into Hoffman's death?"

"No. At least—no. But I can't help being curious."

"Mm." Jack continued to regard his cigarette, before taking another puff. "What makes you think I know anything?"

"I have a feeling you don't miss much, Mr. Everett."

"It's Jack. No, I suppose I don't. All right." He stubbed the cigarette out and leaned forward, the intensity of his gaze belying his earlier relaxation. "Everyone knows the Hoffmans. Where do you want me to start?"

"Anywhere. From the beginning."

"The beginning." Jack lit another cigarette and leaned back. "All right. Well, the beginning is Hoffman's father, old Karl. Came to America from Bavaria before the Civil War, couldn't speak a word of English, but managed to do pretty well for himself."

"Oh?"

"Mm. War profiteering is the same in any language, you know. Supply guns to both sides, and you make a fortune."

Matt's face darkened. "My uncle died in that war."

"A lot of men did. Anyway, Karl got rich, rich enough to send his son to the best schools, rich enough to try to buy his way into society. That's when the trouble started. The first trouble," he amended.

"What kind of trouble?"

"Seems Karl kept a mistress and had a son by her."

"McCabe?"

"Yes. Nothing really unusual in it, of course, except she got greedy. Sued him for paternity. Lost, of course, but you can imagine the effect it had."

Matt nodded. "Yes."

"That ended all of Karl's chances to get into society. He still had ambitions for his son, though, and still had the money to finance him. First thing was to get him married properly, and that's where Adele comes in. Adele Schuyler."

"Old New York family?"

"Going back to the patroons," Jack said, referring to the Dutch who had originally settled New York. "No money, though. Of course."

"So you're saying that Adele married Julius for money."

"All arranged by their parents, of course. Isn't that how it's done?"

Matt took a deep drag on his cigarette. "Not where I come from, no."

"Not my idea of an ideal marriage, either. But then, I can afford my odd notions." He groped for his cigarette case and then put it back in his inside coat pocket. "Smoking too much lately. Old Karl conveniently died a few years later. Conveniently for Julius, that is. Not like his father at all, or so I've been told, except for one thing."

"And that is?"

"Making money. Better at it, actually. His firm's one of the biggest dealing with railroads in New York. One of the best, too." He frowned. "Until recently, that is."

Matt leaned forward, alert. "What happened recently?"

Jack's frown deepened. "Hard to say exactly, but there've been rumors of problems. Rumors that things aren't as solid as they seem, that Hoffman and Langdon have been fighting. There's even talk that money's missing."

"Yet they came on this ship together and were talking about starting a London office."

"True."

"Who would have access to the money?"

Jack raised his glass in a mock toast. "Now you're catching on. No one except the two partners, of course."

"Which would give either one a motive for murder," Matt said, more to himself than to the other man.

"Quite. You should also know that Adele and Richard are supposed to be close." He withdrew his cigarette case again and then, with the little grimace that passed for a shrug, opened it. "Quite close."

"I see." Matt nodded. After the incidents of the last few days, that was hardly a surprise. "Tell me. Have there been any rumors of a divorce lately?"

It was Jack's turn to raise his eyebrows in surprise. "How did you know that?"

"Guesswork. Am I right?"

"I'd heard something, yes, a few months back." Jack's gaze was sharp now. "The rumor is that Adele told one of her friends that if Alva Vanderbilt could leave her husband and then marry Oliver Belmont, she could do the same. But that was months ago."

"Nothing more since?"

"No." He leaned forward. "Can't see Julius agreeing, if you want to know. He doted on Adele."

"And she?"

"Saw him as her income and nothing more."

Matt's mouth tightened. He had rather liked Julius during their brief acquaintance, and now he felt some pity for him. It had to have been hard, knowing his wife preferred another man. Yet, in refusing her wishes, had he set in motion the events that ultimately led to his death? Was that why he had left that cryptic letter in the ship's safe? "Interesting. Not sure what it means, but interesting. Anything else?"

Jack looked up. "Did Brooke tell you about the death threats?"

"Yes." Matt toyed with the end of his cigarette, and then tamped it out. "What do you make of them?"

Jack's shoulders lifted in an infinitesimal shrug, and then, frowning, he adjusted the set of his lapels. "I have no idea. If anyone knows what they mean, it's Langdon."

"Unless he wrote them," Matt said, again to himself.

"Like that, is it?" Jack asked, giving him a sharp look.

"Maybe."

"Well, then." Jack spoke softly, stopping Matt in the act of rising. "If that's the way the wind is blowing, maybe there's something else you should know."

"Such as?"

"Do you know Gregory Tate?"

"I've seen him. Hoffman's secretary, correct?"

"And his assistant. And, until Julia's engagement, in line to marry her."

"Really." Matt slowly sat back down. "Doesn't seem like reason enough to kill someone."

"Reason, no. Cause for resentment, yes. Tate's an ambitious young man. Marrying the boss's daughter would do him good. Except . . ."

"Except?"

"Except that I'd heard he was having trouble with Hoffman. All rumors, of course, but he didn't seem to think he was advancing the way he should. Apparently Julius promised things he didn't deliver. Told Tate he'd make him a broker, and then never went through with it."

"Yet Tate stayed with him."

"Don't know how long he would have lasted. He's been seen at other investing houses and banks. Well, one has to wonder why, doesn't one?"

"Yes, one does—yes, there's something there," Matt

said, catching himself. If he stayed much longer, he'd sound exactly like Everett.

"Not anymore, though. Langdon will need him, to keep the business running."

Matt sat back, thoughtful. "So. You're telling me he could have had a motive for wanting Hoffman out of the way."

"No such thing." Everett appeared shocked. "Not if he planned on working elsewhere."

"You'd be surprised what people have killed for," Matt said, rising at last and stubbing out his cigarette. "Thank you for the information. I should go rescue Brooke."

The corner of Jack's mouth tilted up again as he ambled beside Matt, out of the smoking room. "Shirley's a good kid. Smart, too, or I wouldn't have left her alone." His face sobered. "Not done, you know, socializing with someone from second class."

"I don't see why not." Matt held out his hand as they climbed the stairs leading to the promenade deck. "Thanks. You've given me a lot to think about. I appreciate it."

"Glad to help," Jack said, and, shaking Matt's hand, went back inside.

Smith stomped along the deck, scowling, his rolling gait automatically adjusting to the roll of the ship. Devlin thought he could just come in and take over, did he? Well, he had something to learn. This was Ambrose's ship, his, and he wasn't going to let anyone interfere in the best case he'd had yet. Wasn't much for him to do aboard ship, at least, not in first class. Steerage was another matter, but the problems there were easy to solve. Knock a few heads together, and usually that would be the end of it. This was different, though. This kind of thing, a nice, juicy murder, could be just what was needed to make the muckymucks in New York sit up and take notice. And maybe then they'd admit that they'd made a mistake, forcing him to resign as they had.

He didn't hesitate when he reached the door to the suite around the corner from the Devlins, but instead raised a meaty fist and pounded on it. No matter that it was late; no matter that the people inside had had a trying day. Murder waited for no man, he told himself sententiously.

"Yes?" a woman whispered, peering around the edge of the door. The maid, by the looks of things.

"I want to see your mistress," he said, and pushed the door open before she could react.

"But, m'sieur," she protested, reeling back from the door. "Madame is asleep. You come back tomorrow, *non?*

"No." He rounded on her. "I want to speak to her, toot de sweet. Get it?"

"Claudette, what is it—oh, it's you." Adele appeared in the bedroom doorway. Though she was clad for the night in a nightgown and wrapper, still she looked impeccable, glacial.

"Oh, madame, I tried to stop him, but he just came in—"

"It's all right, Claudette." Adele came into the sitting room and sat down. "Please find Mr. Langdon for me. He should be in his room."

"Maybe," Smith said, sitting down without being invited, as the maid fled the suite.

"What does that mean?"

"Means Mr. Langdon has a habit of not being there when he's needed." Langdon would be there, however. Since McCabe's arrest had gone bad Smith had set a man to watch both Langdon and the Hoffmans, very discreetly. Thus he was aware of their every movement. A smart cop was prepared, he thought, brandishing a cigar. "Mind if I smoke?"

"Yes, I do," Adele said, but to no avail, as he lit the cigar anyway. Her nose wrinkled in distaste. "Really, Mr. Smith, this is rude of you. Couldn't you have waited until morning?"

Smith blew out a thin stream of smoke, making her nose wrinkle again. "Don't you want to see your husband's murder solved, Mrs. Hoffman?"

"Yes, of course I do." The look she gave him was filled with icy disdain. "Now that you've let the obvious suspect go."

"I'll keep my eye on him," Smith said, grimly. "Now. I want some answers from you."

"What is that stench—oh." Richard stepped into the suite, frowning at Smith. "What do you want?"

"Evening." Smith didn't rise. "Interesting that you come running when she calls."

"Mrs. Hoffman needs someone to rely on." Richard sat beside Adele at the sofa. "Are you all right?" he asked her. "I can have the captain make him leave—"

"No." Her voice was firm. "We need to face this."

Richard looked at her for a moment, and then sighed. "I suppose it's inevitable." He faced Smith. "Well? Do you think we did it?"

"Interesting question." Smith studied them. "Guilty conscience, Langdon?"

Richard's face was stiff. "What else would you be doing here at this time of night?"

"Oh, I have my reasons." He leaned forward to flick the ash off his cigar. "Your maid." He stared at Adele. "Does she back you up, that you were here at the time in question?"

"Yes." Adele's head was high. "Ask her yourself, if you haven't scared her to death."

"I will," Smith said, ignoring the gibe. "Be assured of that." He rounded on Langdon. "And you?"

"In my stateroom, as I believe I've said before."

"No, Mr. Langdon." His voice was almost gentle. "You weren't. And before you protest, you should know that I have a witness."

"That's absurd!" Adele burst out.

"Why?" Smith rounded on her. "Were you with him?"

"I—no, of course not."

"Someone came looking for you last night. A passenger, name of Eastman. Sound familiar?"

"I've had business with him, yes," Richard said, stiffly. "I find it hard to believe that he'd tell you anything."

"Oh, he didn't want to." Smith's voice was very soft. "But when I went to your room today and you weren't there, I saw him looking for you. He mentioned that you hadn't been there last night, either. Took a while to get him to admit that." Smith paused, contemplating his cigar. "But I have ways, you see?"

"The third degree? I've heard of the things you cops do."

"They work," Smith said, still in that soft, deadly voice. "Well, Mr. Langdon? Still say you were in your room?"

"What possible reason could I have, could either of us have, for wishing Julius dead?"

"Richard!" Adele exclaimed, aghast.

"The usual ones, Mr. Langdon. Sex and money, you see?" He grinned. "Sex and money."

"That's it." Richard stood, pressing the button to summon the steward. "Get out."

"Plan on making me?"

"If I have to."

Smith chuckled and got up. "If you had to. You couldn't on a dare. But, don't worry, I'm going," he said, as Richard raised his fists. "We'll continue this conversation tomorrow."

"Oh, no, we won't. Who is it?" Richard said, as a knock came on the door.

"Steward, sir."

"Good." Richard flung the door open. "Mr. Smith was just leaving. Will you see to it that he does?"

Startled, the steward looked from Langdon to Smith. "Yes, sir," he said, swallowing. "Mr. Smith?"

Smith laughed again. "As if you could make me, either, if I didn't want to go. Get back to your post."

"Yes, sir," the steward stuttered, and fled.

Smith stared after him, chuckling to himself, and then turned. "I'll see you tomorrow," he said, and went out.

Once on deck, however, his buoyant mood faded. He hadn't broken down Langdon or Mrs. Hoffman, and no matter what he'd said, the captain wouldn't let him use any rough stuff with them. They were cabin class. Special. Like Devlin and his wife. He scowled, his pleasure disappearing completely. Devlin, he thought he'd taken care of. His wife, however, was another matter. Women were nosy creatures, and if she found out something interesting, she'd tell her husband. And he couldn't have that.

No, he couldn't have that, Smith thought, stopping by the railing to light another cigar and glaring in the general direction of the Devlins' suite. And he wouldn't have it. Mrs. Devlin would have to learn not to interfere.

"So what happens now?" Gregory Tate asked, leaning his forearms on the ship's railing.

Julia turned dull, red-rimmed eyes to him. "What do you mean?"

"Are you still going to marry that English lord?"

"Mother wants me to." Julia looked away, gazing over the moon-sparkled sea far below. It was late evening, and few people were about on the promenade deck. Though she knew she should probably still be in seclusion, she had needed to get out of the suite and away from her family, if only for a little while. Her life had turned upside down in the past two days, and she didn't know if she'd ever recover.

"Of course she does," Gregory said, impatience tinging his voice. "But do you want to? That's what I wonder, Julia."

"I don't know."

"I don't think you do, you know. You hardly know the man, and you'll be living far away. You won't know anyone there, and—"

"Oh, stop it!" Julia burst out, covering her face with her hands. "Just—stop."

"Julie, Julie." Gregory slipped an arm about her waist,

and though she stiffened, she didn't pull away. "I'm sorry.
I didn't mean to upset you."

"Didn't you?"

"No." He set her away from him, lips twitching in annoyance. "I want you to think for yourself."

Julia blinked, and then gazed at him, her mind steady at
last. "No. You want to do the thinking for me, Gregory.
You always have."

"That's not true. But I do know what's best for you,
Julie," he said, thus putting the lie to his words as he set
his arm about her shoulders again. Julia let it lie there,
heavy, imprisoning. "And it's not going to live in England
to be married for your money."

But isn't that what you want to do? Almost she spoke the
words aloud, holding back only by great effort. Gregory
was a decent sort, really. She liked him and he liked her.
No denying, though, that he was ambitious, and if he
didn't have eyes for her inheritance, he did for the position marrying her would bring him within her father's
company. Julia was no fool. When Gregory, hired as her
father's secretary, had come courting her, it hadn't taken
her long to figure out why. "I don't know what's going to
happen with the company now," she said, softly.

"I don't give a—a fig about the company," Gregory
said, but the way his arm jerked on her shoulders said otherwise.

"There'll have to be a reorganization, I suppose. Mr.
Langdon will want to take on another partner." Her mind
raced. Of course he would, he didn't have the insight, the
shrewdness about people her father had had, to run the
firm himself. Would he see that, though? And if so, who
would he hire on? Not Chauncey, who was too young and

in any event far more interested in poetry than finance. Not like Julia, who had inherited her father's business acumen. Why not a woman? she thought, her heart pounding. Why not Julius Hoffman's daughter?

"Julia." Gregory cleared his throat. "Do you think you could see your way clear to doing something for me?"

Julia looked up sharply. "What?"

"Richard will need help. If you could remind him how long I've been with the firm—"

"You can well do that yourself," she said, twisting away from him. "You've never been shy about it before."

"Yes, well, this is different. With your father dead, it will look like I'm taking advantage."

She faced him squarely, hands on hips. "Well, aren't you?"

"No! But the firm needs everyone to pull together now. And, face it, Julia. While I worked for your father I was never going to get ahead."

"Yes, and I wonder why?"

"Julia." He looked at her reproachfully. "What a thing to say."

"Is it? My father was no fool, Gregory." She moved away from him. "If he wouldn't promote you, he had his reasons."

"Unfair ones, I assure you. I—"

"Do you? But now that he's gone, so are those reasons, aren't they?"

"For God's sake, Julia! What are you saying?"

Julia stared at him for a moment and then turned away, lips compressed. "I don't know what I'm saying," she said, her voice small. "Please forgive me, Gregory. I didn't mean anything by that."

"I should hope not." He stood stiffly beside her, the very picture of an outraged, insulted male. "I hope you know that I held your father in high esteem, Julie, and that I would never have done anything to hurt him."

"No," Julia murmured, still not looking at him. For the truth of the matter was, someone aboard this ship had wanted to see her father dead, and had done something about it. Perhaps not Gregory, even if he did have a motive, but someone she knew. The thought made her shiver. For, if that were so, who could she trust?

Brooke hurried along the promenade deck, shivering in the cool night air. Shirley had returned to her room some time earlier, and Matt had yet to come back from the smoking room. She didn't think she could forgive him for that; at least, not yet. She hadn't minded being left with Shirley, whom she liked. She did mind being left out of any investigation Matt might be conducting. And he was conducting one, deny it though he might.

The promenade deck had emptied; people were in their staterooms preparing for bed. Hurrying, Brooke turned into the corridor where their suite was located, and came to a sudden stop as a man loomed up before her.

7

"Oh!" Brooke's hand flew to her heart. "Oh, Mr. Smith, it's you. You startled me."

Ambrose Smith took a step closer, the shadow of the wall falling diagonally across him, leaving him half in shadow, half in light. It gave him a sinister appearance that surely must be in her imagination. "I imagine you want to talk to my husband," she chattered, fumbling for the doorknob. "I'm not sure he's back yet, but if you'll wait I'll see—"

"Not him." Smith moved abruptly, his big body pressing her back against the wall. "You."

"M—me?" It came out a croak. She craned her head, trying to see around him. "Mr. Smith, you're scaring me."

"It's what I'm trying to do, girlie."

"What? Why do you—?"

"I seen you, you know. Yeah. Heard about you too, you see? Heard you like to poke your nose in where it doesn't belong." He pointed one stubby finger at her nose, and she reared her head back, desperately trying to avoid his touch. He smelled of stale alcohol and unwashed clothes. "I told your husband, girlie, and now I'll tell you." He leaned his head forward, and Brooke turned away, biting her lips. "Look at me when I'm talking to you, girlie. Look at me." He grabbed her chin, turning her, so that she couldn't break free. "This is my case, do you hear? Mine. And I'll not put up with the likes of you interferin'. You see?"

From somewhere deep within Brooke found her voice, and her courage. "I wasn't interfering."

Smith gave her chin a little shake. "Do you see, girlie?"

"I—yes." She gasped as the pressure of his fingers on her face increased. "Yes, I do, but—"

"Good." He dropped his hand, though he didn't move away. "See that you keep on understandin'. And make sure your husband does, too. Because next time I might not restrain myself." His eyes bored into hers. "You see?"

"Yes." She swallowed, hard. "I see."

"Good," he said, and at last moved away. He rounded the corner of the corridor onto the promenade deck and, as quickly as that, was gone.

Brooke pressed her fist to her mouth to stifle an hysterical giggle of relief. He was gone, and her knees were shaking so badly they barely supported her. Reaching out her hand, she fumbled again for the door handle, whimpering when it slipped out of her nerveless grasp. "Oh, please," she whispered, and this time felt the knob under her hand, felt it turn and the door open. She almost fell into the sitting room, slamming the door closed and shooting the bolt home. She was safe. No one would harm her here.

"M-Matt?" she called, but even before saying a word she knew he wasn't there; the suite felt empty. "Oh, dear heavens." Shaking still, she stumbled over to the sofa and fell onto it, hugging herself. *It's over.* It was over, and she was safe. And, she found to her surprise, angry. Angry? She sat up, trembling, the feeling growing within her. Yes, anger, at the bully Smith was, threatening an unprotected woman and expecting her to cave in. And, for a moment, she had. She'd had no choice, not when he'd been so close that the thought of it made her shudder. He certainly would not have treated her so had she been a man.

The doorknob turned and then rattled, making her jump. "Brooke?" Matt called from outside. "Are you in there?"

"Oh, Matt!" She jumped up, running to the door and pulling back the bolt. "Oh, thank God."

"Hey," he said, as she threw herself against him, his arms automatically going around her. "What's this?"

"Smith," she choked, her anger and courage both deserting her, now that she was no longer alone.

"Smith?" Matt stepped into the sitting room, still holding her, and closed the door behind him. "What about him?"

"He was here, Matt," she said, and in a shaky voice related the events of the last few moments. Matt's eyes turned a stormy navy blue as he listened, pacing the floor with chin outthrust and hands balled into fists.

"The bastard," he said, when she was done, smacking his fist against his palm. "I'll get him for that."

Brooke leaned forward on the sofa, hands clasped tightly. Matt looked in a mood to do murder, she thought, and shuddered. No, not murder, but mayhem, anyway, and if he started a fight he'd likely be hurt. It was the last thing she wanted. "Matt, he's so big—"

"What?" He rounded on her. "You afraid I can't take him?"

"I'm afraid you'll be hurt."

"I've won my share of fights, Brooke," he said, grimly.

Seeing the look in his eyes, she didn't doubt it. "But he'll fight dirty. You know that, Matt." She looked up at him, her face earnest and pleading, trying to get him to see sense. "If he'll come after me, there's no telling what he would do."

"Not if he wants to keep his job. I can't let this go, Brooke."

"I know you can't," she said, after a moment, lowering her eyes. The capacity for violence she saw inside him appalled her, and yet, if he'd reacted any differently, she would have been disappointed. That was appalling, too. "But you don't have to stoop to his level, do you?"

"Why not?" He smacked his fist against his palm. "I'd like to push his face in, the bastard." He broke off, staring out the window, his hands bunched into his trouser pockets, and the anger slowly faded from his face. In its place, though, was something equally dangerous, equally implacable, a crafty look. It should have reassured her. It didn't. "But what I think I'll do instead . . ."

"What?" she asked, when he didn't go on.

"Something that will really pay him back." He turned, and in his eyes was the fierce light of battle. "I'm going to investigate Hoffman's death."

"Are you sure?" Brooke exclaimed, staring at him. "It'll only make Smith angrier."

"I'm sure." His voice carried the ring of conviction. "I

haven't felt right, standing back and watching someone else handle it. As for Smith." His grin widened. "That's the whole point."

"But, Matt—"

"He won't come after you again, I promise." He looked closer at her. "Unless you really don't want me to do this."

"No, no, it's not that." Brooke brought her fingers to her lips and then quickly snatched them away. Biting her nails was a habit she thought she'd outgrown long ago. "I think you should do it, too. At least, I did."

"You've changed your mind."

"You seemed so much not to want to." She leaned forward, her uneasiness fading. "Yes. Yes, I think you should do it. I think you should go to the captain right now and tell him. And I also think you should tell him about Smith."

"No." Matt shook his head. "Under ordinary circumstances Smith is probably capable enough, and I'll need help. I'd rather have him on my side than against me."

"He won't like it."

"I don't like him threatening my wife."

She shuddered, remembering those tense moments in the corridor. "Neither did I. Matt?"

"What?"

"I want to help. No, before you refuse, just listen to me. We're in my world now, Matt, not yours. I know these people, and I can find out things. You know that."

"I do, but—"

"Julia Hoffman asked me to help. I didn't get a chance to tell you that."

"It's dangerous, Brooke."

"It's dangerous for you, too."

"I can handle myself."

"And I can't?"

"Dammit." He rubbed a hand over his face. He did need her help. Because of his background, because of his job, he was viewed as an outsider by the social world. Probably he always would be. It didn't help, either, that because there was no communication between the ship and land, he couldn't get the information he needed in another way. "I don't like putting you in danger."

"I won't be, Matt. Look." She leaned forward again. "There are only four days before we reach Southampton. How are you possibly going to solve this in that time? You need me," she went on as he opened his mouth to speak. "You won't be able to do it without me. You know it, Matt."

"Dammit," he said again, pounding the windowsill with his fist. "I know it, but I don't like it. All right." He turned to face her. "I'll tell the captain I'm taking the case, but I won't tell him about you. That way," this time he held up his hand to forestall her from speaking, "no one needs to know about it."

"That would work." Brooke nodded. Of course everyone would guess, even if her part in solving last summer's murders wasn't generally known. She'd be careful, though, making sure she was never alone. A murderer on the loose was dangerous, not to mention Mr. Smith. "Now. You'd better tell me what you know."

Saturday, April 18

". . . And I'd check into Langdon if I was you," Smith said, rising from the sofa in the sitting room of the suite. Matt stayed sitting at the table he'd had set up to use as a desk, papers spread out before him. "In fact, I'll do it if you want."

"Thanks. Stay with the ones we discussed, for now," Matt said, leaning back. He wasn't surprised to see a flash of resentment cross Smith's face. As of an hour ago Matt had taken charge of the investigation. Smith hadn't received the news well, but after Matt explained some things to him he'd settled down. Matt smiled, grimly. The bruise around Smith's eye was turning a nice shade of purple. Matt's knuckles tingled at the sight. Smith wouldn't bother Brooke again.

The thing was, though, Matt needed the man. The ship was too big and held too many people for him to handle everything himself. He didn't have the resources of the New York, or even the Newport, police behind him this time. Fortunately Smith was smart enough to realize that it would do him little good not to cooperate. He had agreed to interview crew and staff members who had been about the night Hoffman died. That left the passengers to Matt, and to Brooke. He shifted in his chair. On this case he needed her, but he didn't feel good about it.

"Right." Smith carefully folded the paper and put it in his pocket. "I'll get on it right away. Anyone knows anything, I'll find out, you see."

"I see—yes."

"Someone else I'd watch out for. That Snow fellow."

Matt leaned back. He, too, had some questions about

Snow, given what he'd said about Hoffman on the night of the memorial service. "What about him?"

"He's a card sharper. Got himself into a game last night with some gentlemen and did pretty well for himself, so I heard." His face darkened. "We don't like his type aboard our ship. Doesn't do anything for our reputation, you see? But I say if someone's willing to be fleeced, that's his problem."

"Snow's been on this ship before?" Matt asked, though he really wasn't surprised. Nor did he believe Smith's show of indignation. Probably he had pocketed some of Snow's winnings from last night.

"Once or twice. We have to watch out for his type, and con men, too. But it sounds to me as if Snow had a grudge against our Mr. Hoffman, you see?"

"What have you heard?"

"Talk," Smith said vaguely, making Matt look at him with suspicion. No matter how agreeable Smith might appear at the moment, Matt didn't trust him. And, in his experience, the confidence men and card sharpers rarely resorted to violence, preferring instead to rely on their wits.

"I'll talk to him," he said, just as the door to the suite opened. "In fact—"

"Matt?" Brooke called. "It's nearly time for luncheon, and—oh." She stopped, hand on the doorknob, as if poised for flight, staring at Smith.

Matt rose and crossed to her. "Mr. Smith is helping with the investigation," he said, taking her arm. "He'll be asking the crew and staff questions."

Brooke relaxed, though her eyes were still wary. "Oh."

"Glad to help." Smith twisted his cap in his hand.

"Mrs. Devlin. About what I said earlier—hope you'll for-get it? Wasn't myself, you see? But I'm that sorry for it." He looked down at the floor. "Didn't mean to scare you," he mumbled.

"Thank you, Mr. Smith." Brooke's tone was gracious-ness itself. "I'm sure you'll be a great help."

"I'll try, ma'am. Er, Mrs. Devlin. I'll just be going now."

"Report back to me when you're done," Matt said, as Smith edged towards the door.

"Er, yes. Evenin', ma'am. Mr. Devlin." And with that Smith went out, the door banging shut behind him.

Matt grinned. "He couldn't get out fast enough."

"What did you do to him?" Brooke pulled out the long steel pin that kept her hat on her head, and laid the hat on the desk. "He looked as if he'd seen a ghost. And his eye—Matt." She stared at him reproachfully. "You didn't."

"I did." Matt sounded satisfied. "I had to. If he's going to be working for me he has to understand who's boss."

"But you could have been hurt!"

"But I wasn't." And Smith knew that if he bothered Brooke again, he'd get worse. Not to mention that he was in danger of losing his job if he didn't cooperate with Matt. "Investigating can be rough, Brooke. Are you sure you want to stay with it?"

Brooke raised her chin, struck by the challenge, as he'd expected. "I can take it if you can."

He nodded and turned away, lips tight. He needed Brooke's help; he'd admitted that already. He didn't like it, though. One thing was certain: the experience would change them both. And God alone knew if the changes would be for the better, or the worse.

Breakfast was over, and for once Matt, striding along the promenade deck, was facing the day on a full stomach, though the sky was overcast and the sea rough. There was even talk that they might see icebergs. Matt didn't notice. Three days left, and too much to do. But he was starting now. By way of a note, he had made arrangements to speak with Adele Hoffman at last.

A lady's maid, French by her accent, let Matt into the suite Adele had once shared with her husband. His feelings were mixed. On the one hand, he was glad to be starting the investigation, and not beforehand, either. On the other hand, he hadn't particularly liked Adele the few times he'd seen her, nor did he enjoy dealing with members of society. Brooke, dealing with the other passengers, would be taking quite a load off his shoulders with her own investigation.

Adele was lounging on the sofa in the sitting room, wearing a pale blue teagown that exactly matched her eyes. For all the casualness of pose and dress, however, her hair was impeccably coiffed, and her gaze was alert. By the sofa stood Richard Langdon, hands clasped behind his back, meeting each swell and roll of the sea with an ease Matt could only envy. Together they presented a united, formidable front. Getting information from them was not going to be easy.

"I hope this won't take very long," Richard said. "Mrs. Hoffman has taken this hard. She can't handle much more."

"I realize that." Matt fished in his pocket for his notebook, feeling a bit more at ease with the comfortable prop in his hand. Except for his surroundings, he could almost be back on land, doing his job as he always had, wearing clothes that were comfortable and suited him, though Brooke had frowned this morning when he'd put this suit on. "And I'd like to say how sorry I am for your loss, ma'am."

"Thank you." Adele's gaze was stony. "It was a terrible shock."

"You do realize, however, that I have to ask questions."

"I don't know why," Richard put in. "We had nothing to do with Julius's death."

"You can tell me about his state of mind," Matt said, pencil poised over the notebook. His belief that they did, indeed have something to do with the death was something he wouldn't bring up just now. "Was he worried about anything? Angry? Had he quarreled with anyone?"

Adele glanced up at Richard. "No. What does this have to do with anything, Mr. Devlin? My husband didn't kill himself."

"No, he didn't. But he's the logical place to start, ma'am, especially since we have information that makes it seem certain he was murdered."

"What kind of information?" Richard said, sharply.

"We'll get to that. Now, Mrs. Hoffman—"

"No. I want to know. And I'd like to know, Devlin, by whose authority you're questioning us. This isn't New York."

"The captain's authority." Matt kept his voice level. "His word is law while we're at sea."

"That doesn't mean—"

"It means I have the authority to investigate this crime. Is there a problem with that?" His gaze was steady. "I must warn you, if you don't cooperate, it only makes you look guilty."

"I say!" Richard took a step forward. "We haven't done anything."

"Huh." Matt's lips twitched. There they were, the two of them, trying to look innocent, when he knew Smith had all but accused Langdon of murder. Who were they trying to fool? Him, or themselves? "Then you won't mind answering my questions."

"I don't like your tone of voice—"

"Oh, Richard, enough," Adele interrupted, the back of one slender, white hand pressed to her forehead, though she sounded very much in control of herself. "We've been through this before. We do want Julius's death solved, don't we?" Her gaze held Richard's, and some sort of communication passed between them. "It's causing too many complications for us now, hanging over our heads as it is."

"I don't like it," Richard muttered, but he sat down at last. "If any of your questions are out of line, Devlin, I have every intention of talking to the captain."

"Do that." Matt glanced down at the notebook. "Now. Can you tell me about your husband, Mrs. Hoffman? His state of mind, as I said. Was he worried about anything?"

Adele took a moment to answer. "No, not that I noticed," she said, finally. "He seemed much as usual, didn't he, Richard?"

"Yes." Again, that glance passed between them. "If anything, I'd say his mood was good. He was looking forward to opening a European office, you know."

"Business was doing well, then, Mr. Langdon?"

"Yes," Richard said, but his eyes shifted away. So, Matt

thought, watching him. The rumors about trouble in the business might have some basis, if Langdon's reactions were anything to go by.

"I see. Did he have any enemies? Before you object," he held up a hand as Richard opened his mouth to speak, "I already know of at least one."

"Randall Snow."

"You know him?"

"Of course I know him." Richard's face twisted with scorn. "He's always blamed his financial losses on the firm, when it was his own poor judgment that caused them."

"Oh?"

"Yes. The man liked to speculate on the market. When the panic came, he was overextended."

"I see." Matt pretended to consult his notebook. "He did say some bitter things about Mr. Hoffman. It makes me think that, if there was one enemy, there were probably others. It's been my experience that a person doesn't acquire wealth without angering some people."

"Wealthy, are you, then?" Richard taunted.

"No, Mr. Langdon. Observant. Why is this such a difficult question for you to answer?"

Again a look passed between Adele and Richard. "Very well," Richard said, grudgingly. "He did have some enemies. The Panic of '93 beggared a lot of people, Devlin. It's easy to resent those who managed to keep their money."

Matt nodded. "Any names?"

"Of anyone who might be aboard the ship? No. Just Snow."

"What of Gregory Tate?"

"Gregory?" Richard stared at him. "Is he a suspect?"

"Possibly. Since Hoffman denied him promotions more than once. Or so I've heard."

Richard and Adele glanced at each other, and Matt had the impression he'd caught them both completely by surprise. "I suppose he does have a motive," Richard said, slowly. "Especially the way you put it. But I can't see it, you know. He doesn't seem the type." He paused. "Not like Ambrose Smith."

Matt glanced sharply up from the notebook. "What about Smith?"

"Why, didn't you know, Mr. Devlin?" Adele said, a faint mocking edge to her voice. "He lost his job because of Julius."

Matt's mind was racing. That Smith had been fired from the New York police force, he knew; also that Hoffman had been involved in exposing the corruption within the force. Until now, however, he hadn't put the two facts together. "You are certain of this?"

Adele raised her chin. "Of course. Julius seemed rather amused when he realized Smith was on this ship."

"And Smith?" Matt asked reluctantly, not wanting to expose a fellow police officer to scorn, no matter how corrupt he might be.

"Oh, angry, I imagine. He certainly looked it. In fact, he and Julius had words. I'd look at him, Mr. Devlin, before bothering Mr. Tate."

"Huh." Matt pretended to jot down a note, his mind whirling. Smith. Damn. That complicated an already complicated case. "There is, of course, one other suspect you haven't mentioned."

"Who is that?"

Matt looked directly at Richard. "You, sir."

There was silence for a moment. "You're as bad as Smith," Richard said, "making accusations without any evidence."

"No, sir. Evidence has been found implicating you in Hoffman's death." He paused. "Both of you."

Richard jumped to his feet. "That's ridiculous!"

"Of course it is." Adele frowned. "What evidence, Mr. Devlin?"

"Adele, you can't think there really is such a thing—"

"Oh, I do. I doubt very much Mr. Devlin would say so if there weren't. Am I right?"

"Yes," Matt said. "Mr. Hoffman wrote a letter which he left in the ship's safe. In it he said that if anything happened to him on this voyage, to ask both of you about it."

Stunned silence met this statement. "I—don't know why he'd say that," Adele said, her hand fluttering to her throat. "We certainly didn't wish him any harm."

"Yet you wanted a divorce, ma'am."

She stiffened. "Where did you hear such a ridiculous thing?"

"Is it true?"

Richard leaned forward in his chair. "Don't answer that, Adele," he said.

Matt looked at him. "Are you a lawyer, Mr. Langdon?"

"No. But I know enough not to let her answer a question which could incriminate her."

"From what I understand, the problems in your marriage are common knowledge."

"Gossip," Richard said, tersely. "That's all it is. Malicious gossip."

"Yet you and your husband didn't get on well, Mrs. Hoffman. I saw that with my own eyes."

"We had had a quarrel." Adele looked directly at him. "That happens between married couples, sir."

"Mm-hm." Matt frowned down at his notebook. Clearly they weren't going to tell him more on that subject. Not that he'd expected them to. "All right, then. Where were you when your husband died, ma'am?"

"I've answered that question already," Adele said, stiffly. "I was here. If you doubt me, all you need do is ask my maid. Claudette," she called, and the maid who had let Matt into the suite came out from the bedroom, so quickly that Matt suspected she had been listening behind the door. "Where was I the night Mr. Hoffman died?"

Claudette cast a quick glance at Matt. "Here, madame."

"When?"

"All night, madame." Claudette's eyes widened. "But monsieur surely doesn't think madame had anything to do with Monsieur Hoffman's death?"

"What time did I return here from the grand saloon?" Adele said, sharply.

"Early, madame." She faced Matt. "Madame wasn't feeling well. Ocean travel does not agree with her, *comprendez vous?*"

"What time was that, Claudette?" he asked, his voice mild, but all his instincts were on alert. She was lying. He could tell by the way her eyes shifted, by the way her arms were crossed on her body. They were all lying, of course, but Claudette was the only one with nothing to hide.

"About ten, monsieur." She glanced at Adele. "Is that not so, madame?"

"Yes. Thank you, Claudette. You may return to your work."

"Yes, madame." Bobbing a little curtsey, Claudette went back into the bedroom.

"And what does that do to your theory?" Richard said. "Now that you know what there is to know, even you have to admit Adele—Mrs. Hoffman—could not have killed Julius."

"Maybe." Matt looked up at the other man. "But what about you, Mr. Langdon?"

"Me?"

"Yes. Where were you that night?"

"I was in my stateroom, of course," he said, quickly.

"No, Mr. Langdon." Matt's voice was soft. "Smith has talked with me about his investigation, you know. He tells me a passenger named," he frowned down at his notebook, "Eastman went to see you a few minutes after ten, and you weren't there."

"Yes, Mr. Smith mentioned him to me." Richard gazed stolidly at Matt. "We know each other from New York. I don't know why he says I wasn't there—no, wait." He frowned. "That's right. I left the grand saloon with Adele, and then I went on deck to have a smoke."

"Not to the smoking room?"

"No. To tell you the truth," he said, leaning forward, "I was afraid I'd see Julius in there."

Matt looked up, pencil poised over notebook, suspicious of this sudden cooperation. "Oh? Why did that bother you?"

"He would have talked business, of course."

"So?"

"So it was the last thing I wanted to think about. I

haven't had a vacation in years. Besides," his voice lowered confidentially, "there's a young lady I left behind in New York and I was thinking about her. So you can understand if I didn't want to discuss business just then."

"Mm-hm." From the corner of his eye, Matt saw Adele start in surprise. Another lie, he thought. "Did anybody see you, Mr. Langdon?"

"Oh, probably. I believe there were one or two people on the deck, but I didn't see anyone I knew."

"In other words, you can't prove where you were, can you?"

"I'm telling the truth, Mr. Devlin."

The hell he was, Matt thought, but he let it pass. "And after you had your cigarette?"

Langdon's eyes met his levelly. "I returned to my room."

Matt's lips thinned. There was, unfortunately, no evidence otherwise. "What do you know about the death threats Hoffman supposedly received?"

"Death threats!" Adele gasped, her hand going to her throat. For the first time, she looked rattled. "Julius never received any death threats!"

"But he did." Richard let out his breath. "They started a month or so before we left."

Adele stared at him. "He never told me—and neither did you!"

To Matt, that last statement was further evidence of their closeness. "Can you tell me about them, Mr. Langdon?"

"Yes." Richard drew his hands down his face. "There were three altogether. How did you hear about them?" he asked, his gaze suddenly sharp.

"Sources," Matt said, vaguely. "Did he take them to the police?"

"No. I urged him to, but he wouldn't. Said the police couldn't find out anything he didn't know himself. I thought—." He paused. "I still think that he had an idea who sent them. Though they were unsigned, of course."

"You saw them?"

"Only by accident. After he received the third one he discussed them with me—"

"When was this?"

"Three days before we sailed."

"Was he upset?"

"No. He seemed, if anything—amused." Richard's brow wrinkled. "He put the letter down for a minute, so I didn't see much. The handwriting was very quick, with some mispellings. I don't think whoever wrote them was very intelligent."

"What did the letter refer to? Besides a threat?"

Richard frowned. "Investments, I believe. Failed investments, or why threaten Julius? Of course investments fail all the time. Maybe that's why Julius didn't take it seriously."

A failed investor. Matt knew of at least one person who had lost money, and that person was on this ship. What had happened recently to trigger Snow's need for revenge? "Where was the letter from?"

"Julius thought of that, of course. I didn't see the postmark, but he said they were mailed at the Old Post Office."

That was no good, considering the volume of mail that went through that office; yet it also implied familiarity with New York. Snow was looking more and more likely. "And you have nothing more to tell me."

Both Richard and Adele stared back at him, a solid, united front. "Nothing," Richard said. "Why should we? We're innocent."

Huh, Matt thought, but kept his face impassive as he closed his notebook. They had closed ranks against him. He'd learn nothing more from them. At least, not now. Let them stew for a bit. "Thank you," he said abruptly, rising.

"That's it?" Langdon looked up at him. "You're not going to arrest us?"

"No." Matt put the notebook away, ignoring the mockery in Langdon's voice.

"That is a relief."

"Don't be so certain. Thank you," he said again, and went out, closing the door behind him. There. That should give them something to think about.

"Psst! M'sieur!"

Matt turned. Claudette was peering out the door of the suite. "What?" he said, whispering as she had.

"There's something—yes, madame, I'm coming." The look she gave Matt as she closed the door was expressive, but of what, he didn't know. All he did know was that none of the people in that suite had told him the truth. They'd regret that. For he was going to find it out, no matter what it took.

"Mr. Devlin? Excuse me," a voice called behind him, and Matt turned to see a white-jacketed steward approaching, his face furrowed. "May I have a word with you?"

Matt stood, hands in pockets. "What is it?"

"My name is Carter, sir. I'm the steward for the forward cabins on the main deck."

"Yes, well?"

"If we may go someplace private?"

Matt looked hard at him for a moment, and then nodded. "My suite," he said, and turned, assuming Carter would follow. A moment later, he opened the door to the suite.

"Matt?" Brooke called from the bedroom, looking out. Behind her was her maid, fussing with Brooke's clothes.

"Yes, just me." Matt tossed the key to the suite onto the sofa. "And a Mr. Carter."

"Oh?" Brooke came out into the sitting room, her face curious. "Has something happened?"

"I don't know. Mr. Carter has something he wants to talk to me about."

Carter shifted from one foot to the other, clearly ill at ease, though whether at Brooke's presence or because he was in a passenger's suite, Matt didn't know. "If I could speak with you alone, sir?"

"Sybil?" Brooke called to her maid. "Could you press the oyster silk for tonight?"

"But I thought you were planning to wear the blue, ma'am," the maid protested.

"I've changed my mind." Brooke smiled. "I'm sure you won't mind."

Sybil glanced at the three people standing in the sitting room, her eyes curious, and then shrugged. "Of course, ma'am," she said, and left the suite, the silk gown carefully draped over her arm, to find the ship's laundry facilities.

"There. Now we're alone," Brooke said, settling onto the sofa. "What is this about?"

"I don't know." Matt turned to the steward. "Mr. Carter?"

Again the steward shifted. "I was, uh, hoping to speak to you alone, sir."

"You can say whatever you want in front of my wife. I'll tell her anyway," Matt said, as Carter glanced dubiously at Brooke.

"If you say so, sir. Well. It's like this. As I said, I'm the steward for the forward cabins on the main deck. Anyways, this morning I was cleaning like usual, and I come across this."

"What is it?" Brooke asked, leaning forward to peer at the leather object the steward held out.

"A wallet. It was under the bunk. I thought it belonged to the man in the suite. Mr. Tate. Do you know him, sir?"

Matt leaned forward. "Yes, he works for Hoffman and Langdon. Is it his wallet?"

Carter swallowed, hard. "No, sir. A paper fell out, and I seen—"

"Let me see it." Matt held out an authoritative hand, opened the wallet, and let out a silent whistle. "Holy God."

Brooke craned her head to see. "What is it, Matt?"

"It's Julius Hoffman's."

8

Gregory Tate paced back and forth within the confines of his cramped stateroom on the main deck, his tie askew and his celluloid collar hanging at an angle from his shirt. "I didn't do it. I swear to you I didn't."

"Then why was Hoffman's wallet found in your room?" Matt asked mildly, looking up from his notebook. He was sitting at ease in the room's one chair, one leg comfortably crossed over the other. The discovery of Hoffman's wallet had jolted everyone and set the case in a new light. Could the motive for Hoffman's murder possibly have been burglary? And if that were so, was anyone aboard the ship safe?

"I don't know!" Gregory spun around to face Matt. "My God, Mr. Devlin! Do you think that if I'd actually killed Julius I'd be stupid enough to keep his wallet? Or to hide it where anyone could find it?"

"I don't know." Matt sat back, crossing his arms. "I've seen criminals do more stupid things."

"I'm not a criminal," Gregory blurted, but his eyes shifted. Not much, but enough for Matt to note, and to wonder about.

"Then explain how Hoffman's wallet got here."

"I can't." Gregory dropped down onto the bunk, head in hands. "I can't, and that's the truth."

"You can't because doing so would be an admission of your guilt."

"No." Gregory shook his head. "If I had killed Julius it wouldn't have been over his wallet."

"What would have been the reason, then, Mr. Tate?"

Gregory's eyes shifted again. "Nothing. Because I wouldn't do such a thing."

"Mm-hm." Matt opened his notebook, glancing down at the cryptic jottings he'd made after speaking to Jack Everett. "You were Hoffman's secretary."

"Yes. In fact, he was thinking of putting me in charge of the London office."

"Not what I've heard, Mr. Tate. What I've heard is that you didn't get the promotion you thought you deserved. You've been with Hoffman and Langdon for five years, you're apparently quite able, and yet Hoffman never advanced you beyond his secretary." Matt flipped his notebook to a fresh page. "Now why is that?"

"Jealousy," Gregory muttered.

"I beg your pardon?"

"Jealousy!" Gregory glared at him, eyes glittering. "Because he knew I could take over the firm someday, and that was what he wanted for his son. Chauncey," he sneered, "who writes poetry and music."

"You are telling me that you didn't advance because

Hoffman's saving the firm for his son? For a boy who is years away from joining the firm in any capacity?"

"Yes."

"Then why did you stay?"

"I liked my work," Gregory said, without conviction.

"Come, Mr. Tate, I'm not stupid. I've been told you're talented and ambitious. Now why would you stay in a job where you were never going to advance?"

"Because I liked it!" Gregory flung out defiantly. "Because it was good, steady work and I was learning a lot for the day when—"

"When what?" Matt prompted, when Gregory didn't go on.

"When I could own my own firm. Look." He raised his head. "I know things look bad for me, what with the wallet being found here, but I swear to you I had nothing to do with Julius's death. And if I could explain about the wallet, I would."

"Mm-hm." Matt frowned down at the notebook, hearing weary truth in Tate's voice, at least about the wallet. About other things, he wasn't so certain. There was something here. Maybe not the solution to the murder, but something. Yet the evidence against Tate didn't ring true. If he were as clever as Matt had been told, why would he hold onto Hoffman's wallet? It would have been easier, and safer, to dispose of it in the sea.

Matt rose. "Very well, Mr. Tate, if that is how you wish to leave it, then you give me no choice."

Gregory looked up. "You are arresting me, then?"

"No. But you will be confined to this stateroom for the duration of the voyage."

"But I didn't do anything—"

"Would you prefer the brig?"

"No." Gregory lapsed into sullen silence. "No, I'll stay here."

"You see, we have yet to verify your whereabouts for the time Hoffman died," Matt said, almost gently, as Gregory's head came up. "It doesn't look good, Mr. Tate."

"I didn't do it!" Gregory pounded his fist on his knee. "I swear to you, I did not kill Julius."

"We'll see," Matt said, and went out, nodding to the steward who stood outside the door. With authority from the captain, Matt had deputized several stewards to keep watch on Tate until the ship reached Southampton. He was a prime suspect in the case, the best to date. And yet questions still remained. The mystery of what Hoffman's last letter meant had yet to be solved.

Frowning, Matt took the stairs up to the promenade deck at an easy lope, not noticing their tilt. This case had caught him. He'd felt good since he'd gotten involved, alive, aware, needed, as he hadn't since coming aboard.

The thought startled him, slowed his steps, making a man walking behind him swerve to avoid a collision. Though a moment before he'd been eager to share the information he'd garnered with Brooke, now he wasn't. He hadn't been born to the life of the idle rich, and so it wasn't surprising if he often felt out of his element among them. Yet this feeling went deeper. He was at last doing what he was meant to do, what he was best at. And though Brooke was of necessity his partner in this case, in his heart it was his alone. He was going to solve it, he thought, pacing determinedly towards his suite. It was his.

———————

"Is it my imagination, or are you being ostracized?" Jack Everett asked, coming up to Brooke as she stood at the railing earlier that morning, sketching.

Brooke turned to him. "Not ostracized, exactly, but there is something." Standing on deck with her sketchbook, trying to catch the indefinable essence of being at sea, Brooke had, in the last few moments, returned the greetings of people she knew, who then hurried off. It had been different before, when people talked to her about recent events. Then it had been only gossip, and meant nothing. "It's because Matt's investigating. I think people are afraid I'll tell him what I hear."

"Well, won't you?"

"Of course."

"Quite the little detective, aren't you?"

"Don't patronize me, Jack." She lowered the pencil and scowled at him. "This murder has disrupted what is supposed to be a happy time for us. I'd like to see it solved. Besides," she turned and began walking, "Matt is happier when he's working. Not that he'd admit it."

"I'm sorry," Jack said, after a moment. "Didn't mean to insult you."

"I know." She sighed. "But it is hard when people I know avoid me." And yet she'd wanted this, as much for her own sake as for Matt's. "At least you don't do that."

"Never. Particularly as you are at last dressed stylishly." He stepped back, studying her walking ensemble of beige moire taffeta, the jacket closely fitted with huge leg o'mutton sleeves and trimmed with rust-colored braid, the skirt gracefully flared, without a train. Just a hint of a lace-trimmed blouse showed at her throat, and upon her head she wore a hat of natural straw, trimmed again with the rust braid. "That particular shade suits you."

"Thank you. And I must say, I do like that suit. I haven't seen it on you before."

"Of course not. I make it a point to vary my wardrobe."

"Oh? And do you have a different outfit for every hour of the day?" she teased.

"Of course," he said, quite seriously. "To be stylish at sea one requires a minimum of twenty trunks."

Brooke burst out laughing. "You're joking."

"My dear, I never joke about fashion."

"Mm-hm." She glanced up at him, her good humor restored. He was, indeed, serious about fashion. If she didn't know him better, she would think it was the only thing he cared about. "Jack, you hear things, don't you?"

"Of course. Doesn't everyone?"

"But you always seem to know more than anyone."

He tilted his head. "I keep my ears open. Sometimes people think that because one is interested in fashion, one doesn't care about anything else."

"Have you heard anything about Mr. Hoffman's death?"

"That you could tell your husband? No." He ambled along beside her, a stylish lounger in a white flannel blazer and straw hat. Only Brooke, looking up at him, saw the sharp gleam in his eyes that belied the image. "But—"

"What?"

"Plenty of people had reason to dislike Hoffman."

"Why?"

"Because of money, of course. Or losing money."

"Like Mr. Snow? But the panic was three years ago."

Jack's lips tightened. "Who's talking about the panic?"

"What are you talking about?"

"Brooke." He turned to her. "You're not stupid. You know as well as I do that anyone who is as successful as Hoffman makes enemies. If he makes money, others lose theirs. It's that simple."

"You sound bitter," she said, puzzled. "But surely he didn't lose anything of yours."

"Not mine, no. But people I know—yes, that he did."

"Someone who's aboard?"

Jack's lips were a thin slash in his face. "Someone who could not afford passage on this ship in a million years, unless it's in steerage."

Brooke frowned. "Then why mention it, Jack?"

He shrugged. "Just to let you know that if you're looking for suspects, you'll find plenty."

The shrug, so unusual a gesture in a man who hate his clothing to wrinkle, along with the bitterness in his voice, made Brooke's frown deepen. "If I didn't know better, Jack, I'd think you were talking about—"

"Madame," a voice hissed from an adjacent corridor, and, startled, Brooke turned to see a woman approaching. Her simple black dress proclaimed her to be a servant; but its excellent cut, along with her accent and bearing, said that she was of the superior type, most likely a lady's maid. "You are Madame Devlin, are you not?"

"Why, yes." Brooke stepped towards her, not certain whether to be relieved or not. Jack's words had roused an uneasy suspicion in her mind. Had he had reason to wish Julius Hoffman dead? "And you are?"

The woman's eyes shifted from her to Jack. "*Pardon,*

madame, but if I could have a moment of your time? Alone, *s'il vous plaît?*"

Brooke's eyebrows rose in surprise, but her voice when she spoke was calm. "Of course. Jack, excuse us, please?"

"Certainly. I'll see you at luncheon, Brooke." Jack tipped his hat, turned, and left, leaving Brooke to stare after him for a moment.

"Madame?" the woman said, and Brooke turned, shaking her head. Jack couldn't have done it. Of course not.

"Yes. Please come this way, to my suite. We'll be private there."

"Oh, *merci*, madame." The woman followed Brooke into the suite. "I did not wish to speak before the monsieur, *comprendez vouz?*"

"Yes. At least, I think I understand." Brooke settled on the sofa, gesturing the woman to a chair. "You are—?"

"Claudette Lavoie, madame. Lady's maid to Madame Hoffman." Shrewd, sharp black eyes scanned Brooke quickly from head to toe. "A stylish ensemble, madame. The sleeves are a bit too big for you, though, *peut être?*"

"Perhaps," Brooke began, and caught herself. Whatever Claudette had come for, it was surely not to discuss Brooke's taste in clothes. She was a little weary of having that dissected. "What can I do for you, mademoiselle?"

Claudette's hands clenched and unclenched on the lap of her black twill dress. "Your husband is a policeman, *non?*"

"Yes." Brooke sat forward. "Is there something you wish him to know?"

"Oh, madame, I don't know." Claudette wrung her hands together, while Brooke watched in fascination; she had never seen anyone actually do that outside of books.

"I think long and hard before coming to you, *comprendez vous?* But Monsieur Hoffman was kind to me. Someone should know."

"What?"

Claudette glanced away. "You perhaps know about Madame Hoffman and Monsieur Langdon?"

"I've heard gossip."

"Oh, it's quite true, madame," Claudette said, matter-of-factly. "Madame Hoffman, she was not happy with the monsieur. And Monsieur Langdon, he is a handsome man, *comprendez vous?*"

"*Je comprends*—yes, I understand." Brooke kept her composure by a great effort. To hear infidelity discussed so calmly was new to her. "Is that what you came to tell me? No," she went on, quickly, at the look on Claudette's face. "I can see it isn't."

"Oh, madame, I could lose my position over this!"

"No one needs to know you talked with me." If the woman ever told her anything. "What has you so upset, mademoiselle?"

"It is," she swallowed, hard, "I am a good Catholic, *comprendez vous?* I do not like to lie. To me, it is a sin. And besides," her voice hardened, "she has told me that now, while we are in France, I may not visit my family."

"Oh." Now Brooke understood why Claudette was here. "That is a shame."

"It is, and after she made me a promise—eh, *bien*, you don't wish to know that." With a thoroughly Gallic shrug, Claudette seemed to compose herself. "Today your husband asked Madame Hoffman where she was when Monsieur Hoffman died."

"Yes, and?"

"She said she was in her room. But she wasn't, madame." Claudette's face was grave. "Madame Hoffman, she did not return until after midnight."

Brooke leaned farther forward. "Where was she, Claudette?"

"I do not know this for certain, *comprendez vous?* But I think, madame, that she was with Monsieur Langdon."

Brooke sat back, somehow not surprised. "Where?"

Claudette glanced away. "In his stateroom, madame."

"Do you have any proof of that?" Brooke asked, sharply.

"No, madame. But," she looked directly at Brooke, "before we left New York, they had a quarrel, Monsieur and Madame. About Monsieur Langdon."

"What, specifically?"

"I do not know, madame," Claudette said, not meeting Brooke's eyes. "But I think Monsieur Hoffman, he knew—"

"Brooke? Are you here?" Matt called, opening the door to the suite, and Claudette jumped up, her arms flung out, looking like nothing so much as a startled blackbird.

"Yes." Brooke held her hand, palm out, to Matt. "Matt, this is Mademoiselle Lavoie—"

"I must go," Claudette gasped, flying towards the door as Matt stepped into the sitting room. "Madame Hoffman will be missing me." And with that, she was gone, the door banging shut behind her.

Matt stared at the door in mystification. "Was that Adele Hoffman's maid?"

"Yes. Really, Matt!" Brooke sat down, her arms crossed. "You could have waited a few minutes to come in."

"This is my suite, too, Brooke."

She stared at him, and then sighed. "Of course it is. I'm sorry I snapped at you. It's just that I think she had more to tell me."

Matt glanced at her sharply as he sat next to her. "More? Why did she run?" he said, more to himself than to her. "She wanted to talk to me before.

Brooke sighed again. "I think she's scared. Heaven knows the Hoffmans are under a great deal of pressure, Matt." She turned to him, her legs curled up under her. "She told me where Adele was when Mr. Hoffman died," she said, and went on to relate what Claudette had told her. Jack's words, and the suspicions they had aroused, she kept to herself.

"I knew she was lying to me," Matt said thoughtfully, when Brooke was done, and after he had related the events of his morning. "It doesn't look good for Langdon. Or Adele. Or," he went on, "Tate or Snow. This case has too many suspects."

"Matt, how could Adele have done it? She couldn't possibly have the strength to push her husband over the railing."

"Unless she had help. It probably would take two . . ." His voice trailed off. "And no sign of a struggle."

"I don't believe it, Matt," she said, urgently, leaning forward. "I just can't see Adele doing it. It's too cold."

"She's a cold person, Brooke."

"No." Brooke spoke with conviction. "Not if she's having an affair that she must have known would jeopardize everything she had. Not if, for heaven's sake, she wanted a divorce."

"Rumor, Brooke."

"Which we could investigate further." She thrust her chin out. "You should be able to find out if anyone saw Adele going into Langdon's stateroom."

"I could. I could put Smith on it. He's already looking into who was around when Hoffman went over." He looked closely at Brooke. "You really don't believe it, though, do you?"

"No. It seems too—too neat, somehow. As if someone wants us to believe Adele is the murderer. Or Langdon."

"Who? Hoffman put the letter in the safe, Brooke. There's no question about that."

"I know." She blew out her breath in frustration. "And I'm not saying there's no motive. But don't you think that if they did plan to kill Hoffman, they'd make certain they had strong alibis? They aren't stupid, Matt."

"Maybe," Matt conceded. "Otherwise, what good would it do them? But things are starting to add up, Brooke." He reached out to take her hand. "I won't do anything, though, without doing more investigating."

She nodded. "What about Mr. Tate, Matt? Is he really a suspect?"

"With Hoffman's wallet found in his room? Yes, of course. Though I don't like it." He opened his mouth, as if about to say something, and then closed it again. "Smith is checking where he was at the time in question." He rose, pacing the confines of the sitting room. "But it could be Adele, or Langdon. Or both." He rubbed his finger across his mustache. "They were both lying to me." He stopped before the window, looking out. "Langdon could have sent the death threats himself, to lay a false trail."

"Do you think he did?" Brooke said, startled.

"What? No. I don't know. I was just thinking aloud."

"Oh." Brooke looked at him, hard. He sounded remote, distant, and she didn't like it.

"The trouble with this case, there are too many suspects and not enough time—now who could that be?" he said, as a knock came on the door.

"I don't know. By the way, I didn't hear anything of importance this morning, only gossip." She hesitated. "People don't seem to want to talk to me."

Matt nodded as he crossed the sitting room to open the door. "I'm afraid you'll have to get used to that. I—yes?"

"Good evening." The man who stood in the doorway was tall and whipcord lean, garbed in a herringbone greatcoat with several capes attached, and a deerstalker hat, which he swept off with a flourish. "My apologies for disturbing you so near to luncheon, sir. Padlock Homes, at your service."

Matt blinked. "Excuse me?"

"Padlock Homes, sir. Have you not heard of me?"

"Er—" Matt glanced back at Brooke, but found no help there; she was biting her lips, and her eyes were bright with suppressed laughter. "What can I do for you?"

"It is more what I can do for you, sir. May I come in?"

"Er, yes." Matt stepped back, and the man entered the sitting room. "My wife, Mrs. Devlin."

Homes bent over Brooke's hand. "A pleasure, madam."

"Thank you," Brooke said, her voice only slightly strangled. "Are you by chance related to Sherlock Holmes?"

"Oh, no, no." Homes tugged at the legs of his trousers as he sat in a chair facing her. "He's fictional, you know. Actually," he said, and his voice lost its careful British enunciation, gaining a distinctive New Jersey accent, "my name's Ronald Lewis. I'm an actor, but I thought I should come to see you."

Matt glanced at Brooke, seated beside him on the sofa, but she was holding back laughter again. "Why?"

"To help with the investigation. I should explain."

"Yes, I think you should."

"Obviously, I'm not really a detective." Homes got up suddenly and began to pace back and forth, his coat swirling about him, a long-stemmed pipe in his hand. "The American Line hires me to provide entertainment. You do know we plan to have a mock trial tonight?"

"No," Matt said, as Brooke made a choked sound.

"Yes. A very interesting case. Breach of promise. I'm to testify."

"Er, yes." Matt stared at him. "What does this have to do with me?"

"Well, it's like this." Homes dropped into the chair. "I've learned a bit about detecting doing this. Plus I've read all the Sherlock Holmes stories. More than once, I might add. It's important that I play my role right. For example, you, madam." His voice was suddenly clipped, British, again. "You are obviously from the best society, but you are also open-minded. You are from," he frowned, "New York. Yes, definitely New York, but someplace else, as well. Southern New England, I believe. You attended college at Wellesley. You are newly married, you hate the color pink, and you like hats." He stopped, looking at them, and his voice when he spoke was back to normal. "How'd I do?"

Matt and Brooke exchanged looks. "Very well," Brooke said. "How did you know all that?"

His smile was smug. "For the past three days, madam, you've worn every color but pink. It was a good guess."

"And the rest you could have learned from anyone in cabin class," Matt said.

"Maybe I did. Does it matter? What counts is that I was right." He swung around, his coat swirling again. "I am, sir, exactly the man to be of help to you."

"Thank you, Mr. Homes, er, Lewis." Matt rose. "But I have things under control."

"A matter like this, sir, is too important to ignore."

"I agree, but—"

"And you can't trust handling people like Mrs. Hoffman to just anyone."

"What are you saying?"

"I am saying, sir, that Mrs. Hoffman has asked for my assistance—"

"The devil she has!"

"—and to that end, I will be conducting my own investigation into Mr. Hoffman's unfortunate demise."

Matt glanced at Brooke, who no longer looked amused. "Like hell—the devil you will," he said. "The captain has authorized me to investigate, as well as the ship's detective."

"Mrs. Hoffman may hire who she wishes," Homes said, his head held at an imperious angle. "And from what I can see, sir, you need all the help you can get. For example." He gestured with his pipe. "Do you know Gregory Tate's motive for wanting Mr. Hoffman dead?"

Matt's eyes narrowed. "I can guess what it was, yes."

"But it is only a guess, while I, sir, know for certain."

Matt leaned forward in spite of himself. "What?"

"No, no, I am not ready to reveal that. Not until I know more about the man."

"You realize you could be charged with withholding evidence."

"On land, perhaps. But we're at sea, sir. Everything is different here." He turned, his greatcoat swirling again. "I will inform you of events as they proceed. I shall solve this case, or my name isn't Padlock Homes."

"It isn't," Matt said, and heard Brooke, behind him, choke off a laugh.

"No matter. With my detecting skills, sir, and your experience, we will have our culprit in no time." He clapped his hat on his head. "Good day, sir, madam. Thank you for your time," he said, and went out, leaving Matt and Brooke to stare at each other in stunned silence.

Brooke was the first to recover. "Padlock Homes," she gasped, at last letting out the laughter she'd held back. "Oh, Matt! Have you ever heard anything more ludicrous?"

"No." He sat beside her on the sofa. "And it's not funny, Brooke."

"Oh, Matt, where's your sense of humor? He's never going to be able to solve anything."

"No, but he could mess everything up." He rubbed his hands over his face. "Things are hard enough as it is. God help me, Brooke, but there are only three days left."

"I'll help. You know that." Brooke leaned her head on his shoulder, her smile fading as she felt his tension. Something was wrong, something more than just the difficulty of the case, and she didn't know what. There was no time, though, to wonder about it, not with a murderer loose. Three days. Though she wouldn't say so aloud, she shared Matt's doubts. How would they ever figure things out in time?

Julia wandered over to the railing on the saloon deck, staring fixedly down at the sea. The deck was nearly deserted, with everyone being in at luncheon, and that suited her mood. Everything simply hurt too much.

She hadn't expected to miss her father as much as she did. In recent years, as she grew up and became more involved in society, she had come to share her mother's opinion of her father, that he was loud and uncouth and worthy of only the most superficial respect. Now, though, she remembered earlier days, when her adored Daddy always had time for her and her concerns, when he had been the only man she was certain she'd ever love. And he was gone.

Tears puddled in Julia's eyes, and she grasped the railing. Oh, it just wasn't fair! Why did this have to happen to her? Father's death had left her alone, so alone, with no one to talk to who might understand. Mama, for all her show of grief, was determined that things would go on as planned, and that Julia would marry the Earl of Lynton, a prospect she dreaded. Oh, the earl was nice enough, she supposed, but he wasn't for her. He was too old, for one thing, and not at all interested in any of the things she cared about. And his breath was bad. Maybe, Julia thought now with regret, if she hadn't been so cold to her father, if she'd talked to him as she used to, maybe she wouldn't have to marry the earl.

"Julie? I say, it is you," a voice said behind her, and she

looked up to see a young man dressed in a striped flannel jacket and jaunty bow tie, coming towards her.

"Hello, Mr. Norcross," Julia said automatically, her gaze caught by something else. Farther down the deck, a tray balanced precariously on his shoulder, a steward walked along. There was something about him. . . . "I'm sorry?" she said, suddenly aware that Mr. Norcross, now standing beside her, had spoken and was waiting for her reply.

"I said, I didn't think we'd see you again until we reached Southampton." William Norcross reached over to lay his hand on hers, and she pulled it away.

"I just came out for some air, Mr. Norcross. If you'll excuse me—"

"No, stay." He gave her a smile that she supposed could be called charming. He was a good-looking enough man, but his reputation among her set wasn't good. Word was out that his fortunes were low, and that he was seeking a wealthy bride. Rumor, whispered in shocked giggles in ladies' cloakrooms at balls, also had it that he kept a mistress in a little flat in Greenwich Village. Julia hadn't liked him since the time at the Greshams' ball, when he had grabbed her and tried, not only to kiss her, but to grope at her, as well. Why was it that she could not seem to find a moment to herself aboard this ship? Last night it had been Gregory, and now it was this. "You look as if you could use some cheering up."

"Of course I could." Her voice was tart. "My father is dead, Mr. Norcross. Now, please excuse me—"

"But you're not, my lovely Julie." He caught at her arm, and for the first time she caught the distinctive odor of liquor on his breath. "Tell me you're not going to marry the earl, hm?" He was so close she could feel his hot breath on her neck, making her shiver. "You're much too young to marry an old man like him."

"Mr. Norcross! If you don't let me go right this minute, I shall scream!"

"You should stay in America, my lovely Julie. Come, don't struggle. Why pretend? You want this, and no one will see—"

"Is there a problem here, miss?" a voice said beyond them, and Julia took advantage of William's brief surprise to twist away from him. A few steps away stood the steward she had seen a few moments earlier, a mild-looking man with steel-rimmed spectacles. Her eyes widened as she stared at him.

"Go away," William said haughtily. "This is none of your business, and if you persist, I'll see you're—"

"The lady asked to be left alone," the steward said, and to Julia's immense surprise, drew back his arm and hit William solidly on the nose. Without a sound, William fell to the deck, and Julia stared at the steward, stunned and amazed—and wondering why she hadn't recognized him before.

9

Late afternoon, and the day had turned blustery and cold, more like winter than spring, with the seas running high. Matt shivered as he opened the door to the smoking room, wishing he'd thought to put on a topcoat. The wind took the door out of his hand, banging it back against the deck housing, and the gentlemen gathered inside for a pre-dinner drink looked up in some surprise at the noise. The delights of crossing the North Atlantic, Matt reflected, shooting his cuffs and pretending a nonchalance he didn't feel after his dramatic entrance, were vastly overrated by the American Line's publicity.

Matt's afternoon had been busy, spent checking up on crew members and their whereabouts at the time of Hoffman's death. Not that he thought any of them had anything to do with Hoffman; but it was possible one of them had seen something significant and didn't know it. At that time of night, however, only one had been close enough to hear the splash, and he hadn't seen anything. Staff and crew alike were wary, however, something that puzzled Matt, until one of them said something about Smith. Not for the first time, Matt wished for the backing of the New York police force, and a more tactful investigator than Smith. Getting information out of people he'd already questioned was making the investigation more difficult than it already was.

The cold weather had driven most people inside from the normal deck activities, and so the smoking room was crowded. Matt pushed his way past knots of men engaged in conversation, hearing bits of talk about the stock market, the coming presidential election and the silver issue, and, of course, Hoffman's death. At last he reached the long bar that stood at one end of the room and ordered a whiskey, bracing himself against the brass rail as he cradled the crystal tumbler in his hand. Brooke was likely getting dressed for dinner, and as likely swearing, softly and ladylike, but still swearing, as the maid laced up her corset. It had thus seemed wise to him to wait before proceeding to the suite. Spacious though it was, there still was no place there for him to escape to. The wealthy, he had noted, seemed to require a great deal of space in which to live. For someone who'd grown up in a cramped flat in a crowded neighborhood, that usually seemed a waste. Tonight, for the first time, he was glad of it.

Leaning back, Matt surveyed the room, seeing men he knew slightly. Nowhere else was he as aware that he was in a different world than among the men of society, where the talk was all of business and money and Republican politics. He had little in common with them, and that was just as well, he thought, still scanning the room. His gaze passed by a table where several men played cards, and then came back to it. Well, well. Randall Snow, dealing out a hand of poker. Good, fast hands, and—hell, if he wasn't mistaken, that was a marked deck. Snow was cheating.

Setting his drink down on the bar, he made his way across the room. "Randall," he said heartily, clapping his hand on the other man's shoulder. "Good to see you. Remember me?"

Snow looked up, startled, and his eyes took on a wary look. "Devlin, isn't it? Of course I remember."

"Thought you would." Matt's grip on his shoulder tightened. "I was talking about you with some of the fellows I work with, just before I left."

Snow's eyes narrowed. "You were?"

"Yes. Heard you were a whiz at cards."

"I say," a gentleman at the table spoke up. "He told me he didn't play too often."

"I think Mr. Devlin's confused me with my brother," Randall said, rising and palming the marked deck so smoothly that Matt was certain no one else noticed. Snow was a pro, all right. "Now there's a man who can play. But I haven't seen Devlin for a long time, so if you'll excuse me?"

"You'll be back later, won't you?" another gentleman, not much more than a boy, said.

"Maybe. Have fun," he said, slapping a deck of cards onto the table. The unmarked ones, Matt thought. "Damn." His voice was without heat as he turned to walk with Matt. "How did you find me out?"

"At the risk of being insulting, I've seen your type before. Was that a cold deck I just saw you palm?"

"What, me? Play with marked cards? Detective, I'm shocked."

"Uh-huh. Stand you to a drink?"

"Sure. Why not? Since you just cost me my daily bread."

"Religious, Mr. Snow?" Matt said, raising an eyebrow slightly as they slipped into the chairs at the same table he'd earlier occupied with Jack Everett.

"Only when I play." From an inner pocket in his Savile Row tailored suit, he withdrew a fine leather wallet and took out a silver dollar. An ordinary coin, Matt saw, except that someone had drilled a hole at the top. "My lucky coin," Snow explained, casually transferring it across the back of his fingers. "Use it to keep my hands in shape. I had a real pigeon, too," he went on, as a waiter came to take their order, another whiskey for Matt, club soda for Snow. "Ripe for the plucking."

"And how old is this pigeon, Mr. Snow?" Matt took out his cigarettes. "Care for one?"

"A coffin nail? No." Snow made a face. "I don't smoke those things, and neither should you."

To Matt's surprise, he could feel himself holding back a smile. "I'll keep that in mind. How old is the pigeon?"

"The young man that wants to play?" Snow shrugged indifferently. "21, 22. Does it matter? He's old enough to decide for himself. I assure you," he spread his hands, with their neatly manicured nails, "I did nothing to entice him."

"Huh."

"I swear it. I didn't have to. The pigeons entice themselves," he said, smiling disarmingly.

Again Matt had to force his face to stay expressionless.

Snow was a charming man, no doubt about it, as card sharpers and confidence men usually were. In his profession, he had to be, to lure people into their traps. "That's an expensive suit you're wearing, Mr. Snow."

Snow shrugged again and sat back as the waiter set their drinks on the table. "So it is. What of it?"

"Expensive haircut, expensive manicure—it all takes money, doesn't it?"

"I have standards to maintain. And," that smile again, "I have to look the part, or I won't get rich pigeons to play with me. Look, Devlin." He set his drink down. "You know what I am. So let's get down to what you really want."

What Matt had originally wanted was to save an innocent young man from a fleecing. This, however, was an opportunity not to be missed. When it came to being questioned about Hoffman's death, Snow was proving to be remarkably elusive. "You said some hard things about Julius Hoffman the other night."

"Tension." He smiled and spread his hands again. "The tension of the moment."

"And yet you blame him for the loss of your fortune."

"True." He took a sip of his drink. "He was partly responsible for that."

"Only partly?"

"Yes. The truth is, Devlin, I'm a gambler. Always have been. If I'd kept my money in nice, safe boring securities, I'd be okay. But where's the fun in that? The zest?" He snapped his fingers. "Julius had word of a speculative venture that sounded good. A silver mine. He asked me, and a few others, to go in with him. He speculated on his own account, you know," Snow said, his eyes suddenly shrewd.

"No, I didn't."

"And you don't know what that means, do you? Look." He leaned forward. "A broker is supposed to handle stock for his customer and and make his money on the transactions. Julius did that, of course, but he also speculated himself."

"Is that illegal?"

"No, but it's . . . unethical."

"A fine word, coming from you."

"Well, look at it. If you're supposed to be taking care of someone's money but you're more concerned about your own, whose account are you more likely to concentrate on? Your own, of course. Creates a conflict of interest, don't you know."

"Hm." This was a whole new world to Matt, but he understood Snow's point. "So Hoffman was a gambler, too."

"A conservative one, if there's such a thing. He always seemed to know when to get in, and when to pull his money out."

"And he didn't tell you?"

"Oh, he told me." Snow glanced to the side, sipping from his drink. "But I'm a gambler, and the profits were good, on paper at least, so I decided to stay with it. And then the Reading collapsed." He shrugged, seemingly unconcerned. "The rest is history."

History was that the bankruptcy of the Philadelphia and Reading Railroad had started the Panic of '93, ruining a great many people. "You resented him for that."

"Damn right, I did," Snow declared, slamming his glass

down. "Especially when he wouldn't extend credit to me, when he had the nerve to lecture me about speculating." His laugh was mirthless. "I think I hated him, then."

Matt studied the other man's bent head for a moment. "You know what these remarks sound like, don't you?"

"No, what?"

"Like you had a reason to want him dead."

Snow's eyes widened. "Wait a minute. Are you trying to pin his death on me?"

"You had a motive, Mr. Snow."

"For God's sake. After three years?" He stared at Matt. "You're serious."

"Someone killed him, Mr. Snow. You're a likely suspect."

"Well, I may have a motive, but I also have people who can say I was here when Julius went overboard. I was playing cards. We all rushed out together. Ask them." He rose. "And look for someone else he fleeced. Thanks for the drink," he added, and sauntered away through the crowd.

Matt sat on for a moment, finishing his drink, and thinking. Snow had an alibi. He should have seen it. After all, Snow would need to take every chance he could to make money, especially with his high expenses. But still . . . He could still have done it. He could have excused himself to go to the men's washroom, seen Hoffman, and thrown him over on the spur of the moment. That didn't explain the cry of "Man overboard," however—no one yet admitted to yelling it—or the running footsteps. Snow was not a likely candidate for a murderer—but someone had wanted Hoffman dead badly enough to do something about it.

Matt made his way through the smoking room and up to the promenade deck, holding alternately to stanchions and the railing to keep his balance as he walked along. If he didn't find the killer, the question would haunt him for the rest of his life. Who had killed Julius Hoffman?

"How long have you known Jack?" Shirley asked, as Brooke poured out tea for them in her suite. Odd, Brooke thought, setting down the silver teapot, but she felt more comfortable with this girl than she did with people who were supposed to be of her own class.

"Several years." Brooke added cream to her cup. "Since I came to live with my aunt and uncle."

"He's sweet on you, did you know that?"

"Jack?" Brooke eyed her in surprise. "Well, I suppose he was, once, but that was a long time ago."

"Funny," Shirley went on, holding her teacup carefully, her little finger extended. "I've only known him a few days, but it feels like forever." She peered at Brooke over the cup. "Know what I mean?"

"Yes. Some people are like that."

"I know it doesn't mean anything." Shirley set her teacup down with great care, so that it wouldn't rattle on the saucer. "I mean, I know he's not my kind. But sometimes I wish . . ."

"Jack is independent enough to do what he wants," Brooke said, picking her words with great care. "But you do realize that society would give you a difficult time if anything did come of your friendship."

"I know." Her nose crinkled. "Would you still be my friend?"

Brooke leaned over to place her hand on Shirley's, unaccountably touched. "Of course I would be."

"Then that's all I care about. See, society doesn't matter to me, I know I don't belong there and I never thought I would. But I think Jack would mind, after a while."

"I'm not so sure of that. He does pretty much what he wants to do. Although he does keep it quiet."

"Does he actually do anything? I mean, besides change his clothes ten times a day?"

Brooke smiled at the exaggeration. "He does like to be stylish. But, yes, he does do something worthwhile. Hasn't he told you?"

"No. Like I said, we haven't known each other long."

"Well." Brooke took a sip of tea. "I'm not certain I should tell you this if he hasn't, but he works in the settlement houses."

Shirley blinked. "With immigrants? He does? Golly. I'd've never thought it."

"Most people wouldn't."

"Well, that explains that."

"More tea?" Brooke held up the teapot and proceeded to pour. "Explains what?"

"Well, when we heard Mr. Hoffman died—that was when we'd just met—he told me he once invested money for some people who didn't have much, and they lost everything. I wondered how he knew poor people."

Brooke paused in the act of stirring her tea. "I can't believe he'd be so careless."

"Oh, he wasn't. He put the money with someone else, and that person lost it. Well, how was he to know? He thought it was a sure thing. Instead, he had to make the money up himself." She took a sip of tea. "I think he's still mad about it."

Mad enough to kill? Brooke's cup stopped halfway to her lips before she carefully set it down. This wasn't the first she'd heard of an investment going bad. "Who did he put the money with?"

"Dunno. He wouldn't say. But he said he'd done something about it, and that was that. He doesn't talk much about money to me. Maybe he thinks I'm not interested, but I am. After all, I work for it."

"Talking about it wouldn't be polite," Brooke said, her thoughts whirling. Who had invested the money for Jack? And how had Jack taken care of the matter? She had a sick feeling in the pit of her stomach that she knew just what he had done.

Brooke raised her teacup again, this time to shield her face. "When did you meet Jack? On the first day?"

"No, the next one," Shirley answered, and went on to describe the meeting, unaware of the effects of her words. If she had met Jack on the first day, she might very well have spent the evening with him. Instead, what he had done that night was still unknown. And, unless Brooke asked, there was no way to know where he had been when Julius Hoffman died.

With tea over, Shirley rose to go, and Brooke went out on deck with her to see her off. She was about to return to the suite when she saw Matt approaching from the forward section of the ship. She noticed as he neared that he smelled of cigarette smoke. Probably he'd been in the smoking room. "Any luck?" she asked.

He shook his head. "Not much," he answered, and went on to outline all that he had learned that day. "At least I know more than I did. I think Langdon did it, or Adele. If not separately, then together. They were lying to me today."

"Perhaps if I talk to Adele?"

"Maybe, but I don't think you'll get anything out of her. She's tough." Matt crossed his arms on his chest, frowning in frustration. "They've got motive and opportunity and they were probably together that night, but no one saw them. Smith has interviewed just about all the crew, you've spoken to the passengers, and no one can place Adele or Langdon on the deck at the proper time. Dammit." He rubbed at his mustache, roughly. "The only way we'll get them is if they confess, and that's not going to happen."

"No," Brooke murmured, laying her hand on his arm. All she could do just now was listen to him, and support him as best she could. Odd. It might not have been the honeymoon of her dreams, but this investigation was drawing them closer together than most married couples she knew. At least, the parts of it he'd let her share. "What about Mr. Snow?"

Matt stared unseeingly at one of the giant smokestacks before answering. "He has an alibi. The only person who does."

"You don't sound too certain."

"Alibis can be faked, though the people who vouch for him are pretty solid. I think—"

"Mr. Devlin." The plummy British tones projected over the sea breeze, commanding attention and making Matt break off in mid-sentence. Matt turned, to see Padlock Homes, in full costume of greatcoat and hat and pipe, marching towards them, holding the arm of a man wearing white jacket and trousers and propelling him along. "A word with you sir," he said, as he reached them.

"Tell this madman to let me go!" the man Homes held captive yelled at the same time.

"Yes, Mr. Homes?" Matt said. Beside him Brooke was silent, but from the corner of his eye he could see her lips twitching. "What is it?"

"I've found your killer, sir."

"Have you."

"Yes." A crowd of curious spectators had gathered, and Homes's accent grew richer. "If you will give me the authority to make an arrest, I will do so."

"Look, I didn't do anything!" the man burst out. "Ask the chef, ask anyone in the kitchen—"

"Be quiet!" Homes thundered, and turned back to Matt. "Well, sir?"

"I can't give you that authority. It has to come from the captain."

"Then ask him, sir."

"He's crazy," the man said. "One minute I was whipping cream, and the next he was shouting stuff about me being a killer—"

"Be quiet! You'll have your chance to speak."

"Mr. Homes," Matt's voice rapped out. "What is going on?"

"Sir." Homes straightened, in an unconscious response to the note of authority in Matt's voice. "I have here one Gino Guasconi. I found him in the ship's kitchen."

Matt looked from one man to the other. "Yes, well?"

"Look at him, man! He's Italian. Doesn't that say something to you?"

"But I'm American," the man protested. "From Massachusetts."

"Quiet! I know who you are. Mr. Devlin." Homes turned to Matt, his chest outthrust. "You have, I presume, heard of the Black Hand?"

Matt glanced quickly at Brooke, and she could see that even he was having trouble holding onto his composure. "I have, but I don't see what that has to do with anything."

"They are aboard this ship, sir." Homes's voice had lowered. "They are everywhere. This, sir, is a member of the Black Hand. He is," Homes seemed to puff up even more, "the man who murdered Julius Hoffman."

It was too much for Brooke. Hastily she turned away, biting the inside of her lips to keep from laughing. Beside her Matt, in better control of himself, continued to stare at the two men. He knew about the Black Hand; any big-city policeman did. It was a growing problem in the immigrant neighborhoods, where a stenciled black hand meant that money was being extorted for "protection," and woe to those who did not pay. Matt had seen organized crime before, in the gangs that controlled some of New York's less savory districts, but this threat was different. This preyed on the very people it purported to protect. There was no evidence, though, that it had yet become a problem outside of the immigrant communities. "You can prove that, of course," he said.

"Look at him, man!" Homes shoved Guasconi forward again, and this time the man twisted out of his grasp. "He's Italian."

Matt looked for a moment at Guasconi, and then at Homes. "Should that mean something?"

"Sure it does!" Homes's accent had slipped a bit. "Everyone knows about the Black Hand." From one of his capacious pockets he pulled a small book. One glance at the cover, with its lurid illustration of a distressed young woman and a menacing man of obvious southern European background, and Matt recognized it as a penny-dreadful. It was the type of publication that specialized in sensational, and highly romanticized, literature. Not exactly the best source for a detective. "And everyone knows it's Italian."

"Sicilian," Guasconi said, glaring at Homes, "not Italian. My family is from the north of Italy."

Matt looked at him. "But you're American, Mr.—"

"Guasconi. Gino Guasconi, but I prefer to be called John. And I was born in Bridgewater."

Matt nodded. Even if Guasconi hadn't told him, he would have known by his accent that he was a New Englander. "What is your position on this ship?"

"Does that matter?" Homes broke in.

"Mr. Homes." Matt held up his hand. "I'll conduct this inquiry."

"But he did it—"

"We'll get to that." Matt looked at Homes from under his brows, and Homes fell silent. "Now, Mr. Guasconi. What is your position?"

"I'm a pastry chef," Guasconi said, relaxing a bit. "I started off as a kitchen assistant—I've been with the ship five years—and I'm working my way up. Someday I hope to be head chef."

"Did you make the raspberry torte we had last night?" Brooke broke in.

"Yes, ma'am." He glanced at her. "Did you like it?"

"It was wonderful. You have talent, Mr. Guasconi."

"Thank you, ma'am. Look." He turned back to Matt, holding out his hands. "These are my tools. Do you think I'd risk damaging them in a fight?"

"How'd you know Hoffman was in a struggle?" Homes put in.

"Hey, I'd struggle if someone tried to push me overboard. Look, Mr. Devlin. I'm just a cook trying to earn a living."

"Can you account for your time when Mr. Hoffman was killed?" Matt asked.

"I don't know. Probably. They keep us pretty busy in the kitchen." He glared at Homes. "He didn't even ask."

"Don't worry, I will."

"Good." Guasconi nodded. "What's going on on this ship? You going to keep arresting crew members who are innocent? First McCabe, now me?"

"How long have you known McCabe, Mr. Guasconi?" Matt asked, mildly.

"Since I came aboard." Some of Guasconi's belligerence faded. "He's a heck of a nice guy. Quiet. I've never seen him do anything he shouldn't. Oh, he left the ship the day we sailed, when he wasn't supposed to, but he must've come right back on. And I've never done anything wrong, neither. You ask anyone. They'll tell you."

"I will, Mr. Guasconi." Matt nodded. "You can go."

"Thanks," Guasconi said and, after shooting one last glare at Homes, hurried away.

"Hey! It's my arrest," Homes protested.

"Your arrest, Mr. Homes?" Matt's voice was quiet, but there was a note in it that made Homes step back a pace. "On whose authority?"

"On—on—dash it, he's guilty!"

"The only thing he's guilty of is having an Italian name," Matt shot back. "And in the future, sir, remember. There's a difference between Italians and Sicilians."

"All the same to me," Homes muttered, gazing back at Guasconi, now far down the deck. "You just going to let him go?"

"Yes."

"You've got your nerve, Devlin." Homes faced him. "I'm trying to solve a murder here."

"You're an actor, Lewis, not a detective," Matt snapped. "And you have no authority."

"Oh, yes, I do." Homes puffed up again. "Remember, I've been hired by Mrs. Hoffman."

"And you're an embarrassment to her," Matt shot back.

Homes drew himself up, scowling. "At least, sir, I am doing something about finding out who killed her husband." His British accent had returned with his confidence. "And rest assured, I shall continue to do so," he said and, greatcoat swirling about him, turned and stalked away.

There was silence for a moment in the wake of his leaving. "Good heavens," Brooke said, finally.

"Damned fool," Matt muttered. "He'll have to be stopped, before he messes everything up."

"You don't think Mr. Guasconi had anything to do with it, do you?"

"Of course he didn't. That's just Homes's stupidity. All it means is more work." He pulled out his watch and glared at it. "Nearly time for dinner, dammit, and there's still so much to do."

"It will keep, Matt."

"Yeah. Yeah, I suppose it will." Taking her arm, he led her into the suite, his face grim and preoccupied. Too much still to do, and so little time. In two days they would be docking at Southampton, and the passengers would go their separate ways. He had to find the murderer by then. If he didn't, God help him.

Randall Snow weaved unsteadily down the dimly lit corridor to his stateroom. It was good enough, he supposed, but not what they had up in cabin class, no sir, and not at all what he was used to. Only the best for him, or so it had been, before he'd had the misfortune to meet Julius Hoffman. A sound man on railroad securities, or so Randall had been told. Everyone knew railroads were the way to go, had been for years. And there'd been the other investments Hoffman had suggested, silver out West, for one. Well, look what had happened. The Philadelphia and Reading had gone bankrupt, the price of silver had crashed, and he, Snow, had lost everything. Not Hoffman, though. Oh, no. His type prospered on disasters such as that. His only consolation was that Hoffman had gotten what was coming to him.

Randall grinned, a sour smile, and lurched against one of the walls. Damned rough sea today. Of course, he might have had one too many whiskey and sodas. Usually he didn't drink, preferring to keep a clear head when he played cards, but things had gone wrong this afternoon. There he'd been with a winning hand, until Devlin had come along and interfered. It was a good thing he had an alibi for the night Hoffman died; otherwise he suspected

Devlin would try to pin the murder on him. But that wasn't Randall's problem. Winning back his fortune was, and tonight he had a chance at it. The young man who had been playing cards with him when Devlin interrupted him was still game; they had made plans to play again tonight, after the amateur theatrical.

This afternoon, though, was ruined, and he couldn't afford to waste a moment, not with his fortunes to mend and everything costing so dear. After all, if he wanted to fit in with cabin class people he had to dress like them, and that didn't come cheap. Nor did a stateroom on the *New York*, even in second class, deep in the ship, with no window and barely enough room in which to turn about. And, worse, he had to share his quarters. Someday, he vowed, he'd have it all back, and they'd pay. All of them.

Fumbling in his trouser pockets for his keys, he saw a steward come out of the stateroom next to his. Small man, receding hair line, heavy mustache, and glasses. Randall saw and catalogued every characteristic automatically, so used was he to judging people quickly. Not a good mark for a game, he thought. Too meek to take the chance, and no money. At least . . .

Randall looked up, and the keys dropped with a metallic jangle. "Let me get those for you, sir," the steward said, bending down. "Is everything all right?"

"Yes." Suddenly, sharply sober, Randall gazed at the steward. "McCabe, isn't it?"

"Yes, sir. I'm Edward McCabe. How did you know?"

Randall put the key into the lock. "Everyone on the ship knows about you."

"Oh. Of course, sir."

"Been a steward long?"

"Yes, sir, quite a few years, now." McCabe paused. "If there's nothing you need, sir, I have things I have to do."

Randall waved his hand in dismissal. "Go on. We'll talk more later, you and I."

McCabe stared at him a minute, his eyes behind his wire-rimmed glasses unreadable. "Yes, sir. Good day, sir," he said, and turned.

"Good day—McCabe," he said, and saw the other man's shoulders stiffen, before he walked on. Smiling to himself, Randall went into his stateroom, throwing himself onto the bunk. Edward McCabe, he thought, looking up at the ceiling, a little smile on his face. Well, well. An innocuous steward on the surface, beneath most peoples' notice. But not Randall's. Because he knew who McCabe really was, and he intended to use that knowledge to his advantage.

Grinning, he stretched out. Not such a bad night, after all. At long last, his fortunes were about to change.

10

Ambrose Smith was not a happy man. Here he was, in clover, with a murder to solve that would go a long way towards shining up his tarnished reputation. Or, rather, he had been, until that Devlin fellow had come along. Had a hell of a nerve, he did, barging in on Smith's own case. It wasn't supposed to be that way. Cops stuck together, even hick cops like Devlin. But, no. Wanted all the glory for himself, he did, and so Smith was reduced to checking who was where when Hoffman had gone over the side, and what they might have seen. Fat lot of good it would do, if you asked him. He knew who the murderers were and what the motive had been. Sex and money. It always came back to that.

So now he was down in the crews' quarters, way down in the ship where passengers never went, talking to staff who'd been topside that night, and finding out little he didn't already know. A thankless job, this, somethin' he was doing only because Devlin wanted him out of the way.

Well, Ambrose Smith was no one's fool. There was one bit of information he hadn't given to Devlin yet, and he wasn't certain he was going to. He'd find a way to make good on this somehow.

Going up one level, he stumped down a corridor until he came to the door he sought and pounded on it. It was finally opened by a man with sleep-puffed eyes, wearing a wrinkled white jacket. Smith pushed into the stateroom past the man. Save for the two of them, it was empty, the four bunks lining the walls unoccupied, with only one rumpled to mar the tiny room's neatness. "Sleeping on the job now, Davies?" he asked.

"No, sir." Owain Davies, first class night steward, tried to straighten his jacket. "This is my time off. I always catch a nap if I can." Smith grunted in response, continuing to prowl the room. "What is it you want?"

"Got some questions for you, you see?" Smith turned. "The night Hoffman died—"

"I didn't see anything, I told you that."

"Oh, you saw something. Or, rather, you didn't see something." And what he'd seen could change everything. It could restore Smith's reputation.

"Excuse me?"

"'Excuse me?'" Smith mimicked. "Gettin' all hoity-toity, are you? And you from Five Points. First class rubbin' off on you?"

"I don't have to take this." Davies's face had darkened. "You might be the ship's bull, but I don't have to take this from you or any other cop."

"Oh, yes, you do." Smith whirled around, surprisingly lightly for a man of his size. People never expected that of him. "You'll take whatever I dish out, until I get the truth.

You see?" Davies didn't answer, and so Smith resumed pacing, hands folded behind his back. "Now. You say that Langdon was in his stateroom that night. Still want to stick to that story?"

"I do," Davies said, stiffly.

Smith frowned. Langdon claimed to have been in his stateroom at the time of Hoffman's death, yet Smith had heard conflicting information. How much more convenient it would be if he hadn't been. Then Smith would be the one to solve the case, not Devlin. "You're sure of that?" he said, softly.

"Yes. He called for me at ten to eleven."

"Oh, did he? Strange you didn't tell me this before." Davies stayed silent, and so Smith went on. "Explain to me, then, why he didn't answer when a passenger knocked on his door a few minutes earlier."

"I don't know. All I know is he asked for a bottle of champagne, and I brought it to him."

"A whole bottle? For himself?"

Davies shrugged. "It's what he asked for."

"Unless you're mistaken, Davies." Smith loomed over him, scowling. "You brought it to another room, didn't you?"

"No, sir," Davies said, stubbornly. "It was Mr. Langdon who asked for the champagne, and Mr. Langdon who got it."

"Going to stick with that story, are you?"

"It's the truth."

"Oh, is it." Smith leaned forward. "And why didn't you tell me this earlier?"

Davies glared at him. "Because I like Mr. Langdon, sir, and I do not like you."

Smith let out a bark of laughter. "I don't much care what you think of me, you see? Now. How much did he pay you to say that?"

"Nothing."

"You're lying." Smith hauled the other man off his feet by his lapels. "I'll have the truth from you, boy, if I have to beat it from you."

"You've had the truth!" Davies wrenched away, his fist held high. "Langdon was in his stateroom. You don't believe me, you ask whoever was in there with him. And if you threaten me again," Davies stepped towards him, not at all cowed by Smith's size, "you'll get what's coming to you."

In the act of raising one meaty fist, Smith stopped. "Who was with him?" he asked, mildly enough.

"I don't know, and I don't care." Davies glared at him. "Just you keep away from me from now on, or you'll regret it."

"Oh, I will, will I?" Smith's smile was humorless. "So how do you know there was someone there, Davies? Or are you making this whole thing up?"

"Because I heard voices before I knocked, and when Langdon opened the door, he stood so I couldn't see inside."

"Man or woman?"

Davies hesitated. His face was still flushed with anger, but the threat of violence appeared to have passed. "A woman."

"A woman." Smith grinned. This was better than he'd expected. Langdon had been in his stateroom ten minutes before Hoffman's death, in spite of what Smith had been told, but he hadn't been alone. And Smith could just

guess who'd been with him. Mrs. Hoffman. The two of
them could have easily gone on deck and pushed Hoffman
over together. "Good lad," he said, clapping a heavy hand
on Davies's shoulder. "Next time don't be holdin' out on
me, or I might have to beat you. You see?"

"I'd like to see you try," Davies retorted.

Smith laughed and went out, slamming the door behind
him. His step was lighter as he walked down the corridor
to the stairs. He had them now, Langdon and the Hoffman
woman both, and see if they could get out of this one.
They'd done it, no question about it, and he, Ambrose
Smith, was the one to break the case. Let's see what Devlin
thought of that.

Matt tugged on his bowtie and leaned forward. "I think
I'd better go," he whispered into Brooke's ear, just as the
lights in the grand saloon dimmed and the orchestra near
the makeshift stage set up a lively tune. "I can't stay to see
this."

Brooke quietly swiveled her chair around to face him,
placing her hand on his arm. "What are you going to do?"
she whispered. "You've talked to everyone you could
possibly talk to."

"Except McCabe."

"Who isn't involved. Seriously, Matt. You've interviewed the crew and the staff and every possible suspect.
What more do you expect to find tonight?"

"Are you telling me not to work?" His voice rose, and
she frowned.

"No. But I do think you're working too hard."

"You're the one who wanted me to take this case."

"I know. Matt, sometimes when I paint I get so frustrated by one detail that I forget my original idea of what I'm doing. But if I go away for a while, I see things more clearly."

He frowned. "I don't have the time to spare, Brooke. God help us, there are only three days left, and too many people who had reasons to want Hoffman dead. Adele and Langdon, Tate, Snow, McCabe—"

"And Smith."

"And Smith," he agreed, heavily. "Actually, this would be a good time to talk to him—"

"Oh! Good evening, Julia." Brooke reached her hand across the table to Julia Hoffman who was just slipping into her seat. "I didn't think we'd see you here."

"My father was to have taken part in this," Julia said, wistfully, and settled back in her chair, her eyes on the stage. The last notes of the overture were dying away and the curtain was opening; in the sudden expectant silence all chance to carry on a private conversation were gone.

Matt shrugged and began to rise, and Brooke's hand tightened on his arm. "Stay," she mouthed, cocking her head towards Julia. He glanced at Julia, rigidly facing forward, and frowned again. Shrugging, he sat back in his seat. Brooke was right. He did need a break from the case, though he wished he'd thought of it himself. And maybe he'd have a chance to talk with Julia later.

The play, a condensed version of *The Masked Ball*, was lively and entertaining, if not particularly well-acted. The amateur performers obviously enjoyed what they were doing, and that enjoyment transferred itself to the audience. For Matt much of the fun lay in seeing the transformation of people who had become familiar over the past few days. Amazing how makeup and false hair, combined with acting a role, could change a person. If Randall Snow were present, he might be getting some ideas he could use in his career fleecing people.

Julia rose as the play ended and the lights came up, obviously intending to escape. Before she could, however, she was accosted and surrounded by well-wishers, preventing her leaving. The glance she shot at Brooke, as she gathered up her gauzy silk shawl, was filled with desperate appeal. Brooke glanced at Matt, who nodded, and together they pushed their way to Julia's side.

"Come, Julia," Brooke said, taking her arm. "We'll walk you back."

"Yes, we promised your mother we'd get you back at a reasonable time," Matt said from Julia's other side.

"Oh, thank you!" Julia's voice was low but fervent as they finally were able to cross the grand saloon. "I did think for a moment there that they wouldn't have let me go." She made a face. "They mean well, I suppose."

"They're nosy," Brooke said bluntly. "You probably shouldn't have come tonight."

"Yes, I know. But Father was so looking forward to being in the play, I had to come."

"I remember now, seeing him in a play in New York. He was quite good."

"Yes, he loved it. When I was young we would always stage our own plays. We had trunks in the attic filled with clothes for costumes, and we'd all take part. But that was a long time ago," she said, her voice small.

Brooke patted her arm. "It will pass, Julia," she said, gently. "It will take time, but it will pass."

"Will it?" Julia's face went remote. "Bad enough what

happened to my father, but Mother won't tell me why she wasn't in the suite then."

"What?" Matt and Brooke exclaimed together.

Julia started. "Nothing. Excuse me, I must go," she gaped and, before they could stop her, had turned and was nearly running up the stairs.

Matt and Brooke stared at each other. "Did she just say—damn, she has to explain that!" Matt said, setting his foot on the bottom stair.

"No, Matt." Brooke's hand on his arm held him back. "Not now."

"But, damn, Brooke, if Adele wasn't there—"

"I know, but she won't tell you, Matt. Not like this. She might tell me, though."

Matt stared at her and then stepped back. "Huh. Yeah, you're probably right. Besides," his gaze sharpened, "there's Randall Snow. I want to talk to him."

"All right. And I'll see to Julia." Giving him a distracted smile, Brooke headed up the stairs.

For once there were quite a few people on the promenade deck, heading to their staterooms and suites after the play. Brooke paused by the door, frowning. She could see no sign of Julia anywhere. Logic told her, though, that Julia would have headed toward the Hoffman's suite, near Brooke's own. Disregarding other people and the convention that the part of the deck near the deck housing was reserved for steamer chairs, not people walking, Brooke strode quickly along, the wind tugging at her hair and whipping her skirts about her. There was a young woman ahead—but, no, she was with someone, a young man who held her arm. Not Julia. Could she have reached her suite so quickly? Unless . . . Brooke stopped near the corridor where Julia had once approached her. Unless Julia had decided to hide from any pursuit. "Julia?"

There was a rustling noise that might only have been the wind, and then a shadowy figure stepped forward. "How did you know I was here?" Julia asked from the corridor.

"I guessed. Julia." Brooke stepped forward, and there was another rustle of cloth as Julia backed away. "I don't want to scare you, but you can't say what you just did and then expect us not to ask about it."

"I didn't say anything."

"But you did, you know." Brooke kept her voice gentle. "It's cold here. Would you care to go along to my suite? We could talk—"

"No! It's talking that's gotten me into this fix—"

"And talking that will get you out. What did you mean, Julia?"

"I don't know what you're talking about."

"You said your mother wasn't in the suite when your father died. That was around eleven. Was she there, or wasn't she?"

"Eleven?" Julia's voice was high-pitched. "Oh, that explains it!"

"What?"

"My watch," Julia babbled. "It was fast. Well, remember that they told us to set it back about an hour every day? I always get confused, and I put it ahead instead. So it was only ten, not eleven."

"Julia, it was only the first day of the cruise. No one had set their watches yet."

"I did, so I wouldn't forget the next day," Julia said, stubbornly. "And then when I found out what I'd done, I had to reset it. Not that it mattered by then."

"You're sure about this?"

"Yes. I was wrong about the time, and nothing you say will make me say anything different. Now if you'll excuse me, I want to go to bed," she said and, head held high, pushed past Brooke, her skirts rustling.

"Julia," Brooke called, and then stopped, letting her breath out. It was no good; she'd get no more from Julia tonight, if ever. And, she thought, walking out from the corridor herself, she couldn't blame her. If she thought someone in her own family were implicated in a crime, she would want to protect that person. Even if she was a cop's daughter.

Standing on the deck, Brooke glanced back in the direction of the stairway leading to the grand saloon, and then made a decision. It was late, and Matt likely wouldn't welcome her presence when he was questioning a suspect. The best thing for her to do would be to return to the suite. There, perhaps, she could think of a way to convince Julia to tell the truth. Adele's maid had already told them that Adele hadn't been in the suite when Hoffman died, and that meant that one thing was certain. Julia was lying.

"Mr. Snow," Matt said, just as Snow opened the door to the saloon deck. "May I have a word with you?"

Snow stopped, his shoulders rising and then falling in an exaggerated sigh. "And I was this close to getting away."

In spite of himself, Matt felt the urge to smile. "We didn't finish our discussion this afternoon."

"As far as I'm concerned, we did."

"Your alibi checked out."

"I didn't expect it not to."

"I doubt that you did, or you wouldn't have said anything. Still." Matt gave him a hard look. "I have the feeling, Mr. Snow, that you know things you're not telling me."

"And I'm still a suspect, alibi or not. No, don't answer that. You know," he went on, "you'd be pretty good at cards, but you've got a few things that give you away."

"You said some bitter things about Mr. Hoffman at the memorial service."

"I admit it. But then, I despise hypocrisy. And I think—no, I know—that you haven't looked at everyone as closely as you should."

"Meaning?"

"Meaning don't take everyone at face value. Mr. Smith, for example."

"What about Smith?"

"Did you know he was in the smoking room not long before Hoffman went over? He rousted me from my game, you know. And that's something you can check."

"I already have, Mr. Snow."

"Oh?" Snow's eyebrows rose. "You are thorough, aren't you? So tell me, Mr. Devlin. Where did Smith go afterwards?"

"If you know something, Mr. Snow, why not just say so?"

Snow held up his hands in a gesture of innocence that didn't fool Matt for a moment. "I know only what everyone else knew."

"Which is?"

"That Hoffman claimed to be doing very well, and yet

his firm was losing money. Don't tell me you haven't heard that. And there are only two people who could have anything to do with it."

"First Smith, and now Langdon. Are you accusing them of murder, Mr. Snow?"

Snow held up his hands again, his guileless expression deepening. "I'm not accusing anyone of anything. That could be dangerous, when I'm not even sure Hoffman was murdered."

"What do you think happened to him, then?"

"God knows. But wherever he is now, he's laughing at us. You can be sure of that."

An odd thing to say. "So you're saying you have no grudge against Hoffman?"

"I did once, but now?" He shrugged. "What would be the purpose? I'm doing well enough, and my prospects are good."

"If you can still find people to play with you," Matt said, and at that moment Snow went very still, staring beyond Matt, his eyes suddenly wary. Matt turned, but all he saw were people chattering, and stewards removing empty glasses from a table. "What is it?"

"Why, nothing." Snow smiled, his poker face firmly in place. "Thought I saw someone I played cards with last night. The man had the gall to accuse me of cheating."

"Imagine that," Matt said, dryly. "All right, Mr. Snow, I'm done with you. For now."

"But don't go anywhere?" Snow's voice was mocking. "Where would I go?"

"Don't worry, Mr. Snow." Matt remained calm. "There are people watching you."

"For all the good that will do them," Snow said, and

slipped away, joining the throngs still climbing the grand stairway, until he was just one of many.

Matt frowned, and then turned to follow. An odd interview, and he wasn't sure he'd learned anything that could help him. Snow knew something, of that he was certain. Whether it was anything that would help solve the case, however, was another matter.

"Matt?" Brooke called as he opened the door to the suite.

"Yeah, it's me."

Brooke came to the bedroom door as he pulled off suit jacket and tie. "Did you have any luck?"

"No. You?"

"No. Julia denied what she said. I don't know if I can ever persuade her to explain it." She paused. "Did Snow have anything to say?"

"Nothing helpful." He frowned. "He was different tonight. He seemed a lot more confident."

"Does that mean anything?"

He shrugged. "Probably not. He probably has some deal going we don't know about. Remember, he is a gambler—now, who's that at this time of night?" he said, as a knock came on the door of the suite.

"Steward," a voice called.

Matt frowned. "Did you call for a steward?"

"No."

"Go back into the bedroom and close the door," Matt said, approaching the door to the suite carefully.

"Matt, you don't think there's any danger—"

"I don't know. I do know we're in the middle of a murder investigation, and I'm not too popular right now. Go."

Brooke hesitated and then, nodding, went into the bedroom, leaving the door open a crack. Matt stared at it a moment, and then opened the door to the suite, peering around the edge. A steward did indeed stand there, one Matt hadn't seen before. In one hand he held a tray with a wine bottle and two glasses. "Yes? What is it?"

"The wine you ordered, sir."

"I didn't order any wine."

"For God's sake, let me in," the steward said, his voice dropping to a hiss. "If Smith knows I'm here there'll be the devil to pay."

"Smith. Huh." Matt frowned, but he opened the door wider. The steward slipped inside. "You'd better have a good explanation for this."

"I do. Whew." The steward set the tray down and wiped his brow. "It's that Smith, sir. He's got everyone on staff that scared of him."

Somehow, Matt wasn't surprised. "And you are?"

"Oh. Didn't I say? Owain Davies. I'm a steward on the saloon deck." He paused. "Where Mr. Langdon has his stateroom."

Matt tensed again. "Oh?"

"Yes. There's something I didn't tell you, sir. Rather, I didn't tell Mr. Smith, but he found out, anyway. Now I don't know what he's going to do."

Matt stood with his arms crossed on his chest. "About what?"

"About Mr. Langdon, sir. You see, I told Smith I didn't see Mr. Langdon that night, I mean the night Mr. Hoffman died."

"Yes, and?"

"I lied, sir."

"Oh, did you." Matt gestured Davies to a chair and sat down on the sofa. "And why did you do that?"

"Because none of us like Smith. But I don't want Mr. Langdon to get into trouble, even though," he swallowed, "I think he may be."

"Why?"

"Because he called for me just before eleven that night."

Matt sat up straighter. "The devil he did!"

"Yes, sir. He wanted champagne. And, sir."

"Yes?"

"He wasn't alone. There was a woman with him."

"Who?" Matt said, sharply.

"I don't know, sir, I didn't see her. But I heard—oh, Christ!" This as another knock came on the door.

"Devlin!" Smith called from the deck. "Need to talk with you."

"Oh, Christ!" Davies said again, jumping to his feet. "If he knows I'm here—"

"In the bathroom." Matt waited while Davies stumbled across the sitting room to the lavatory. "This is turning into a farce," he muttered, slowly crossing the room to open the door yet again, at last letting Smith in.

"Sorry to disturb you so late." Smith staggered in, glancing at the bedroom door. "Got some things you should know."

"Such as?"

"I talked with Owain Davies tonight."

"Davies." Matt frowned. "Steward in first class. Langdon's steward?"

"That's the one. I don't trust him, you see? He's Welsh, and I never trust the Welsh. Didn't think he was telling

me the truth when he said Langdon was in his stateroom,
but he was. At least, I couldn't shake him on it."

"And I imagine you tried," Matt said, drily.

"Oh, that I did." His glance fell on the bottle of wine.
"Am I interrupting somethin'?"

"No. Is that it?"

"It's enough. I say we go talk with Langdon about this,
and Mrs. Hoffman, too."

"No. Not tonight."

"Aw, come on, detective. Let's do it. Or, better yet. Let
me do it. Yeah." He leaned forward, as if he'd just now
thought of this. "Let me have Mrs. Hoffman. I'll find out
what she's hiding."

"No," Matt said, sharply. "This has to be handled
right."

Smith's face darkened. "And you don't think I can do
it?"

"Frankly, no."

"Not good enough for you, am I, detective? I do all your
dirty work, but you won't give me any of the credit."

"If you deserve credit, you'll get it. And, by the way,"
he said, stopping Smith as he was about to open the door
to leave. "Where were you when Hoffman died?"

Smith turned from the door, and the look in his eyes
would have made another man quail. "What was that, detective?" he asked, his voice deceptively soft.

"You heard me." Matt held his ground. "Where were
you?"

"Doing my job."

"Which was?"

"Making sure all was secure."

"Where?"

"Wherever I was needed. Is that all, detective?"

"You had a motive," Matt said, quietly.

"Be damned, and suppose I did?" Smith erupted. "And the means, too, I suppose you'll say, as well as knowing my way around the ship! But where are your witnesses, detective?" Smith leaned forward, his nose almost touching Matt's. "You tell me that."

"They're all scared of you," Matt said, not giving an inch, and had the satisfaction of seeing Smith blink in surprise.

"Who?" he demanded. "Who are your witnesses?"

"D'you think I'd tell you, so you could scare them into silence?" Matt glared at him. "No."

"I'm part of this investigation, detective."

"Not of this part."

"Be damned." Smith stomped back towards the door, and then stopped. "You don't have anyone, do you? No one. And I know you, detective." He half-turned back to Matt, an odd little smile on his face. "You won't accuse someone if you don't have the evidence to back it up."

"I'll find it, Smith," Matt said softly. "On whoever did the murder."

"Not on me. You'll never find it on me, detective," Smith said, and, giving a jeering laugh, stomped out of the suite, slamming the door behind him.

"Dammit," Matt said into the silence left by his departure. "Damn, if he's not guilty of something—"

"But, murder, Matt?" Brooke stepped out of the bedroom. "Would he go that far?"

"He wants his job back in New York."

"Murder isn't the way to get it."

"It might be in his mind, if the victim is the man who could keep him off the force."

Brooke frowned. "Matt, you don't really think—"

"I don't know what I think, Brooke." He turned towards her, shaking his head, and his gaze sharpened. "Damn. I forgot about Davies. Mr. Davies. You can come out."

It took a moment, but the door to the lavatory at last creaked open, and a wide-eyed Davies stepped out. "Did Smith do it?" he blurted.

"I don't know," Matt said, sharply. "If you know what's good for you, Davies, you'll forget you ever heard that."

"You sound just like Smith, sir."

Matt grimaced. This was the second time someone had told him that. "It's for your own good," he said, his voice milder. "How do you think Smith would react if he knew you were here."

"Badly, sir. So you can rely on me. I won't say a word." He cast a quick glance at Brooke as he reached for the door. "Enjoy your wine, sir, ma'am," he said, a smile at last lighting his face, and went out.

"Good heavens," Brooke said into the silence.

"Yeah. Things are more tangled now than ever." He paced the room. "I've got to do something about this."

"Not now. It really is too late to see Adele."

"Yeah. But what do you want to bet it was her with Langdon? And, dammit, she'll never admit it."

"You never know. Something will happen, Matt. You've got enough people stirred up now."

He shrugged. "Maybe."

"In any event, you can't do anything more tonight."

He was silent for a long moment. "No," he said, finally. "I can't do anything more tonight."

Sunday, April 19, 1 A.M.

Late at night, and the great ship slept. At least, the passengers did. James Turner was glad of that fact as he crept along the corridor towards his second cabin stateroom. It was deuced awkward, having met a lady who appealed to him on this voyage, and to have to be so discreet about their meetings. After all, she had her reputation to consider, since she was a very proper widow, on her way to Europe with a friend. And he was on his way to England on business for the Mitchell Import-Export Company, who employed him, so that he had to be careful of his reputation, too. Thus he and Clara, his lady love, had taken to meeting at strange and inconvenient places and times. And all because neither of them had a private stateroom. Clara shared a stateroom with her friend, an old battle-axe of a woman who had disliked James on sight; the feeling was mutual. As for him, Mitchell's had refused to pay for a private room, and so he had to share with another passenger.

Most of the time, that wasn't a problem. His roommate managed to spend a great deal of time in first cabin. He was a cardsharper, and made no secret of the fact, practicing shuffling and dealing on his bunk for hours at a time. James's lips curled in a sneer. He didn't hold with such things. Not that he was an angel, but never in his life had he fleeced someone of his money. He hadn't expressed his disapproval, though; it was really none of his business. He'd be glad when this voyage was over. Perhaps, then, he and Clara could be more open about their feelings. Maybe he'd even marry her . . .

His stateroom door swung ajar as he put the key in the lock, startling him. Probably Snow was back, he thought, frowning, and likely he'd have questions about where James had been. As if that was any of his concern. Closing the door more firmly than necessary, James reached for the lightswitch. After all, a man couldn't get undressed in the dark, and he didn't intend to, even if it disturbed Snow. In the few seconds before he flipped the switch, however, he was aware, on a level just below conscious thought, that there was something odd about the stateroom. Only later would he realize what had caused that impression: the feeling of something soft underfoot, perhaps a piece of clothing, and the absence of a man's heavy breathing in sleep.

Turning on the switch, James stepped towards his bunk, and then stopped, staring. Clothes and other items were scattered about the room, on the floor and the bunk and the dresser. Heart thumping, James turned, and, to his eternal disgrace, became thoroughly, messily sick. Because, lying on the floor on the far side of the room, was Randall Snow, his eyes staring and a pool of blood spreading from his head. He was very dead.

11

"Christ almighty." Matt took one step into the second class stateroom and stopped. He'd seen his share of violent death, but never would he become accustomed to it. Snow, to whom Matt had spoken just a few hours earlier, lay in a crumpled mass on the floor in a thickening pool of blood, his eyes blank and staring and the back of his head curiously flat. It could have been an accident; the corner of the nearby bureau was stained with what looked, even at a distance, like blood and hair, but Matt had a sinking feeling in his stomach that it wasn't. Snow had known something, that Matt had seen for himself. And whatever it was, he'd taken it to the grave.

He glanced away from the body, and instantly his temper rose. "Dammit, Smith!" he roared, as Smith, without a thought of preserving any evidence, rummaged through dresser drawers. "Stop that. You should know better than to touch anything."

Smith turned his head, his face impassive but his eyes

shining with a strange light. "Someone did for him, you see? And I intend to find out who it is."

"What you will do," Matt said, his voice surprisingly even, "is step back from that dresser. Now."

Smith turned, and his fists came up. "D'you plan to make me, detective?"

"If I have to." Matt remained still, his gaze boring into Smith's, and it was the big man who looked away first.

"The captain should know about this," he muttered, stepping back from the dresser. "I'll report to him." Not looking at Matt, he crossed the stateroom and went out.

Matt let him go, closing the door behind him and thus shutting out the curious and frightened passengers who thronged outside, wearing wrappers and dressing gowns, and whispering in excited speculation about what had occurred. Reporting to the captain was Matt's job, and he would have liked another pair of eyes to study the scene, but not Smith. Besides, Matt realized, with an undeniable quickening in his blood, this crime scene was his now, and his alone.

He pulled open the door again, and the passengers surged back. "You," he barked to the steward. "Clear all these people away from here."

"Yes, sir," the steward said, craning his head to see inside the stateroom. "Is he dead, sir?"

"Yes. Clear those people away, and summon the ship's doctor."

"He's on his way, sir."

"Good. Let him in when he comes," Matt said, and closed the door again, shutting out the commotion. He was left alone, at last, with the late Randall Snow.

For a few moments he did nothing, but just looked. The

stateroom looked as if a whirlwind had gone through it. Dresser drawers were pulled out and overturned, their contents scattered about the room. Someone had been looking for something, or wanted it to appear that way.

The body looked almost calm in contrast, huddled on the floor. That a struggle had taken place was undeniable; toilet articles, rolling with the motion of the ship, were scattered on the dresser and the floor, and a corner of the bedspread was clutched in Snow's hand, as if he'd grabbed at it to save himself. Who had Snow fought with? Someone he'd fleeced, or someone more sinister?

The door opened, breaking into his thought. He turned to see a distinguished-looking man of middle years come in. Apparently he'd been roused from sleep, as Matt had, for his hair stood on end and he was in shirtsleeves. A heavy black bag was held in one hand. To his credit, he blanched when he looked at the body, but otherwise showed no distress. "Martin Dunn," he said, holding out his hand. "The ship's surgeon."

"Matt Devlin." Matt gestured towards the body. "I don't imagine you've had to deal with anything like this before."

"You'd be surprised, sir. Where shall I put my bag? I don't want to disturb any evidence."

"You've worked crime scenes before?" Matt asked in surprise.

"Once. When I was in practice in New York. One of my patients was murdered and I was the one the family called first. Not a pleasant experience." He set his bag on the floor. "A ship is like a floating city, detective. All sorts of things happen on it. Although I must admit this is a bit extreme." He started to step over a piece of clothing on the floor, and then stopped. "May I examine the body?"

"Yes. I need to know how he died."

Dunn nodded, peering down at the body without touching it. "Obvious, I should think, though you'd probably want an autopsy to be certain. A blow to the head."

"By?"

Dunn crouched down. "Something angled, I'd think," he said, looking up and staring at the corner of the dresser. "He may have fallen against that."

Matt nodded. "Could it have been an accident?" he asked, curiously detached. He had distanced himself from the body now, seeing it no longer as a person, but as an object. It was easier that way.

"Possibly." Dunn was still peering over the body, still not touching it. "If the ship was rolling and he was caught off guard, it could have happened that way. But by the looks of things in here, I'd doubt it." He looked up, his eyes sharp and shrewd. "I suspect you've already thought of that."

"Mm." If Snow had been involved in a fight, he could easily have been pushed against the dresser. It still could be an accident, in that the death had been unintentional, but it would still be murder.

It wasn't surprising. Snow had behaved oddly earlier this evening, as if he knew something, something that was to his advantage and someone else's disadvantage. But would that have been motive enough to kill him? "Depends what it was," he muttered, and Dr. Dunn looked up.

"May I turn him over?" he asked.

"Not yet." Matt stepped closer to the bed, forcing him-

self to look down at the body, forcing himself to forget
that, just a few hours earlier, Snow had been alive, assured
and confident of his future. "Any idea how long he's been
dead?"

"Now that, I can't tell you. Rigor is just setting in in the
hands, see?" He tried to flex Snow's fingers, but they remained stiff. "But it's warm in here, so that would affect
it. If you knew when he was last seen alive—"

"I saw him myself around eleven," Matt interrupted,
"and as it's now after two I'd say it probably happened
between eleven and one." And on a ship this size, that
didn't narrow down the number of suspects by much.

"Probably," Dr. Dunn agreed.

Matt felt carefully inside Snow's jacket, searching the
pockets and finding nothing. "His wallet's missing."

"Burglary?"

"I don't know." Matt rose, looking down at the body.
In spite of the missing wallet, he doubted that burglary
had been the motive in this killing. Snow had known
something; on that Matt would stake his life. Unfortunately, Snow had already done so, taking the biggest gamble possible, and he had lost. And Matt, in pursuing the
investigation, had, indeed, stirred things up.

The news spread quickly through the ship: a burglar
was aboard, one who wasn't afraid to kill to get what he
wanted. The purser was assailed by people wishing to
leave their valuables in the safe, while the passengers
began to look at each other in suspicion. The possibly ac-
cidental death of a passenger was one thing; Snow's was

quite another. With it they had become aware that no one was safe.

Two days left. No matter that it was Sunday, and that there would be a religious service in the grand saloon. Matt was working. After returning to the suite for a hasty change of clothes and an even hastier breakfast, he headed for Smith's office, which he had temporarily taken over. The challenge ahead was difficult, and yet he was more optimistic today. The killer had made a mistake. Had he stayed quiet, hidden, chances were he would not have been identified before the voyage ended. Now, though, the investigation had taken a new turn. Find Snow's killer, and Matt thought he might just find Hoffman's as well.

The passengers whose rooms adjoined Snow's were being interviewed by a sullen Ambrose Smith, who hadn't forgotten Matt's accusation of the evening before. For the first time, Matt spoke with Snow's roommate, James Turner, who had little to add. What he did find, after patient and careful questioning, was where Turner had been that evening, and how long he'd been out of his room, narrowing the estimated time of death still further. It was something, at least, Matt thought, as, his face pale, Turner left the office. Find someone with a motive and the opportunity, and maybe, just maybe, he'd find his culprit.

Leaning back, hands clasped behind his head, Matt closed his eyes. Instantly, the memory of Snow's stateroom sprang into his mind, as if he were still seeing it. The chaos in the stateroom that indicated a struggle bothered him. Would Snow have fought so hard to save his wallet, if doing so meant he would die? Matt doubted it. Cardsharpers usually tried to avoid violence, not just because they disliked it, but because it would draw attention to themselves. No, Snow, being a gambler, would likely have considered the wallet just another loss, and plotted a way to make it up. Complicating matters, no one interviewed so far had heard any sound of a struggle; and there was no sign that the lock on the stateroom door had been forced. It all led to one conclusion. Snow had probably let his killer in, and, if that were the case, it was likely someone he'd known. Someone he'd known something about. The question was, who?

Matt opened his eyes. He was right, he thought, reviewing his logic. Snow was a survivor, a man who lived by his wits, as witness his occupation and the way he had recovered from losing his money. He was not a man to be caught offguard. However if the murderer were someone Snow didn't suspect, someone he thought he could best in some way—Matt grimaced. Yes, Snow could very easily have been caught that way, and the only way to find out which of Snow's acquaintances was capable of such a thing was to talk to them all. Including everyone he'd played cards with.

He was grimacing again when there was a knock on the door. "Come in," he called, and Padlock Homes stalked in, his greatcoat swirling about him. "Good morning, sir. I am here to offer my assistance."

Matt almost groaned. "Thank you, but that's not necessary," he said, curtly.

"Indeed, it is, sir. With so little time left and so much to do? I tell you," Homes leaned over the desk confidentially, "the Black Hand is involved in this."

Matt was staring up at him, speechless, when the door opened again. "Sir?" a timid voice said. "You wanted to see me?"

Matt looked past Homes to see a steward, neat in white jacket and black trousers. "You are?"

"Edward McCabe, sir." McCabe looked uncertainly from Matt to Homes. "I can come back."

"No." Matt rose. "Mr. Homes was just leaving. Weren't you?"

Homes's lips tightened. "For now, detective. But, never fear. You need my help, and I shall provide it." And with that he was gone, his greatcoat swirling again, leaving the other men to stare at the closed door in bemusement.

"God," Matt muttered, and sat down. "Sit down, Mr. McCabe. You were the steward for Mr. Snow's room?"

McCabe sat across the desk from Matt. "Yes, sir."

"Mm-hm." Matt studied the other man. So this was McCabe. He didn't look much like his half-brother; unlike Hoffman, his build was weedy, with sloping shoulders. A thick mustache bristled on his face, while his eyes were hidden behind thick spectacles. Nor did he have any of the vitality that had impressed Matt about Hoffman.

"Edward McCabe." Matt pulled a piece of paper towards him. "Yes, I wanted to talk with you. Where are you from?"

"Brooklyn, sir."

Matt looked up at that. "Really? You don't sound it."

"My mother was very particular about my speech, sir."

Matt nodded. McCabe's speech was precise, almost accentless, as if he had indeed worked hard to perfect it. "My condolences on your brother."

"Thank you, sir," McCabe said, his voice toneless.

"I'll have some questions for you about him later. For now, though, did you know Mr. Snow?"

"Only as a passenger, sir."

"And?"

Matt wasn't certain, but he thought McCabe blinked. "And what, sir?"

"What was he like? Was he demanding? Loud? Neat? Messy? Did he spend much time in his stateroom, did he have a lot of guests—?"

"Oh, no, sir." McCabe sounded shocked. "Guests aren't allowed in the staterooms."

"Really? Even of the same sex?"

"Well, yes, of course. But didn't you mean if Mr. Snow had any female guests—?"

"No. Not particularly. Anyone, Mr. McCabe."

"Well . . . yes, there were some people who came to see him. Most of the times he wasn't in. He didn't spend much time in his stateroom, sir, and when he did, he practiced with his cards." Animation flitted across McCabe's face for the first time. "He was skilled with those, sir. Could make them dance if he wanted to."

"Then you know what he was doing."

"Yes, sir." McCabe's voice was wooden again. "He's traveled with us before, you see."

"Mm." Matt noted that down. Maybe McCabe had some information, after all. "Tell me. A man like that, making his living gambling—he must have made many people angry at him."

"I suppose so, sir."

"Huh." He felt like cursing at the man's lack of response, of interest. "Well? Did any of them confront him?"

"I'm sure they must have, sir." Animation returned to his features again. "I certainly wouldn't want to lose money in such a way."

"Are you saying that Snow played cards with you?"

"Oh, no, sir! Such a thing is not allowed. Besides," his lips pursed, "I'm very careful with my money."

Somehow, Matt could believe it. "So no one came to his stateroom to confront him."

"Oh, I didn't say that, sir. Only that Mr. Snow wasn't in."

"For God's sake." Matt threw down his pen. "Did someone come to Snow to complain about his game, or didn't he?"

"Why, yes. I believe there was someone—now, let me see." McCabe poked at the bridge of his spectacles, settling them more firmly on his face. "Was it last voyage, or this one? They do all run together, you know, when you've been working in the same place for so long. Yes. Now I remember." He sat back with an air of triumph. "It was this voyage."

"What happened on this voyage, Mr. McCabe?"

"Why, didn't I say? You asked if anyone came to complain, and I thought I said that someone did."

Matt's lips thinned in an effort to keep his patience. "When? And who was it?"

"That I can't tell you, sir. A gentleman, of course. Let's see." McCabe's face furrowed. "I was just starting to turn the beds down for the night. Yes. The gentleman was knocking on Mr. Snow's door, just as I came out of Mr. Leslie's stateroom across the hall. He seemed most agitated."

"And?"

"He demanded to know where Mr. Snow was. Well, I didn't know, and so I told him."

"When was this?" Matt asked again, when McCabe continued to sit quietly, his hands folded in his lap.

"When? Oh. Was it last night—no, no, of course it couldn't have been. The night before, perhaps? Yes. That was when it was. Around nine, I think, since that's when I turn the beds down."

"What did he look like?"

"Oh, dear." McCabe's face furrowed again. "I'm afraid I didn't pay too much attention, so much work I had yet to do. He wasn't terribly old, I do know that. At least, I don't believe so. His hair wasn't gray. It was . . ." He pursed his lips. "Brown." McCabe beamed at Matt. "Yes. Brown."

"Eye color?"

"I didn't notice, I fear."

"Was he clean-shaven? Did he have a beard or mustache?"

"Oh, dear. I just don't know, sir. It was very quick, you understand, and I was busy." He paused. "Perhaps a mustache. Oh! And he wasn't terribly tall, sir. Taller than me, but not as tall as you. And not very big. He was wearing—I believe it's called a tuxedo?"

"Mm." Matt noted that down. For someone who claimed not to notice much, McCabe had just given him a full, if sketchy, description. "Would you know him again if you saw him?"

"I don't know, sir." McCabe leaned forward. "Would I have to identify him?"

"Maybe. Depends on what he said."

"Didn't I tell you?" McCabe blinked. "Oh. Well, it wasn't so much what he said, as how he said it, if you take my meaning. He seemed very annoyed that Mr. Snow wasn't there, and then he said, 'You tell him I came to see him, and I want my money back,' and he walked away. Quite frightening, sir, the way he looked at me." McCabe shivered. "When he found out Snow wasn't there I thought I was in danger."

"Mm-hm." Matt wrote that down, too, though he didn't quite believe it. McCabe was an inoffensive little rabbit. It was hard to believe he would do anything to incite anyone to anger, let alone violence. "Is that all you remember?"

"Yes, sir. Is that all, sir? I really must get back."

"I understood you weren't on duty."

"Not at the moment, sir, no. I work primarily at night. But I do like to be available in case the day steward needs me." His face sobered. "And Mr. Snow's room will take some cleaning."

"Later. I need to ask you about your brother."

McCabe blinked. "Half-brother, sir."

"Does that matter?"

"It always did, before."

Matt sat back in his chair, regarding McCabe, who remained stiff and still. "It sounds like you didn't like him much."

"We weren't raised together, sir."

"I'm aware of that. Tell me. Did you know he was going to be on this ship?"

"No, sir." McCabe blinked again, and then pushed his wire-rimmed glasses higher on his face. "Not until sailing day. Sir, Mr. Smith already asked me these questions."

"Bear with me, Mr. McCabe. We now have two deaths to deal with. Do you have any idea who killed your brother?"

McCabe frowned. "Wasn't it the Black Hand?"

"No, Mr. McCabe." Matt's voice held weary patience. Homes's mistaken idea had spread throughout the ship and taken hold.

"Oh. Then I don't know, unless it was that frozen goddess he married."

"You don't like Mrs. Hoffman."

"No, sir, I do not." He shook his head decisively. "And she doesn't like me."

"What about Hoffman?"

McCabe blinked again. "What about him?"

"Well, he got everything, didn't he? Didn't it gall you, McCabe, seeing him come on this ship, living the high life, while you have to work for a living? And you don't even have the benefit of his name."

"Look." McCabe leaned forward. "I don't—didn't—have any grudge against my brother. He was a good man. As soon as he found out about me, he made sure I was all right. My mother, too, and God knows she had it hard. He even helped me get this job."

"And you didn't resent that?"

McCabe hesitated. "Maybe in the beginning. When I think of the life my mother lived—no, Mr. Devlin. If I have a grudge against anyone, it's my father. He's the one got my mother in a fix and then wouldn't acknowledge me. But Julius was always decent enough." He reached up to his glasses again, pushing them higher, and then took them off, polishing them with a handkerchief. For the first time, Matt could see a resemblance to Hoffman. A slight resemblance. "He was the only family I had. The ice queen won't even let me see her children." He put his glasses on again. "That poor girl."

"Who?" Matt asked.

"Julius's daughter. Having to marry someone she doesn't want, and all because of her money."

"How do you know that?"

McCabe blinked. "Julia told me."

Matt frowned. "When?"

"The other day."

"How did she know who you were?"

McCabe hesitated, and then shrugged. "Adele doesn't know this, but Julius made sure Julia and Chauncey knew me. But do you know why she came to see me? It was because she knew it would get her mother upset. Look, Mr. Devlin." He leaned forward. "Do you think I want to get involved with them? Adele would make my life miserable if she could. She probably will, now," he added, gloomily.

Matt looked down at his notebook. "So you don't know anyone on this ship who wanted to harm your brother."

McCabe pursed his lips. "Only Mr. Langdon."

"And why is that?" Matt asked, leaning back.

"I don't think they were getting along too well, from what Julius said."

"Which was?"

"Nothing definite, sir. Just a tone of voice, and the way he looked. And Adele did ask for a divorce."

"Ah." Matt nodded at this confirmation of rumor. "And you think she wanted it so she could marry Langdon."

"I think it's possible." He shifted in the chair. "Look, sir, I really do have a lot of work to do, and I've answered these questions already. Can I go?"

Matt stared at him for a moment, hard, and then reluc-

tantly nodded. McCabe might be meek, but his lips were
set in a mulish pout that told Matt he wasn't going to get
much more out of him. Not now, anyway. "Yes. But I'll
be wanting to talk with you again."

"Yes, sir," McCabe said, and, standing, left the office.

Left alone, Matt picked up his notebook, and then
tossed it down again. Damn, he wasn't getting anywhere.
Two more days before they reached Southampton. If he
had the case cleared up by then, it would be a miracle.

"But I don't want to marry him, Mother!" Julia exclaimed.

Adele pressed her fingertips to her throbbing temples.
With Julia raging on so, the suite seemed shrunken,
cramped. Oh, this terrible, interminable journey. Would
it never end? "Don't shriek so, Julia. I can hear you."

"But you won't listen! I told you in New York I didn't
want to marry the earl—"

"Julia, please. I've such a headache. Must we discuss
this now?"

"Your mother's going through a hard time, Julia,"
Richard said, standing behind Adele's chair. "It's selfish
of you to bother her at a time like this."

"There's no time left!" Julia whirled about. "Oh,
Mother, please! In just a few days we'll be in England and
I'll have to face the earl again—"

"It's a good match, Julia, and I'm tired of your com-
plaints. I—ooh." The breath went out of her as she rose
and was immediately assailed by dizziness. She was aware
of Richard's hand on her elbow, supporting her, and of

Julia, still whining. Dear Richard. What would she do without him?

"Now see what you've done," Richard was saying. "You know your mother isn't well."

"Maybe if she hadn't had that third cocktail with luncheon she'd be feeling better," Julia retorted.

"Julia! Apologize to your mother this instant."

"You're not my father, Richard," Julia said, in so sharp a tone that Adele looked up. With her pale hair and oval face, Julia resembled her. Everyone said so. But there were also times when it was obvious that she was Julius's child, as now, when her voice took on that mulish note. "And just where were *you* when my father disappeared?"

"Julia!" Adele gasped, appalled. She and Richard had been discreet, she knew they had. Yet the implications of Julia's question were frightening. "Apologize to Mr. Langdon."

"I will not!" Julia rounded on her. "And where were you, Mother? You won't tell me that."

"All these histrionics are unnecessary," Richard said, sounding bored, and Adele, who had been too stunned by Julia's attack to react, stared at him. "If you would think a moment, Julia—and I know you are a bright girl—you would realize that there is a simple explanation for that."

"What?" Julia challenged, fist on her hips. "Tell me."

He quirked an eyebrow at her. "Shall I, Adele?"

"I—yes." Dear lord, he surely wasn't going to tell Julia that they had been . . .

"We were taking a turn on the promenade deck."

"Richard—"

"I don't believe you." Julia stared at him. "If you were, you would have said so before this."

"How could we? Think, Julia." He came around from behind the chair, crossing the room to her. "Think what people would say if they knew, of how it looks."

"But if you're innocent—you are, aren't you?"

"Really, Julia!" Adele said, recovering some of her spirit. "Such a thing to say."

"Of course we're innocent," Richard put in. "But people will talk, Julia. If they learn your mother and I were alone on deck together, they'll put the worst possible construction on it. And with the coincidence of your father dying at that time . . ." He shook his head. "What do you think people would say? Including the police?"

Julia looked uncertain. "But you're innocent."

"Don't be naive," Adele snapped. "Since when has that stopped rumor?"

Julia looked at Adele. "Then what about last night?"

Adele stiffened, on guard. "What about last night?"

"When Mr. Snow was killed."

"That has nothing to do with us. Now, about your marriage—"

"I won't marry him, Mother! And nothing you say will make me!" Julia cried, and flung out of the suite.

Heedless of the other passengers, Julia flew across the promenade deck until she reached the railing. She didn't know if the moisture on her cheeks was from spray or tears. What was she going to do? She raised her face to the heavens, beseeching she knew not what. Just a few months ago her life had been ideal, normal, and now everything was ruined. Everything. Mother was more distant than ever, preoccupied with what had happened and her plans to marry Mr. Langdon, now that she was free—and if she thought Julia didn't know about *that*, she was wrong. She was going to be forced into marriage with a man she actively disliked, and there was no one on her side. Father might have supported her, but he was lost to her. Now, far too late, she realized what he'd meant to her.

A wave of melancholy swept over Julia, so deep that she nearly dissolved into tears right then and there. But she didn't. She was her mother's daughter, and one thing she had long ago learned was that a display of emotion was unseemly. How much more unseemly it would be if she gave into impulse and climbed up the railing, swinging her legs over the side and . . .

No. She shuddered. That wasn't the way. At least . . .

Julia whirled around, her back to the railing, an incredulous smile lighting her face. Of course! That was the answer. For she was her father's daughter as well, and when he'd been in an intolerable situation, he'd found a way out. She could do the same.

Nodding once, decisively, Julia strode away from the railing, her melancholy gone. Her life was in her hands now, and that was what she wanted. She had a purpose, a plan, and soon she would put it into action, as her father had. And then no one would ever be able to tell her what to do again.

It was some time before Richard considered Adele calm enough to leave her. Things were a mess, he thought as he walked along the promenade deck to his own room. It was true that he'd wanted Julius out of the way, so that he and Adele could be together, but not like this. Never like this. He and Julius had been good friends at one time, and had made a success of their partnership. True, money was missing mysteriously from the firm, but Richard had his own thoughts on what had happened to that. He hadn't taken it; therefore, Julius must have. And that only deepened the mystery more.

Frowning, he unlocked the door to his stateroom, pulling off his tie as he went inside. Another day gone, with little progress apparently made towards solving the killings, and the cloud of suspicion still hanging over him and Adele. Unless the real killer was caught before they docked, day after tomorrow, that cloud would always be there. As things were, Richard worried whether his relationship with Adele would survive.

It was quiet, the only sounds those of the ship's engines and the restless sea, slapping against the hull. Richard yawned as he opened a dresser drawer to put away his tie, and came coldly, completely awake at the sight of what was in the drawer. A wallet. Lips tight, Richard flipped it open, finding some money, a tattered playing card, and a passport. It was Randall Snow's wallet.

12

Monday, April 20

Gregory Tate met Matt at the door of his stateroom with a smug smile on my face. "Well? Are you now going to say I murdered Snow? I don't have his wallet, by the way."

"Sit down, Mr. Tate," Matt said, taking out his notebook. Tate couldn't have murdered Snow, not with someone guarding Tate at all times. Which still left the question of how Hoffman's wallet had come into his possession. It was just barely possible that there were two murderers aboard, though Matt doubted it. "I know you were here when Snow died, unless the stewards are lying."

"Oh, no." Tate leaned back in the chair, legs crossed, and lit a cigarette. "They were here, Mr. Devlin. And so was I. And," he leaned forward, gesturing with the cigarette, "I didn't kill Julius. Even Mr. Homes agrees I couldn't have."

Matt's head snapped up. "When did you see him?"

"Yesterday." Tate looked surprised. "He said something about the Black Hand. He is part of the investigation, isn't he?"

"No." Homes would have to be dealt with; if he continued interfering he would be more than a nuisance. "You had reason to want Hoffman dead."

Gregory returned Matt's gaze. "Did I?"

"Yes."

"Then what was it? Oh, I know. That Julius wouldn't promote me. That I wouldn't be allowed to marry his daughter. I don't think," he took a long drag on his cigarette, "those are reasons enough for murder. No. Not for me, at least."

"And what would be your reasons, Mr. Tate?"

Gregory let out a laugh. "No, you'll not catch me that way, Devlin. I suggest you talk to the people who really benefited from Julius's death."

"Who are?" Matt said, though he knew.

"Langdon and Mrs. Hoffman, of course. Who else?"

Who else, indeed. Though as yet Matt couldn't see a connection between Langdon and Snow. "Thank you, Mr. Tate."

"I am free to go, then?"

"No." Matt turned from the door. "You are not."

Gregory bounded up from the chair, relaxed no longer. "But dammit, man, I'm innocent! What more does it take to convince you?"

"Proof," Matt said, almost gently, and went out.

Proof, he thought to himself, climbing the stairs to the promenade deck. Proof that one of the people with motives to kill Hoffman actually had. So far all he had was surmise and deduction; his only piece of hard evidence,

Hoffman's wallet, had been found in the hands of someone who could not be tied to Snow's death. And there was only one day left in the voyage.

Proof. Smith was still very much a suspect; he'd had a grudge against Hoffman, and Snow had implicated him. Knowing this, Smith could easily have gone after Snow, as well. It fit, but there was no proof. Nor was there any proof against McCabe, who had an alibi for both killings and no real motive. Only the fact that he had been on the same ship as his half-brother made him a suspect. Tate? Though he had been incriminated by the possession of Hoffman's wallet, he clearly couldn't have killed Snow. That left only Langdon and Adele.

Here his case was stronger. First it appeared that Langdon had not been in his room when Hoffman was killed; now it seemed as if he had been, but not alone. Julia had said that Adele hadn't been in the suite at the time, either; and though she had recanted, the testimony of the maid backed her up. They had motives, as well: the personal one of wanting to be together, along with the still-unanswered question of what had happened to the money missing from the firm. Either way, Langdon had a motive: to cover up his own acts, if he'd taken the money; or as a way of disposing of the real thief. No one, however, had seen Langdon or Adele commit the actual crime; nor had they been seen anywhere near Snow's cabin, although once again they had no alibis. Circumstance. That was all his case was, and, without proof, it might very well be all it ever was. Unless he could get either one of them to confess.

Matt knocked firmly on the door of the Hoffman suite, and the door was opened by Langdon. "Oh. It's you," he said, stepping aside. He was, as usual, well-dressed, in an expensive suit of wool flannel, but his hair needed a trim and his face looked strained. "Come in, though I don't know what you want."

"Just a few questions." Matt stepped into the sitting room, to see Adele sitting ramrod straight on the sofa. Good, so they had both obeyed his request to meet him here. It would probably be the easiest thing he achieved all morning. "Mrs. Hoffman."

Adele nodded frostily. "Mr. Devlin."

"I don't know why you want to see us," Langdon said, crossing the sitting room to stand beside Adele, one hand on her shoulder. She shifted to avoid his touch, a movement Matt didn't miss. "We've answered all your questions."

Slowly, deliberately, Matt took out his notebook, licking his fingers as he turned the pages, as if looking for something. "All but one." He looked up. "Where you were the night Hoffman died."

"Oh, for heaven's sake!" Adele exclaimed. "We've told you that. I was here. Ask my maid."

"I have, Mrs. Hoffman," he said, ever so gently, and had the satisfaction of seeing her face pale. "I think you know what she told me."

"She's lying!" Langdon put in.

"Oh?" Matt, sitting apparently at ease in the arm chair, looked up at him. "Then Mrs. Hoffman wasn't here, sir?"

"I—I—of course she was."

"Huh." Matt leaned back. "You thought the maid told me Mrs. Hoffman wasn't here. I wonder why." He waited, but neither answered, staring stonily back at him. "Is it because she wasn't?"

"I was," Adele said, but her voice lacked conviction.

"Were you? Or were you up on deck, waiting for just the right moment? You knew your husband would be there, didn't you?" he said, attacking. "You'd been to sea with him before and you knew it was his habit to take a stroll before turning in."

"So what of it?" Langdon challenged.

"So you waited, Mr. Langdon. Oh, yes," he said, as Richard started. "I don't suspect Mrs. Hoffman alone. She wouldn't have the strength to push her husband overboard by herself."

"She didn't! I didn't—"

"And so you waited, hidden, of course. You didn't want anyone to see you. That would mean disaster. When Mr. Hoffman came by you went to speak to him. He wouldn't suspect anything, would he? His wife and his business partner. It must have been easy to catch him offguard, push him over before he knew what was happening—"

"No!" Langdon burst out. "It wasn't like that!"

"Richard!" Adele gasped.

"It wasn't—I mean, we didn't do any such thing."

"Did he struggle?" Matt asked, focusing on Richard, who was patting at his forehead with a pristine white handkerchief. "Did he realize in the last moments he was being betrayed? And what did it feel like when you heard the splash? Your friend, your business partner—"

"He was stealing money from me! For God's sake, man, you have to believe we didn't kill him."

"Oh, for heaven's sake, Richard." Adele glared up at him. "Don't beg. It's so beneath you." She kept her contemptuous gaze on him for a moment, and Langdon seemed to shrink under it. "Since Richard has managed to incriminate himself—and me—quite neatly," she looked back at Matt, "I think perhaps I should tell you what really happened.

Matt sat very still. "I think that would be wise."

"Yes." She arranged the skirts of her ice-blue tea gown gracefully about her, but her eyes were steely. "First. We did not kill Julius."

"No?"

"No."

"Not even to get rid of a husband who wouldn't give you a divorce?"

"Oh, he would have done so eventually, Mr. Devlin," she said, calmly. "He resisted, of course, but he would have come around." She paused. "I would have seen to it."

She spoke with such assurance that, for the first time, Matt felt a prickle of doubt. "Then where were you?"

She stared back at him. "I think you know."

He didn't. Not anymore. "I'd rather you tell me."

"Oh, very well. Richard, do sit down. I detest it when you hover over me like that."

Langdon's face was gray. "But, Adele, surely you're not—"

"Sit down, Richard," she snapped, and Langdon sat.

Secretly amused, Matt referred to his notebook. "Your daughter has said that you weren't here at eleven o'clock that night."

"When did she say that?" Adele demanded, face wary.

"Yesterday, Mrs. Hoffman. She denies it now, but she did say it." He looked up. "She was telling the truth, wasn't she?"

Adele glanced at Richard, and then nodded. "Yes."

"Well, then?"

"I was with Richard." She kept her gaze steady, straight. "In his stateroom."

"For God's sake, Adele," Richard burst out.

"Face up to it, Richard! Mr. Devlin's not stupid. He knows there's something between us." She looked back at Matt. "Don't you?"

Matt nodded. "I'd suspected, yes. I have to tell you, ma'am, no one saw either you or him go into his room."

"Of course not, we took great care not to be seen! I may have wanted to divorce my husband, Mr. Devlin, but I did not want scandal."

"And you think this won't cause a scandal?" Richard said from behind his hands, held up before his face.

"Richard and I have been lovers for some time," Adele went on, ignoring him. "It's no secret my marriage was unhappy. Of course, we've been very discreet."

"Mm-hm." Matt jotted down some notes. She could be lying, but he didn't think so. Her voice was too flat; her eyes, too weary. He suspected he was at last hearing the truth. "Was it your idea for Langdon to travel with you?"

"Heavens, no! We had the trip planned already, since my daughter is getting married, but it was Julius's idea for Richard to come along. Wasn't it, Richard?"

Richard shook his head. "God, I don't believe you're telling him this."

"What choice do I have? I'd rather be accused of adultery than murder. No, it was Julius's idea," she repeated. "Whether he really planned to open a London office or not—"

"He did."

"Well, regardless of that, we couldn't imagine why he

wanted Richard along. He was perfectly capable of handling the business itself. We thought it might be a trap of some kind."

"If so, it wasn't very wise of you to be together," Matt said.

"No." Adele seemed lost in thought. "No, I suppose it wasn't. If Julius was planning a trap, he would have caught us easily enough." She looked up. "I confess I would have been rather relieved."

"Adele!" Richard exclaimed, aghast.

"Wouldn't you?" she asked, looking at him for the first time since starting her confession. "To have all the hiding over, all the subterfuge? All the lying."

"Yes, but in such a way!"

"We'll never know now, will we?" She looked back at Matt. "So there it is. We were together when Julius died. Perhaps we can't prove it, but it's the truth."

"God, Adele." Richard reached into his inner pocket. "I need a cigarette."

"Not in here." She glared frostily at him. "I told you the other night to smoke outside." She returned her attention to Matt. "We did not kill Julius, Mr. Devlin."

Matt said nothing; merely wrote in his notebook again. What to believe? What Adele had said carried the ring of truth, enough so that his own doubts had increased. Even if they hadn't, however, he was facing the same tough problem he had begun with. Proof. "Then who did?" he said, finally, looking up.

"I think it was McCabe," Richard said, unexpectedly. His face was still strained, but some of his color had returned.

"Why do you say that?"

Richard glanced quickly at Adele, who made a little face. "That man," she said. "I'd believe it of him. I don't care if he does have an alibi."

Matt frowned; McCabe hardly struck him as the homicidal type, though he knew well that appearances could be deceiving. "Then you do know him."

"Of course I know him." She looked back at Matt. "We may have given you the impression that Julius had little to do with McCabe. The truth is, the two were actually very close."

Matt looked up from his notebook. This was the first time he'd heard this. "Oh?"

"Yes. Not that Julius ever discussed him with me. He knew I didn't approve."

"Julius once told me he'd gone looking for McCabe as soon as he found out about him," Richard put in. "That must have been about, oh, thirty, thirty-five years ago. He didn't have any brothers or sisters, so he wanted to know the one he had. The half-brother, at least."

"You say they were close?" Matt asked, looking at him intently.

"I'd say so," Richard said, after exchanging another glance with Adele. "They always saw each other when McCabe was in New York—Julius got him this job, by the way—and sometimes he'd come by the office. McCabe would, that is. His money was invested with us."

"You never told me that," Adele said, surprised.

"Company policy, m'dear," Richard muttered.

"If they were close," Matt said, ignoring for the moment the financial issues, "did it seem to you McCabe ever resented his brother?"

Yet again, Adele and Richard exchanged looks. "When

he visited our house," she said, "—and I assure you, that only happened once!—he seemed awed, but not resentful. Julius told me once that McCabe was happy doing what he did, that he loved the sea and didn't want anything else. I don't think he's particularly smart," she added.

"Then if he had no quarrel with Hoffman, why do you suspect him?"

"I didn't say he had no quarrel," Richard said. "Actually, they did have quite a row, a few days before we left."

"You never told me that, either," Adele said, accusingly.

Matt leaned forward. "What was it about?"

"I don't know. It was in Julius's office with the door closed. We could hear the shouting, of course, but that was all. When McCabe came out his face was red and he was muttering something about getting his own back."

"Hoffman didn't tell you what that meant?"

"Of course not!" Richard appeared shocked. "Family business, sir. I wouldn't have presumed to ask. Good lord. Did McCabe kill Julius?"

Matt shrugged. "If he did, why would he kill Randall Snow?"

Richard started. "That was a burglary," he stammered. "For his wallet."

"Was it?" Matt frowned. "Does Snow's death bother you, Mr. Langdon?"

"No." Richard had regained some of his composure, but he was still pale. "Why should it? Surely it had nothing to do with Julius."

"I believe the two killings were related." Matt sat back, regarding Langdon, his curiosity aroused. Something was going on here. "Did Snow know who McCabe was?"

Richard's brow furrowed. "I don't know. Snow might have seen him in the office—yes." He looked up. "I think, no, I'm almost certain, that Snow was there one day when McCabe came in. Snow was a nosy bugger—sorry, Adele—he would probably have made it his business to find out."

"So Snow would have recognized McCabe on this ship."

"Probably." His frown deepened. "Does that matter?"

"I don't know yet."

"There seems to be a lot you don't know."

"Mm." Matt looked down at his notebook, refusing to be goaded. So McCabe may have had a motive for both killings. Unfortunately, he also had an alibi. "Just a few more questions, Mr. Langdon," he said, looking up.

"You're not arresting us?"

"Good heavens, Richard, try to have some spine," Adele snapped.

"No, Mr. Langdon, I'm not arresting you. Yet," he added, and let it hang for a moment, let it sink in that he might very well have evidence against them, evidence he would use. Langdon was the weaker of the two. If anyone was going to break, it would be him. "Have you been embezzling money from the firm?"

"Good God, no, that was Julius!" Richard blurted out.

"Richard!" Adele gasped, her face pale.

"I'm sorry, Adele." Langdon was sweating again. "But I'm not going to be accused of something else I didn't do. And I didn't. I swear it." He looked earnestly at Matt. "There was money missing. I don't know how you knew that, but there was. Julius said he'd made some bad investments, but . . ."

"Did he have anything to back that up?" Matt asked.

Richard shifted uneasily in his chair. "Yes, he had certificates, and our books balance, but—you get a certain feeling about people when you deal with their money, Mr. Devlin." Richard straightened, more in command of himself now. "You learn which ones are honest, which don't know anything about the market, which ones would cheat if they could get away with it. And I tell you, there was something about Julius. I can't put my finger on it, but it was there."

"Why would he take money from his own firm, Mr. Langdon?"

Langdon looked blankly at Adele. "I don't know. Do you?"

"No," she said, clearly stunned. "I didn't know anything about Julius's financial affairs. Even if I'd asked, he wouldn't have told me. Good heavens."

Good heavens, indeed. "You seem upset about Snow's death, Mr. Langdon," he said. "Why?"

"Upset? No, why should I be? No, no, I'm not upset at all, except about this whole investigation." Langdon rose, his face suddenly red. "We're innocent, I tell you, and yet you harass us like common criminals! I've a mind to complain to Mr. Morgan about how matters are conducted on his shipping line!"

"Do so." Matt's tone was genial as he regarded Langdon, now pacing the suite. "Why does this upset you so much?"

"I tell you, I am not upset! Now." Richard flung the door open. "I've had quite enough of this, thank you. If you would leave."

It was a command, not a request. Matt gazed at him for

moment and then rose, flipping his notebook shut. He
wasn't going to get anymore out of these people just now,
no matter how hard he pressed. But he wasn't giving up,
especially not after seeing Langdon's reaction to being accused of killing Snow. It was too strong, almost inappro-
priately so—unless he knew something. Later, Matt
thought. He'd get Langdon alone later. Apply the right
amount of pressure, and, without Adele there to support
him, Langdon would break. At least, Matt hoped he
would. "There's one more thing," he said, crisply, ad-
dressing Adele. "Fire Padlock Homes."

"Why should I?" she demanded, her chin raised. "At
least he's trying to find out what happened."

"He's also already made one mistake. And he might
find out things you don't want known, Mrs. Hoffman,"
Matt said, ignoring the insult to himself and focusing all
his attention on her. To his satisfaction, he saw her pale
just a bit. "Can you trust him to be discreet?"

"I—I'll think about it."

"Do that." Matt reached for the doorknob. "This isn't
the end of it." He turned and gave them both hard, searching looks. "When we reach Southampton—it's not the
end."

"It had better be," Langdon said, and slammed the door
behind Matt.

On deck, Matt gazed speculatively at the door for a moment. Something strange here. *Maybe it* was *you, Langdon,*
he thought, and turned away, a new determination to his
step. He was close, now, very close, and he wasn't about
to give up. Whoever had killed Julius Hoffman, Matt
would find him. He was determined. He would find him.

One day left in the voyage. Brooke glanced out to sea
again, and then, sighing, gave her attention to her sketch
book. Her role in the investigation, small to start with,
was almost over. She'd heard all the gossip and discussed
the case with her acquaintances, all to no avail. With the
exception of what Julia had said, and her own half-formed
suspicions concerning Jack, she'd learned nothing that
could help Matt. That Matt was having as difficult a time
was little consolation. At least he was doing something.
She, on the other hand, was mostly left to her own de-
vices. When she had encouraged Matt to take the investigation, she hadn't expected this would be the result. She
hadn't thought she'd feel so left out. Partners, indeed.

"Your drawing's improved," a voice said behind her.

"Oh! Jack!" Brooke gave him a quick, nervous smile,
startled that he had appeared just as she was thinking
about him. "Thank you." She bent her head again, intent
on capturing the feeling of being at sea, along with the
other sketches she had done, of people in deck chairs
bundled against the cool North Atlantic wind or energetic
young people playing shuffleboard. Along the railing, a
solitary stroller, looking pensively at the sea, caught her
attention. Good heavens, it was Julia Hoffman, Brooke
realized, lowering the sketch book.

"Have I done something to offend you, Brooke?" Jack
asked, just as Brooke turned towards Julia.

"What? No, of course not." She gave him a distracted
smile and glanced back at Julia. Julia knew more than she
was letting on. Maybe if Brooke talked with her she could
learn what that was, and she wouldn't feel quite so useless.

"All alone again?" Jack went on, leaning against the railing.

"Yes—no. How can I be alone with all these people about?"

"And your husband?"

"Investigating someone—oh, drat!"

"What?"

"Nothing," she said, frowning. Julia had, in the few moments of Brooke's conversation with Jack, left the railing and disappeared.

"What is it, Brooke?"

"Nothing. Jack, if you'll excuse me—"

"You've been avoiding me, Brooke." He took her elbow in a grip that was surprisingly strong and began to walk, almost dragging her along. "I don't know why."

"That's silly, Jack," Brooke babbled, wondering how to break free, uneasy in the presence of the grim-faced stranger Jack had suddenly become. "I've been busy helping Matt."

"And have you found out anything?"

"No."

"Didn't think so." His grip loosened, and Brooke slipped free. "No, don't go. Unless my presence is so repugnant to you."

"Jack." She brushed back a strand of hair. How did Matt stand it? she thought suddenly. How did he deal with the constant suspicion of people, the wondering at hidden motives and causes? But then, Matt had never, so far as she knew, suspected a close friend of murder. "I am sorry. But this whole thing has been very upsetting."

"I can imagine. Especially since your husband is never anywhere around."

"He's working." Brooke drifted over to the railing. Jack, for all his appearance of being easy-going, could be stubborn. She wouldn't be rid of him until he had an answer. "How well did you know Mr. Snow?"

"Randall Snow?" Jack's voice rose a bit in surprise. "Well enough, I suppose. Saw him about town, you know. One usually does."

"He blamed Mr. Hoffman for losing his money."

"Someone like him usually does."

"Someone like what?"

"Someone who sees the world as focusing on himself. When things go wrong, it's always someone else's fault. I have no sympathy for them." His voice was bitter. "I have little for Snow."

"But he was killed—"

"He made his living cheating people. So did Hoffman. If you ask me, Snow deserved what he got."

"Jack!"

"It was someone he cheated who killed him, wasn't it?"

"I don't know." She stared at him. "I've never seen you like this, Jack."

"Haven't you?" He tilted his head to the side, grimacing. "I suppose you haven't. My apologies. I'm not in the best of moods today." He stopped, gazing out over the sea. "I care about you, Brooke."

"Jack—"

"Surely you know that?"

Brooke let out a deep, shaky breath. This was the very last thing she'd expected. "I—don't know what to say."

"You don't have to say anything." They began to walk again. "I just wanted you to know."

"I—thank you," she said, feeling perfectly wretched.

She cared about Jack, too, but not in the way he meant. Not in the way she cared about Matt. It only made matters worse. "I must go. Matt will be returning to the suite for luncheon—"

"Brooke." He stopped her, his hand on her arm. "Are you going to tell him what we discussed?"

She stared fixedly down at his hand. "I don't know."

"It doesn't matter, you know." His tone was gentle. "He already knows."

Brooke's breath caught. "That you feel as you do about Snow?"

"Snow? What does he have to do with this? No. You and me, Brooke. He suspects, if he doesn't actually know."

"There's nothing for him to know. Anyway," and the words were forced out, "he cares more about the murders than that just now."

"I doubt that. As far as whoever killed Hoffman and Snow—I don't care if he's ever caught." He stared down at her, his gaze piercing. "Do you understand me?"

Brooke swallowed, hard. Because she was suddenly, terribly certain that she did understand. "I must go," she murmured, and fled.

So, Matt thought as he walked aft along the promenade deck, heading for the section reserved for those traveling second cabin. McCabe had come into Hoffman's office often enough for Langdon to know him. Often enough, perhaps, for Snow to have seen him? Maybe. It was time he got some answers out of Edward McCabe, about not only Hoffman, but Snow and Langdon. Beyond that, his own actions were suspicious, and he'd had a motive for wishing his brother dead. Moreover, alibis could be faked.

"Mr. Devlin," a voice called, as Matt opened a door, ready to go in and down to the second cabin staterooms, where he would find McCabe. "A word with you, please?"

Matt looked around the edge of the door. A youngish man was approaching him, dressed in brown tweeds. Not the best cut or materials, Matt noted, and frowned. What did that matter? "Yes, Mr. Turner, what is it?"

"Please, not so loud!" He glanced nervously around. "I wasn't sure you'd know me."

"You found Mr. Snow's body," Matt said, neutrally.

"Yes." Turner twisted his bowler hat around and around in his hand. "Have you found him yet?"

"Who?"

"Whoever killed Snow."

"We're close." Matt opened the door. "If you'll excuse me."

"May I have a word with you?" Turner stepped behind him into the stairwell. "Please?"

Matt glanced at the stairs, impatient to be away. "About what?"

"I—" Turner looked around, wetting his lips. "Not here. Who knows who might hear?"

"Hear what, Mr. Turner?"

"The murderer." Turner leaned forward, whispering now. "I think he's after me."

Matt's first impulse was to shrug that off, but a look at Turner's face stopped him. The man was pale and sweating, though the day was cool. "Why do you say that?"

"I, uh . . ." Turner peered down the stairs, checking to be sure they were alone, and then reached into his pocket. "I found this this morning."

Matt looked down, careful to keep his face expressionless. In Turner's hand was a silver dollar, the face worn but legible. It looked like any other dollar, except that a hole had been drilled at the top. Matt recognized it immediately. It was Snow's lucky coin.

13

"Where did you get that?" Matt asked, sharply.

"I, uh that's the problem. It was in my dresser drawer." Turner leaned forward. "Mr. Devlin, the murderer's trying to get me."

"You realize that Snow kept that in his wallet?"

"Yes. I saw it enough. He used to flip it between his fingers, to keep them in shape."

"And his wallet is still missing, Mr. Turner."

"I didn't take it, sir!"

"No?" Matt looked at him hard, and then shook his head. He had been dealing with guilty people for so long that Turner had become just another suspect. "No, I don't believe you did, Mr. Turner." He also didn't believe Turner was a target for the murderer. Not unless he knew something he wasn't telling. "When did you find this?"

"This morning, sir. I don't mind telling you, it was a shock."

"Mm. All right, Mr. Turner. Is there a place we can talk privately?"

"Yes." Turner took out a handkerchief and mopped at his brow. "My stateroom. I changed rooms, of course," he said, leading Matt down the stairs, his voice echoing hollowly. "After what happened I couldn't stay there, even if they'd let me. I'm in with another fellow, now. He didn't want to share, so he's not too pleasant, but it's better than before. Here. I'm on this corridor."

"He won't be here?" Matt asked, as Turner took out a key and unlocked a door, after taking several quick, furtive looks around.

"He's on deck, and it'll be time for lunch soon."

Matt followed him into the stateroom, compact and confined. Two men could sleep here, but it was close, the one porthole giving little light and less ventilation. "What did you want to tell me?"

Turner put his head outside the door, looking both ways down the corridor, before coming back and throwing the bolt on the door. "There. I think we're alone." He mopped at his brow again. "I don't mind telling you, sir, this whole thing has been very trying. Very trying."

"Yes." Matt took out his notebook. "How well did you know Randall Snow?"

"Not well at all." Turner sat on a bunk. "But I've already told you all I know about him."

"You didn't know him before this voyage? In New York?"

"No, why would I? I'm from New Jersey. What chance would I have to meet gamblers?"

"Mm." Matt flipped a page over in his notebook. "Then why do you think you're in danger, Mr. Turner?"

"I don't know!" he burst out. "I didn't know Snow, ex-

cept for sharing a stateroom with him. We barely talked
to each other. When we did—"

"What?" Matt prompted, when the other man stopped.

"We only talked generalities. Like the weather and
such."

"That's not what you were going to say. Is it?" he said,
pressing forward on instinct. "Snow did say something to
you, didn't he?"

"No! At least, nothing I thought was important."

"Mr. Turner." Matt made his voice patient. "You
asked for my help. How do you expect me to give it to you
if you won't answer my questions?"

"I—I'm afraid," he burst out. "If they find out I've told
you—"

"They?"

"The killer. If he finds out—"

"That you told me what? You'd better say what it is."
Matt loomed over him. "If you don't I'll have you put in
the brig. Oh, yes, Mr. Turner, I can do that," he went on,
as the other man shrank back. Tough tactics, these, but he
was tired of people being evasive with him. "Not a pleasant experience, and what will 'they' think? They'll think
you've talked." He shook his head. "I wouldn't want to be
in your shoes right now."

"But I don't know anything! Not really." Turner licked
his lips. "Just a few things Snow said. You wouldn't put
me in the brig for that, would you?"

"Don't test me, Mr. Turner." Matt's voice was danger-
ously quiet. "What did Snow say to you?"

"I—" Turner's eyes darted back and forth. "Can I trust
you?"

"As much as you can trust anyone."

"I—all right." His shoulders sagged. "But you'll protect me?"

"Yes, Mr. Turner. What did Snow say to you?"

"Not so much, really. Could you please move away? You make me nervous, standing there. God," he said, wiping at his brow as Matt moved back a pace. "This isn't supposed to be happening. This was supposed to be a quiet business trip—"

"What did Snow say?"

"Nothing. No, I mean he said things, but it wasn't really what he said. It was more the way he looked."

"Which was?"

Turner frowned. "On top of the world. Like he'd made his fortune. He was sitting on his bunk, in the other room, of course, practicing his dealing. He was always practicing dealing, always trying to get me into a game, but I'm no fool."

"So?"

"So I said something about it wasn't much of a way to make a living." Turner licked his lips again. "He said he wasn't going to have to do it anymore, gamble for a living, he meant. That he was getting into a new line and he was set for life."

"When was this?"

"The—the night he died."

Matt's interest sharpened. "What was the new line?"

"He didn't say. But after he was killed, I figured maybe he knew something about the killer." He shuddered. "Maybe that's why he was killed."

"Mm. Did he say anything else?"

"No—yes!" Turner looked up. "Now you ask it, there was something. I'm not sure I remember." He frowned.

"He said that he knew something that would, let me see, want to remember exactly what he said. Yes. He said I knew something that would turn the whole ship upsid down. Then he stopped talking, and I couldn't get any thing more out of him. I thought he was just making thing up."

"He may well have been." Matt pretended to no down what Turner had said. Snow had known somethin of that he had no doubt. He'd hinted at it to Matt, ar then, apparently, to Turner. Not very smart in a car sharper, to let his poker face slip in such a way. "He ga no hint what he knew?"

"No. Just that it was something someone didn't wa known, and it would make his fortune. I didn't believ him, though."

"Did you notice anyone Snow spoke with? Anyone seemed to know?"

"I've told you all that already," Turner said, wearily.

"Yes, I know, Mr. Turner, but tell me again, pleas You may have forgotten someone. No, not on purpose he said, holding up his hand to forestall Turner's protes "but because of the shock."

"I—I see." Turner sat back, thoughtful. "Honestly, M Devlin, I can't remember seeing him with anyone in pa ticular. He didn't spend a lot of time in second class. N one here was worth his while."

Matt nodded; this was about what he'd expected. "A no one came to the stateroom?"

"One of the men he played cards with, a young ma but that I told Mr. Smith about. That was about it. I talked to me, of course, and the steward."

"About anything special?" Matt asked absently, looking down at his notes and frowning.

"No. Just the usual. Weather and what was on the menu. Oh, he did say something once about investments."

Matt looked up at that. "To you?"

"No. To the steward."

Matt sat very still. Turner was excitable and imaginative, the type of witness who could easily be led to a conclusion. That was the last thing he wanted. "Who was the steward?"

"You've seen him." Turner's brow wrinkled in an earnest frown. "Mr. McCabe."

"What did Snow say to him about investments?"

"I'm not really sure." His frown deepened. "I simply thought it an odd thing to discuss with a steward. Not that Mr. McCabe answered—he said he didn't know anything about it. And then there was a really strange thing. Snow laughed."

"Mm-hm." Not so strange, really, considering who McCabe was. Snow would be the type to taunt someone who couldn't fight back. "Was he friendly with McCabe?"

"Do you mean, did he know him?"

Matt looked up. That wasn't what he'd meant, but if Turner had noticed something, it might be worthwhile to hear about it. "What makes you think that?"

"I don't know. Something about the way he said his name. 'McCabe.' Like he knew him, or—Mr. Devlin!" Turner sat bolt upright. "Could he be the killer?"

"I doubt it." Though Matt now had more questions for McCabe, when he caught up with him. "He was with

someone both times. He didn't do it." Matt flipped th
notebook shut. He was tired of Mr. Turner, and his inter
pretation of things that Snow had said. Turner was proba
bly capable of making himself and others believe in thing
that had happened only in his own mind. And yet,
seemed that Snow had known McCabe, as witness the tal
about investments. A strange topic to discuss with a stew
ard, indeed, and something McCabe had lied about. H
hadn't been at all forthcoming about knowing Snow

"Thank you for your time," he said, turning to the door

"Wait!" Turner's voice rose several octaves. "Yo
promised you'd protect me."

"Yes, Mr. Turner. I'll see to it."

"Thank you." Turner rubbed at his forehead. "I need
cigarette," he muttered, and turned away, as Matt opene
the door and went out.

A cigarette. That sounded good, Matt thought, stridin
along the corridor to the stairwell. Funny how whe
under stress smoking was appealing. Langdon had mer
tioned wanting one——.

Holy God. Matt stopped, his hand on the knob of th
door leading to the stairwell. Langdon. He'd said h
wanted a cigarette, and Adele had said she'd told him th
other night to go outside. What other night? Since Hof
man's death the two had been watched, and if they'd bee
together at night, it would be known. The only time Adel
could have said such a thing to Langdon was the night
her husband's death. *Holy God*, Matt thought again. Lan
don had been on deck, with no one to vouch for him,
the time of Hoffman's death.

Excited now, Matt jerked open the door and ran up th
stairs, heedless of the way they tilted with the waves. H

had it now, all the pieces he needed to put together a case. Hoffman's letter. The relationship between Adele and Langdon. The missing money from the firm. It all added up, it all pointed to Langdon. What he had to do now was confront him and break him down, without Adele present. Langdon was the weaker of the two, he'd break easily, especially after making the slip about the cigarette. As for Adele—maybe he'd enlist Brooke to talk with her, and get her to admit that Langdon had not been with her all the time he'd claimed. Holy God. He'd cracked it.

Matt rounded the corner of the deckhouse in time to see Brooke at the door of their suite. "Brooke," he called, holding his hand up in a wave. "I was just looking for you."

"Were you?" Brooke turned to wait, for once not particularly eager to hear his news. He had been investigating this morning, while she—well, she had been worse than useless. Not only had she not helped with the case, but she might have alerted a possible suspect. "Matt, I wanted to ask you—"

"It's Langdon," he said at the same time, his voice very low, as he reached her. "It's Langdon, by God, but I don't have the proof." He thumped the doorframe in frustration as they entered the suite. "The only way I'll get it is if either he or Adele breaks down."

Brooke, sitting on the sofa, closed her eyes in mingled relief and apprehension. If Langdon had indeed committed the murders, then her suspicions about Jack were groundless. But what if they weren't? "Do you think they will?"

"Langdon might, if I get him alone. Adele's a different story. Unless you talk to her."

"Oh. Then you actually want my help."

Matt frowned at this first blow to his euphoria. "Of course I do."

"Then you had better tell me what has happened."

Matt needed no prodding, but, pacing the sitting room, launched into a recital of the morning's events, ending with his own deduction. "It all fits," he said when he was finished. "Motive, opportunity, means—it's all there."

Brooke's lips were pursed. "Ye-es."

Matt turned. "You don't sound so certain."

"Oh, it does all fit, Matt, and yet—it doesn't feel right."

"Why not?"

"It's too neat." Brooke brushed her hair back from her face. "Don't you think so? All the things we've found out about Mr. Hoffman, Adele and Mr. Langdon, and that letter in the safe—that bothers me."

He turned to look at her. "Why?"

"I don't know, Matt, but it does." She frowned. "If Mr. Hoffman suspected them of something, why did he let them sail on the same ship?"

Matt pondered that. "Good point. Adele herself said that he could have handled the business in London himself, and let Langdon stay home to take care of New York."

"Yes, and why put his wife in such a situation? Unless." Her frown deepened. "Unless that was what he wanted."

"Why?"

"It seems monstrous, but—Matt, what if he wanted to catch Adele with Langdon? Then he'd have evidence to divorce."

"So he set her up," Matt murmured.

"Excuse me?"

"He put her in a position where she'd betray herself. It's possible."

"No one saw them on deck at the proper time, though, Matt. Your case is all circumstance and guesswork."

"I know that, dammit. But they did it, Brooke. I know they did."

"Then why did they kill Mr. Snow?"

"He knew something. Dammit, Brooke, why are you arguing with me? You know this is the answer."

"No, I don't know it, Matt. I admit that things add up, but there are some things you're ignoring."

"Such as?"

She held up her hand, ticking off the points one by one as she listed them. "Such as Mr. Hoffman's wallet being found in Mr. Tate's room. Such as Mr. Smith's motive, and where he was. You told me about that yourself," she said, as he frowned. "And Jack—"

"What about Jack?" he interrupted, in an ominously quiet voice.

"I was talking with him today."

"Oh, were you."

"Yes, and why not? You weren't around."

"I was working! Dammit, Brooke." He stared at her, hands bunched. "You wanted me to take this case."

"And I wanted to help!"

"You did."

"How? By listening to gossip? And then when I really do try to help you, you don't even listen to me."

"Dammit." His voice was quiet. "I didn't even want to come on this cruise."

"You decided on it, Matt."

"No. You decided. You and your aunt."

"And you agreed! You knew it would mean certain
things. Not murder, I realize that, but socializing with my
friends and behaving in a certain way—"

"I didn't think it would mean seeing my wife with an
other man," he snapped.

"Good heavens, what are you saying?"

"How do you think it makes me feel when I go off to
work on something I never wanted, and you spend all
your time with Everett?"

"That's ridiculous!"

"Oh, is it."

"Yes, and you know it!"

"Huh. I've seen you with him enough."

"At least he treats me like a person," she retorted.

"What is that supposed to mean?" Matt asked, his
voice suddenly quiet, heavy.

"I mean that I offer my opinions and you brush me off
like a fly! I don't deserve that. I thought we were equal
partners in this, Matt."

"We'll never be equals," he snapped, and silence fell
heavily between them as Brooke stared at him, appalled.
An equally appalled look spread across his face. "Brooke,
I didn't mean—"

"I know what you meant." She turned her back, fight
ing to control the sudden tears that threatened to choke
her. They had had squabbles before, even quarrels, but
this was worse. This struck deep to the heart of their mar
riage. "A woman should know her place, shouldn't she?"

"Dammit, Brooke." He stepped closer to her. "You
know I didn't mean that."

"Didn't you?" She turned, the threat of tears now past, and with it, her anger. In its place was a deep, vast weariness. "It's all very well for me to play at being detective, isn't it? But when it actually comes to my sharing the work, sharing the glory—"

"I don't give a damn about glory."

"Neither do I! I just want to be respected, Matt. Treated as an equal." She paused. "If I were a man, I'd be every bit as good a cop as you are."

"But you're not a man," Matt said, almost gently, and she whirled around.

"I thought you were different," she said, her voice muffled. "I thought—oh, never mind what I thought, it obviously wasn't true!"

"Brooke. I didn't marry you to get some kind of partner in crime."

She didn't answer right away. "But there's no honeymoon for death, is there? And some things are always going to come first for you."

"You wanted me to investigate this case, Brooke."

"I know." *I wanted to investigate it!* "I'm not hungry, Matt. I don't think I'll go to lunch."

"Dammit, Brooke, what do you want from me?"

"Go to lunch, Matt," she said, and closed the bedroom door behind her very quietly, very firmly, shutting Matt out. Just now she didn't want to talk to him, didn't want to see him. Their marriage had been split apart, exposing the basic, fundamental flaw at its heart. She didn't know if it would ever recover.

———

Matt stared at the closed bedroom door for a moment and then turned on his heel, slamming out of the suite. Fine. If she wanted to sulk, let her. He had a case to solve, and he'd do it without her help. What the hell did she expect, anyway? he fumed, stalking along the deck, ignoring greetings from people he knew and scaring others off without realizing it. That marrying him automatically made her a partner, automatically made her a cop? Hell, no! She had investigative skill, he'd grant her that; if not for her, he wouldn't have anywhere near the amount of information he needed to solve this case. But if she thought that made her his equal, she was mistaken. His partner in marriage, maybe, though of course he was head of the house; but in crime solving, never. That was his, and his alone.

As far as this nonsense about equality. Matt turned abruptly towards the railing, cutting across the path of an elderly gentleman who exclaimed in surprise, though Matt didn't notice. He didn't know where Brooke had gotten that notion, he thought, opening his cigarette case and lighting a cigarette with a snap of his lighter. Men and women weren't equals. Never had been, never would be. Certainly he and Brooke weren't.

He shifted uneasily from one foot to the other, taking a drag on his cigarette. No, they weren't equals, though Brooke came closer than any woman he'd ever known. She was right. If she'd been born male she'd be a cop, but the fact was, she wasn't. And he was glad. God knew he treated her a lot more fairly than his father had ever treated Ma. They never seemed to talk to each other, and he couldn't remember Da ever telling her any details of his cases. Ever. Brooke was lucky he wasn't like his Da; at least he talked to her. If he didn't talk about his work, maybe it was because he wanted to shield her from the worst aspects of it. And maybe, a little voice whispered inside him, he wanted something that was his, and his alone.

She'd just have to understand that, Matt decided, tossing the cigarette overboard and walking again, calmer now. It was the way he was and he doubted he could change. When he returned to the suite, when they'd both calmed down, he'd explain things to her. He'd apologize for the things he'd said about Everett. For now, though, he had to find Langdon, and at last get the truth from him.

"Mr. Devlin," someone called, and he turned, to see a steward coming towards him. "The captain's compliments, sir. He'd like to talk with you."

Matt nodded. "Fine. I'll follow you," he said. Six days on this ship, and he'd never find his way alone, he thought, following the steward inside and along a maze of corridors. The captain probably wanted a report on progress. At the moment, Matt wasn't certain what to tell him.

Captain Wood was standing at the broad table in his stateroom when Matt was shown in, poring over a chart. "Mr. Devlin." He straightened, holding out his hand, and then gesturing Matt to a chair. "A drink, sir?"

"No, thank you." Matt sat in one of the deep, comfortable leather chairs. "You wanted to see me?"

"Yes." The captain sat across from him. "I had a visit from Mr. Langdon a while ago."

"Oh?"

"Yes. He's most disturbed. Oh, not about you. He says you've been doing your job as you should."

"Kind of him," Matt drawled.

"No, he's concerned about whether the killer will be

caught in time." He peered at Matt. "You realize we reach Southampton tomorrow?"

"I'm aware of it, yes. I have an idea of who committed the murders, though I don't think you'll like it." Clearly and concisely he reported the events of the morning, ending with the case against Langdon. "He could have done it. He has no alibi, and he had motive in both cases."

The captain was frowning. "Even for Randall Snow?"

"Snow claimed he had knowledge that would turn everything upside down. He knew McCabe, by the way, as well as Hoffman, and—my God!" Matt shot to his feet. It was unbelievable, it was impossible, but what if—. "Upside down. We've been looking at this all upside down."

Captain Wood stared at him. "Mr. Devlin?"

"Dammit, it fits. It's fantastic, but it fits." Matt began to pace back and forth, his strides long and quick. "When you think about it—McCabe leaving the ship on sailing day. Why? Hoffman embezzling from his own firm." He turned and stared at the captain. "Again, why?"

"I've no idea."

"Yes, and the mustache, and the letter in the safe—yes. It all fits. Captain." Matt came to a stop. "I know who the murderer is."

14

Brooke glared at the bedroom door. Well! So she wasn't his equal? Maybe that was how society viewed things, but she had thought Matt was different. She'd thought her marriage was different. True, in the marriages she'd seen, one partner was dominant. Look at her own parents, for example, Mama fretting because Papa was home late, and then, when he did come home, not talking to her. Brooke could understand that, a little. She could understand the stresses of Papa's job that had made him occasionally taciturn and surly. She hadn't thought Matt would be like that, though, and she had no intention of being like her mother. No. If she were to emulate anyone, it would be Aunt Winifred, who had things very much to her liking.

And still wasn't happy. Frowning, Brooke bundled her hair up and jammed her hat onto her head. What she was going to do about her marriage, she didn't know, but one thing was certain. She wasn't going to sit in the suite, moping.

Once outside, however, Brooke hesitated. All very well and good for her to declare her independence, but what, precisely, was she going to do? The promenade deck was empty, nearly everyone being at lunch. She could join them, though the idea filled her with distaste. She wasn't particularly hungry, nor did she wish to face everyone when she and Matt were in the midst of a quarrel. Sighing, she wandered listlessly along the deck, stopping at the railing to look down at the sea. One day left in this interminable voyage. Would matters improve once they reached Europe?

"Brooke? Oh, sorry, I didn't mean to disturb you," a voice said behind her, as Brooke turned, startled.

"Shirley," Brooke said, secretly pleased to see her. "How nice to see you."

"Thank you." Shirley's eyes darted nervously back and forth. "I know I shouldn't be here, in first class and all. Do you think anyone will say anything?"

"If they do, I'll answer them," Brooke said firmly, linking her arm with Shirley's and walking with her. "In fact," she went on, taken by a sudden mischievous impulse, "have you seen the ladies' drawing room?"

Shirley's eyes grew round. "Golly! Do you think I could?"

"I don't know why not."

"But won't they want to throw me out?"

"They may, but they won't." Brooke led the way inside, to the landing above the stairs leading down to the saloon deck. "Let's thumb our noses at everyone, shall we?"

Shirley giggled. "You're all right, Brooke. For a toff."

Brooke looked at her in surprise as they reached the landing. "I'm not a toff."

"Sure you are. Golly." Shirley stared down the grand staircase leading into the dining saloon, the sounds of conversation and cutlery clinking on china drifting up to them. "I ain't never—I mean, I've never seen anything like this."

"It is amazing, isn't it? The drawing room is right in here." Brooke opened the door off the landing and let Shirley in, listening with some amusement as the other girl exclaimed over the brocade sofas and divans, the panelled ceiling with its gilt fretwork, the fine piano. As Brooke had suspected, the room was empty, as most people were at lunch. She was glad. She had no desire to see Shirley humiliated. "Let's sit over here," she said, leading her to a sofa near the window overlooking the grand saloon.

"Golly," Shirley said again. "I'd sure like to live like this."

Brooke smiled. "Are your friends still ill?"

"Oh, them." Shirley's face twisted with scorn. "No, they're better, but all they do is complain."

"About what?"

"About everything, the food, the service, everything. Like they're so used to servants themselves." She sank back against the plush, overstuffed sofa, and gave a sigh of pure bliss. "Wonderful. But Europe's not going to be as much fun as I thought."

"I'm sorry," Brooke said, softly, remembering her own earlier gloom. "I hope your friends become more pleasant."

"Yeah, so do I. You and Mr. Devlin, you're going to see everything, I guess?"

"That's what we've planned." Brooke sat back, some of her pleasure in this conversation fading. There was a flaw deep in the heart of her marriage. How could she ever fix it?

"What's wrong?"

"Hm? Oh, nothing." Brooke fixed a bright smile on her face as she saw Shirley watching her, eyes sharp and shrewd. "Matt and I had a little argument. It's nothing."

"I thought you seemed upset, when I seen—saw you. I almost didn't speak."

"I'm glad you did."

"Yeah, me too." She paused. "Is Jack seeing anyone in New York?"

"Not that I know of, no."

"Oh." Shirley played with the fingers of her glove. "Thought he was. It'd make things a lot easier."

"Good heavens. You'd prefer that?"

"No. But I gotta be honest, with myself, anyway." Shirley's face was determined, yet vulnerable. "A man like that, he's not going to want anything to do with me."

"Jack does things his own way," Brooke said, glancing away uneasily. Because she still had her doubts about Jack, and she didn't know if they'd ever be settled. This afternoon, she thought, she'd have to talk to Matt about her suspicions, even if it did seem disloyal.

"Maybe. But I know I'm not his type. Except for one thing."

"It's not fair, is it?" Brooke stretched out her legs, contemplating the toes of her kid walking boots. "Men make the rules and we have to follow them."

Shirley shrugged. "I don't know who makes the rules. I just know that that's the way things are. The most I could ever be to someone like Jack is a mistress."

Brooke glanced up at her. "You'd accept that? So unequal a relationship?"

Shirley shrugged again. "Who cares about equality?"

"I do."

The look Shirley gave her was unexpectedly shrewd. "We'll never be equals, you and I."

"And that's not fair."

"Maybe not, but," she smiled, "who wants to be equal? We can get things our own way."

Brooke scowled. "I've never been particularly good with feminine wiles."

"You're trying to be a cop," Shirley said, with that disconcerting shrewdness. "Ain't you?"

"No. Not exactly, but—"

"But you got ways of doing things your husband don't. Don't you?"

"Yes," Brooke said after a moment. She had found out things Matt never would have on his own, and not just because of his position in society. Would she have found out McCabe's alibi if she weren't a woman? Nor did she have Matt's hard-edged manner of interrogation. A distinct advantage, that. She wasn't a cop, and she never would be. If she wanted to be Matt's equal, in marriage and in crime solving, she would, indeed, have to use her own ways. Even if he never acknowledged them. "Yes, you're right. I can do things he can't."

"Course, you can. You're a woman, ain't you? You got advantages he never even dreamed of. Think your man is stewing right now about your marriage?"

"No," Brooke said, wryly. "He's probably thinking of ways to find evidence against someone. Probably Mr. Langdon, or Mr. McCabe."

"Oh, no!" Shirley sat upright. "You think McCabe done it?"

"Oh, dear. I shouldn't have said that. You won't repeat it, will you?"

"No, not if you don't want. I can keep a secret. But Ellen was with him. You don't really think he killed those men, do you?"

"I don't know if he did, there's no real evidence. But since he's Mr. Hoffman's half-brother, Matt has to ask him questions, if nothing else."

"Darn." Shirley sat back. "I like him, don't you?"

"I don't know. I've only seen him from a distance."

"Oh, he's a nice man. Got to say, I didn't think so at first, the way he was always winking at me."

"He winks at you? Shirley!"

"No, it's not like that! After I caught him at it once too often, he apologized. Said it was a nervous mannerism, tic, he called it, and he had it for years."

"Isn't that funny. His brother had the same thing—my good heavens!" Brooke sat upright.

"What?"

"What—good heavens—what do you think are the chances of two half-brothers having the same nervous tic?"

"I dunno, but—"

"They weren't raised together, they didn't work together—heavens, they're in entirely different jobs! But they were both on this ship, and they look alike, and that tic—good lord!" She stared at Shirley. "I've got to find Matt."

"I don't know what you're talking about," Shirley complained.

"I know. It doesn't matter. But, oh, this would explain everything." She grabbed Shirley's hand and rose. "Thank you. You don't know what you've done for me."

"You're welcome," Shirley said, sounding bewildered.

Brooke, already halfway across the room, didn't answer. She didn't know where Matt was, but she had to find him. He had to know about this. Opening the door, she flew out onto the landing, and collided solidly with a man standing there.

"Hey!" he said, and "I'm sorry," she said, and then they looked at each other, Brooke recovering first. "Matt! Oh, I've got something to tell you—"

"I was looking for you," he said at the same moment.

"I—you were?"

"Yes." His eyes glowed with excitement. "I was with the captain—he asked to speak with me—damn." This as people, leaving the dining saloon, pushed by them on either side. "We can't talk here."

"In the library," Brooke said, and they pushed their way through the stream of people to the door on the opposite side of the landing, into the library. The air was thick, liquid with colored light, but neither noticed. All that mattered was that the room was empty. "Matt, I think I know what happened. I think McCabe—"

"McCabe left the ship in New York on sailing day," Matt interrupted. "What if he never came back on? What if—"

"Hoffman took his place?"

Matt stared at her. "How did you guess?"

"Shirley just told me that McCabe has the same nervous tic as Mr. Hoffman. A wink."

"Damn! So he does. I should have noticed that. And if

Hoffman used theatrical makeup to change his appearanc
he'd look like his brother."

"Matt, do you think—?"

"It all fits, doesn't it? When you think about it? Wh
would Hoffman embezzle from his own firm? To ge
money to start a new life. Why leave that letter, except t
set it up that he was actually killed? And we never did fin
Hoffman's body."

"And Snow might have recognized him as McCabe—"

"I'm almost certain he did."

"Which gives him a motive." She stopped, staring a
him. "You were looking for me? To tell me this?"

"Of course," he said, surprised. "Why wouldn't I te
you?"

"Because—good heavens." She broke off as a scream
high and piercing, cut through the air. "What was that?"

"It came from outside." Matt grabbed her hand, pullin
her out of the library and onto the promenade deck. /
group of people had gathered just outside the doorway
blocking their view, though Brooke craned her head t
see. "What is it?" Matt asked a man standing near him.

The man turned. "There's a girl on the railing, threaten
ing to jump."

"Good heavens!" Brooke exclaimed, as Matt pulled he
by the hand again, dragging her through the crowd. "Wh
is it—?"

"No, I won't come down, Mother!" a high, shrill voic
cried. "I won't!"

"Good heavens, that sounds like—"

"Julia, how can you do this to me?" another femal
voice wailed. "After all I've been through."

"That's Adele," Brooke gasped to Matt, just as the

roke through the last of the crowd to see what was happening for themselves. There was a space between the rowd and the railing, and there, as if on stage, were the rincipal players: Adele, Richard Langdon, and, precariusly straddling the railing, Julia. "Oh, good heavens!"

"I'll jump, Mother, I swear I will!" Julia shouted, and a murmur of astonishment and horror went up from the rowd.

"Go to Adele," Matt said brusquely, releasing Brooke's and.

"What are you going to do?" she asked.

"I'm going to get her down. Keep Adele back."

"I'll try." Brooke scurried across to Adele, all the time eeping her eyes on Julia. Her hair had come down and er position on the railing showed an immodest amount f leg, but she didn't seem to care. The look in her eyes as wild, desperate. Julia meant it, she thought. She really ould jump, for heaven alone knew what reason. Adele," she said in a low voice, touching the other oman's arm.

Adele swung towards her. "I don't know why she's oing this to me," she said, her voice high and thin. "She's ever been like this before."

"I won't marry him, Mother," Julia called. "I won't!"

"We were talking about the earl and her wedding, and ue next thing I knew, she was on the railing. It's all non-nse, of course." Adele surged forward. "Julia, come own from there this instant!"

For answer, Julia loosened her already tenuous grip on ue railing, bringing another gasp from the crowd. "I'm ot joking, Mother."

"Let Matt handle this," Brooke said, pulling Adele

back and indicating Matt with a jerk of her head. He w
approaching Julia from a different angle, near the raili
and out of her direct line of sight. "He'll know what
do."

"I hope so! Such an ungrateful child, when I've gone
such trouble to arrange a marriage for her—"

"A marriage she obviously doesn't want," Brooke sa
tartly, wanting to shake the other woman.

"But I only want the best for her—"

"Julia," Matt said, and Julia, who had been shifting h
gaze from her mother to the sea below, whipped her he
around. He was leaning on the railing several feet fro
her, apparently calm, but Brooke could see his should
muscles tensing. At a moment's notice, he would be rea
to spring.

"Keep away," Julia said to him, "or I will jump, I swe
it."

Matt glanced over the railing. "It's a long way down."

"I don't care! I—"

"Do you know what happens when someone jum
from such a height?" he said, almost conversational.
"No? Then I'll tell you. When you hit the water, Julia,
you don't go in just right it's like hitting concrete." H
gaze flicked toward Brooke. "You know what will ha
pen?"

"Your bones will break," Brooke said, as if on cue, a
saw Matt give her a quick, approving glance. The startl
look Julia gave her was equally brief, but it was lo
enough for Matt to take a step forward.

"I don't believe her," Julia said, defiantly.

"Oh, but it's true," Matt assured her. "Do you swim
Julia's chin jutted out. "I'm a very good swimmer."

"You won't be, with both legs broken."

"Oh, why is he saying such horrible things?" Adele
id, her voice ragged with hysteria.

"So if you change your mind, Julia, it will be too late,"
latt went on. "You'll drown for sure."

"Maybe it's what I want," Julia said. "Like Ophelia in
amlet."

"All covered with flowers? I don't think so," Matt said,
irprising Brooke, who didn't know he'd read Shake-
peare. "It's not a romantic way to go. Do you know what
appens when you drown? The water rushes into your
ngs, and you can't breathe."

"I'll float!"

Matt shook his head and glanced towards Brooke again.
Not right away."

"Not for several days," Brooke said. "My father told
e once that when drowning victims reach the surface,
ey're all bloated." Beside her Adele sagged, but she
ade herself go on. Julia had looked toward Brooke as she
poke, and that gave Matt time to take another step.
Usually the fish have gotten at them, too. It's not a pretty
ght."

"I don't care—keep away!" Julia said, seeing that Matt
ad drawn nearer. "If you come any closer, I'll jump."

"Go ahead," Matt said, studying his fingernails, and
rooke saw a fleeting expression of surprise cross Julia's
ce. Why, she didn't really mean to jump. "By the way,
hy are you doing this?"

"Because she," a venomous glance at her mother,
wants me to marry someone who's twice my age, just be-
iuse he's an earl, and she won't listen to me when I say I
on't want to."

"Oh, Julia," Adele moaned.

"You're listening now, aren't you, Mother?"

"Only come down, Julia, and we'll discuss it."

"No! Not until you say the wedding is off."

"I can't—"

"Then I'm staying here," she declared, her eyes glittering, and Brooke realized that she was right. Julia had no
intention of jumping. But what a way she had chosen to
get her mother's attention.

"It's dramatic," Matt agreed, as if reading Brooke's
mind.

Julia looked back at him. "I don't want to marry him."

"Then I don't think you should."

That seemed to startle her. "No? Really?"

"Really." Again his gaze flicked towards Brooke. She
opened her mouth, wondering what in the world he
wanted her to say now, when she felt a touch on her shoulder. She looked up to see Edward McCabe, a finger to his
lips as he pushed past her. With his shoulders squared
and his spectacles removed, he no longer looked like the
meek steward, but instead was unexpected confirmation
of her theory. Good heavens.

"No," Matt went on, his concentration all on Julia, as if
willing her to keep looking at him, while McCabe crept up
behind her. "I don't think anyone should marry someone
they don't want to. Why make things harder than they
have to be?"

"Yes!" Julia leaned forward, gripping the railing with
both hands, and all the time McCabe advanced, one quiet
step at a time. Now he was four feet away, now three . . . "I
don't want an arranged marriage. I want a real marriage,
like you and Brooke have. I want—" Her voice rose in

shriek as McCabe caught her around the waist, and she struggled, clinging to the railing and kicking at him with her near leg. "No, Daddy!" she cried, just as he gave a mighty heave and pulled her backwards, onto the deck and safety.

"Daddy?" someone said, in the hush following the rescue.

"Daddy?" Langdon echoed.

"My God," Adele whispered, her face suddenly pale, staring at the man who now held Julia in a protective embrace. "My God, Julius!" And with that she collapsed, a sudden deadweight, sagging against Brooke. Brooke grabbed for her, her attention diverted, but not before she saw the steward's eye twitch in the familiar fashion, not before she realized that her theory was indeed, true. For it was not Edward McCabe who stood on the deck, the hero of the moment. It was instead, most improbably, Julius Hoffman.

15

"But I'm still not sure I understand," Mr. Tuttle complained, taking his glass of seltzer water from the steward in the captain's stateroom. It was late afternoon. Julius Hoffman was confined in the brig, Adele and her family were in seclusion, and Matt and Brooke could at last relax. They sat together on a sofa across from the captain, their quarrel forgotten. For now. For now there was a new closeness between them. "Why did Hoffman do it? Why impersonate a steward?"

"I told you McCabe was the one who did it," Smith put in. He was leaning against the wall, and the look on his face could only be described as smug. "Turns out I was right."

"In a way," Matt said, exchanging a swift, amused glance with Brooke. Let Smith take the credit, if he wanted. What mattered to Matt was that the murderer had been found, and caught, in an entirely unexpected way. "Since it turns out he and Hoffman were one and the same."

"Dear, dear. Not at all good for the ship, no, not at all," Tuttle fretted, and J.P. Morgan, his massive frame folded into an armchair, snorted.

"The ship's reputation won't suffer because of this," he said, taking a sip of his whiskey. "I assume you're certain of your facts, Mr. Devlin?"

"Mr. Hoffman admitted it," Brooke said, not as content as Matt was to let credit for solving the case slip away. He deserved it, after the superb job of detecting he'd done. As, she thought, sipping her sherry to hide her expression, did she. But only Matt knew that.

"What is this world coming to," Captain Wood said, shaking his head. "I know he confessed, but it still is hard to believe."

Matt set his drink down on a table. "I suppose from his point of view it made sense. And, to give him his due, he didn't expect anyone to be hurt. Things didn't happen as he planned."

"But why?" Mr. Tuttle wailed. "And why choose our ship to do it?"

"The ship was the perfect place. He had a brother working here, a brother who, by the way, resembles him. McCabe's mustache fooled me, until I remembered that Hoffman was involved in amateur theater and knew how to use makeup. And what better way to get rid of a body than to tip it overboard?" He reached for his drink. "Or to pretend to tip it over."

Captain Wood was shaking his head. "Someone did go over, that first night."

"No. Hoffman threw a deck chair into the water, then yelled 'man overboard.' And then he disappeared." He sipped from his drink. "He's the one I heard running away. It was a good plan, actually." Matt set his drink on the table again, leaning back. "Julius Hoffman wanted to begin a new life, and he saw this trip as his chance. His life was falling apart—his wife in love with another man, his business partner in love with his wife, and his children were distant from him."

"We saw that ourselves, the first night," Brooke put in, softly. "Poor man. I felt rather sorry for him. I always liked him."

"So did I," Morgan put in, unexpectedly. "Never expected this of him, either."

Matt nodded. "No one did. That worked to his advantage, of course. He had reason to want to change his life. This wasn't a spur of the moment plan. He knew he'd need money, so he started putting away what he could, taking it from the firm's accounts and his own investments. He even sent himself death threats, to set it up that he was in danger. Once he reached London, he intended to begin again under his brother's name."

"And the real Edward McCabe?" the captain asked.

"Paid well to leave the ship in New York. I would imagine that when you return you'll find he's disappeared. In any event, he left behind his keys and his stateroom for Hoffman. And, more importantly, his identity. Hoffman needed a place to go, once he put his plan into effect. A steward in second class was the perfect disguise."

"He didn't fool me," Smith growled.

Matt and Brooke exchanged another swift, amused glance. "Everyone assumed Hoffman was the one missing, and not a steward," Matt went on. "I imagine if you check with the rest of the staff they'll say they couldn't find

McCabe on sailing day, but since he was around afterwards, probably no one thought anything of it."

"We're looking into that," the captain said grimly. "If Hoffman had any help, we'll find out."

Matt shook his head. "I doubt he did, except for Ellen Reilly. I suspect if you talk to her you'll find out she's known Hoffman for some time. Other than that, Hoffman wouldn't have wanted his real identity to be known, not when he was supposed to be dead."

"Then she's an accomplice to the crime."

"Yes. Still, the only real accomplice he needed was his brother, and he's an ocean away. It was a good plan," he said again. "What he didn't bargain on was a second-class passenger who'd done business with him seeing through his disguise."

"Randall Snow."

"Exactly. Randall Snow. He blamed Hoffman for the loss of his money, so he had excellent reason to hold a grudge against him. Plus he knew Hoffman's brother, and that they look alike. Mr. Langdon confirmed that." Matt took a sip of his drink. "Snow recognized Hoffman. I was aware that Snow knew something, he was obvious about it. Hoffman claims he never meant to kill Snow, but he did want him to keep quiet. He says that while they were fighting the ship rolled, and Snow fell against the dresser. Whether it was an accident or not, though, it was murder." He paused. "It was learning that Snow had said he could turn everything upside-down that made me look at things differently."

"And I realized they both had the same nervous mannerism," Brooke put in. "Still, it seemed like such a fantastic theory, I could hardly believe it."

"Me, either." Matt shook his head. "Until Julia Hoffman forced his hand."

"But what about the missing wallets?" Tuttle demanded. "Are you certain there's not a burglar on the ship?"

Matt shook his head. "That was meant to throw us off. It nearly did, too. Hoffman wanted us to think the motive was burglary, and where Snow was concerned it was a possibility. But he also wanted to implicate Langdon, which is why he put his own wallet in Langdon's stateroom."

The captain frowned. "But that, sir, was found in another passenger's room."

"Yes. I'll admit that had me confused, until Langdon confessed what he'd done. When he found it in his room—and Snow's wallet, as well—he panicked. He knew he had to get rid of it in some way, so he put it in Gregory Tate's room. That Tate also had a motive to want Hoffman dead was an advantage. Though we'll probably never know exactly what it was."

"Dear, dear," Mr. Tuttle said, taking off his pince-nez and polishing them. "People lying and cheating and trying to get others into trouble—and a young lady climbing onto the ship's railing! Such a way to behave. What this will do to the ship's reputation, I hardly dare think."

Morgan snorted again, casting Tuttle a scornful look. "Can't help it if the girl acted foolishly."

"Poor girl," Brooke murmured. "It was the only way she felt she could get her mother's attention. She didn't want to marry the man her mother chose for her, you see."

"But, my dear lady! He's an earl!" Mr. Tuttle exclaimed.

Brooke bit back a smile. "Regardless, she didn't want to marry him. Probably she got the idea of staging a suicide attempt after she realized her father was alive. She recognized him, too.''

Matt nodded. "Probably if things had gone on a little longer, Adele would have given in and agreed to break the engagement.''

"But Hoffman was still keeping an eye on his children,'' Brooke said. "And when he saw Julia in danger, he acted, no matter what it did to his disguise.''

"Must give the man credit for that,'' the captain said.

"Yes.'' Matt nodded. "He didn't want anyone to be hurt, but the fact remains that someone was.''

"And that letter he left in the safe?''

"Revenge. It was meant to do exactly what it did: throw suspicion on his wife and Langdon, and make their lives difficult. I'm not sure he expected either of them to be arrested, he claims he didn't, but it came close to that.'' He paused to take a sip from his drink. "Even if they hadn't been, it would have followed them for the rest of their lives.''

"Sometimes I wonder how well we ever know somebody,'' Brooke said. "I always liked Mr. Hoffman, and yet—this.'' She shuddered. "It's so cold-blooded.''

Morgan had risen to freshen his drink. "Hoffman always has been cool. A hard man in business,'' he said.

"And now he's forfeited it all,'' the captain said, and a heavy silence fell. The case had been solved, and the killer would be brought to justice, but at a high cost. One person dead, a family shattered, and a new marriage strained.

"Dear, dear.'' Mr. Tuttle fussed with his pince-nez again. "I hope we can avoid adverse publicity on this.''

"Not likely.'' Morgan's tone was grim. "We'll bring Hoffman back to New York to stand trial. Murder cannot go unpunished." He glanced at Matt. "You'll be returning with us."

Brooke reached out her hand to Matt, her lips tightly compressed. If he had to return in the line of duty, then of course she would go with him, no matter her personal feelings. There was, indeed, no honeymoon for death. "No," Matt said, taking her hand. "I'm on my honeymoon, in case you've forgotten."

"But this is murder, sir!" Captain Wood exclaimed.

"Smith can handle it." He twisted his head to look at Smith, leaning against the wall behind him. "Can't you?"

"Course I can." Smith pushed himself off from the wall. "I'll bring that murderin' bas—dastard back to New York and see he stands trial. I'm still a good cop, you see?"

"Yes, Mr. Smith, I see," Matt said, gravely, and rose, holding out his hand to Brooke. "That should explain everything. Neither of us had lunch today, so if you'll excuse us."

"I'll make sure something is sent to your suite," Captain Wood escorted them to the door. "I owe you a great debt of gratitude for this," he said, his voice lower. "Rest assured I'll be discussing the matter with Mr. Morgan. I wouldn't be surprised if there'll be a reward in it for you."

"Thank you, sir." Matt shook his hand, and he and Brooke went out.

In the corridor Brooke stopped, looking up at him. "Whew!" She blew out her breath, lifting a wayward strand of hair away from her face. "It's really over, isn't it?"

"Mm." Matt took her arm as they walked along the corridor. "Do you know how to get back to the suite?"

"Yes, along here and to the stairs. You don't sound ry happy."

"I am," he protested, as they came out onto the prome-de deck. Instantly they were hailed by passersby want-g to know all the details of the day's shocking events. It ıs only after a few minutes of answering questions that ey were at last able to break away, moving over to the ıling.

"I am happy," Matt said, when they were alone again.

Brooke looked up at him. "What?"

"I said, I'm happy the case is over."

"Mm." She looked down at the water. So much had anged, in so short a time. At least she knew Jack was ınocent, though she'd learned again that people weren't ways what they seemed. "This is where it all started, 't it? From this deck and this railing."

Matt slipped his arm through hers. "Feeling let-down?"

"A little, yes." She looked up. "How did you know?"

"Because I am, too. Usually do after a case."

"Well." Again she blew out her breath. "Thank heav-s we don't have to worry about it anymore."

"Amen to that."

"And what will we do with our time?"

Matt's grin was slow, and wicked. "I imagine we'll think something."

"Matt," she reproved.

"It's our honeymoon, Brooke. At last." His smile ded. "I couldn't have done it without you, you know."

Her eyes searched his, seeing there only respect and ad-iration. He did see her as his equal, whether he would lmit it, or not. "I couldn't have done it without you," e said, softly, admitting a truth of her own. Maybe she

would have joined the police force had she been a m
but she wasn't. She was a woman, and if that meant fi
ing a way to work within society's limits, then so be it.
long as she knew what she had accomplished. "Partner

He grinned, holding out his hand to shake hers. "P
ners," he agreed, and together they turned to walk tow
their suite.

Tuesday, April 21

The *New York* steamed majestically into the Solent, the n
row passage of water between the Isle of Wight and Engl.
proper, giving those aboard their first glimpse of land
nearly a week. Passengers, chatting and pointing, crow
the railing to see the land slip by, the green hills of
island, the quaint town of Cowes, the bulk of a castle o
headland. Gulls wheeled overhead, squawking and cry
other boats blew their horns in salute, and the scent;
grass and trees and people, almost forgotten after a weel
sea smells, wafted out to them. The voyage was nearly o

Matt and Brooke stood with the others at the rail
strangely quiet, their clasped hands their only commu
cation. But it was enough. All that needed to be said l
been said, yesterday and last night. One phase of their
together was over. Another was starting.

No honeymoon for death, Brooke thought, moving ;
a bit closer to Matt as she was jostled by an overexuber
passenger. What she had expected to be a time apart, i
lic, perhaps even a little unreal, had turned into someth
else. She had hoped to grow closer to Matt during
voyage, and she had, but in such a way. Real life did
stop, even for newlyweds. Perhaps especially for nev
weds. For in investigating the tragedy that had befallen

offman family, she had learned much about herself, and
er husband. She thought he had, too.

The ship's horn gave a mighty blast, and Matt turned to
er, grinning, seeming to enjoy the voyage, now that it was
early over. "What do you think we'll run up against in
urope?" he asked.

"Savile Row tailors," she said firmly, slipping her arm
rough his. "You need more than one good suit."

"Yes, yes," he said, but without any anger. "I thought I
ight also stop in at Scotland Yard or the Surête and see if
ey need a hand with anything."

"Matt," she began, before realizing that his eyes were
winkling. "Scotland Yard can take care of itself."

"True, but they don't have me."

"Conceited, vain, bullheaded mick—"

"Or you."

"Hm." She thought that over. "No, they don't, do
ey? Their bad luck."

He grinned. "They wouldn't know what hit them."

She looked up at him, suddenly serious. "Do you?"

"Yes." The teasing gleam had left his eyes. "Very much
. And—"

The ship gave another blast of its horn, drowning out
e rest of his words. It didn't matter, Brooke thought. In
way, Matt had just acknowledged the partnership be-
ween them. It was enough that he saw her as his equal.
he didn't need to prove herself any longer.

"I promise I will never interfere in your work again,"
e said as the din lessened, hugging his arm exuberantly.

Matt looked down at her in surprise. "Never?"

"Never."

And, at the time, she meant it.

Epilogue

Newspapers littered the sitting room of the suite in Lo[n]don's Connaught Hotel, from the staid London *Times* [to] the very worst examples of England's yellow journalis[m]. The two people lounging about in wrapper and dressi[ng] gown were absorbed, catching up on all that had happen[ed] during their week at sea.

"Listen to this," Brooke said suddenly. "It's from t[he] *Gazette*, the ship's newspaper. Printed in mid-Atlant[ic,] April 21, 1896. 'And so we bid a fond adieu to the passe[n]gers of the S.S. *New York*. We hope your voyage with [us] was pleasant and eventful, and that you will sail with [us] again . . .' "

"Eventful. Huh," Matt snorted, folding back the pa[ge] of his newspaper. "I'll top that. This is today's Lond[on] *Times*. 'High Seas Murderer to be Returned to N[ew] York,' " he read.

" 'High Seas Murderer?' "

"It's a newspaper. They have to call him somethi[ng]

ow, listen. 'Julius Hoffman, who beat fellow passenger
andall Snow to death aboard the American Line steam-
ip *New York,* will be returned to the United States
oard the same ship, Mr. Tuttle, spokesman for the line
nounced today,' " Matt read. " 'Speaking from South-
mpton, Mr. Tuttle said that Mr. Hoffman's actions were
trimental to the *New York,* and had caused his family
eat distress. Mr. Hoffman, a New York stockbroker,
as confessed to the murder, as well as to embezzling from
is firm, Hoffman, Langdon and Co. Mr. J.P. Morgan,
aveling on the *New York* on his annual trip to Europe,
d no comment on the events.

" 'Mr. Hoffman will be returned to New York to stand
ial for the murder. He is currently under guard by the
ew York's detective, Ambrose Smith . . .' "

"And Mr. Smith probably hopes to get back on the
ew York force," Brooke said.

"Heaven help us. My God," he said, suddenly staring at
e paper.

"What?"

" 'By telegraph from New York. The death of Mr. Gil-
ert Warren, curator at the Metropolitan Museum of
rt, was ruled a homicide today at a coroner's inquest.
Ir. Warren was killed when he apparently surprised a
urglar in the act of stealing paintings at the museum. His
urderer remains at large . . .' " He put the paper down.
That's the case I was working on when we left."

"But I know him," Brooke said, shocked. "My uncle
nd aunt are involved with the museum, and—"

"I wonder what happened. If I send a telegram—"

"Ahem." Brooke cleared her throat and rattled her
aper. " 'Arrivals from New York,' " she read. " 'Mr. and

Mrs. Matthew Devlin, of New York City, New York, w
be staying at the Connaught Hotel in London, before er
barking on an extended European tour . . .' "

"God help me." Matt grinned at Brooke, New Yor
temporarily forgotten. "You're sure you won't let me ı
to Scotland Yard?"

"I'm sure." She twined her arms around his nec
"We're on our honeymoon. And so is death."

But she did wonder about Mr. Warren . . .

Author's Note

hope it goes without saying that this is a work of fiction,
d that the events and people contained herein are com-
letely made-up. The *New York* was a real ship, and I have
ied to be as accurate as possible in describing it. In some
stances, however, I did change the setting to suit the
ory. J.P. Morgan did own the *New York*, and since he
so traveled to Europe each year in the spring, placing
im aboard was a reasonable assumption. I do not know if
e actually traveled on that particular ship on that date.
uriously enough, the only other character with any basis
fact is Padlock Homes. At around the time this book is
t, the Cunard Line's *Etruria* held a mock trial, at which
Padlock Homes" gave testimony. The Padlock Homes in
is book is fictional, as are all the other characters. I
uldn't make up *that* name.

Although the Mafia came to the United States in the
880's, it was not generally known in New York until after
e turn of the century. For purposes of the story I have

changed the time frame. Its practice of leaving note
signed with a stenciled black hand for the victims of exto
tion earned it the obvious name.

Finding information on the *New York* was difficult, bu
I was helped by many people. First and foremost, the sta
of the New Bedford Free Public Library, especially Eilee
Michaud and Bill Schneller of the Interlibrary Loan d
partment; also Virginia S. Wood, of the Library of Co
gress and the North American Society for Ocean
History; Don Lynch, of the Titanic Historical Societ
The Steamship Historical Society of America at the Un
versity of Baltimore; Marie Lore at South Street Seapo
in New York; Blair Benjamin, curator of the Nation
Maritime Historical Society; Mary H. Getchell at the M
riners' Museum in Newport News; Frank O. Braynar
noted expert on ocean liners; and the staff at New Yor
Public Library. Any mistakes in this book are, alas, min

Thank you again to my mother, Madelyn Sweene
Kruger, for reading the manuscript for flaws and spottin
the murderer in the beginning (*again*). Thanks also to m
friends and neighbors who allowed me to use their name
And a big thanks to Jennifer Sawyer, for helping me mak
this book the best it could be.

I enjoy hearing from my readers and will gladly answe
all letters. Please write to me care of:

> RWA/New England Chapter
> P.O. Box 1667
> Framingham, MA 01701-9998

Please turn the page for
an exciting sneak peek of
Mary Kruger's next
Gilded Age mystery

MASTERPIECE OF MURDER

now on sale wherever
hardcover mysteries are sold

Prologue

New York, April 1896

Late night, and the Manhattan Museum of Art was dark and quiet, all visitors gone, all staff left for the day. Joseph Warren, assistant director and curator of the paintings department, paced impatiently along the second floor gallery, lighted only by the reflected glow from the offices at the far end. In the gloom, shadows played off the stiff pleats of the burgundy draperies; light glinted on a gilded frame, while leaving another in darkness. It was unusual for Warren to work late, but his position in the museum precluded questioning. If he were to illuminate the gallery, though, the watchman would take heed, and that must be avoided. At all costs, there must be privacy for this meeting.

It was a mess, all of it, the whole sorry business, and he wished he'd never gotten involved. Too many people were asking questions; too many wondered if the disappearance of paintings from the museum's collection was as random as it seemed. Warren stopped pacing for a moment, standing with hands in pockets and glaring sightlessly at a Turner landscape. It hadn't seemed like such a bad idea at the time, but now it was all crashing down on him. After tonight he'd have no more of it. Anything would be better than living in this constant hell of anxiety, of fear that his actions would be discovered. Never mind the scandal, or the likelihood that he'd go to prison. After tonight he'd confess to what he'd done, and face the consequences like a man.

A footfall at the far end of the gallery made him turn. "There you are," he said, his voice pitched low as the figure, backlit by the electric glow from the offices, approached him. "Why did you want to meet me here, when I could—hey! It's you."

Warren's companion took a cigarette from his pocket and lit it with quick, practiced motions, waving out the match. "You were expecting someone else?"

"Yes, dammit. Put that thing out. Smoking damages the paintings."

"Ah, your beloved pictures. I've heard of them."

Warren went still. "What have you heard?"

The cigarette dropped to the parquet floor and was ground out by a hard leather heel. "Enough to know you're holding out on me," his companion whispered, and flicked out a knife.

"What are you doing with that?" Warren said sharply.

"Getting what's owed me." And with that the man lunged.

It was over in a moment. Warren was quick on his feet for so large a man, but not quick enough; the long, thin blade pierced him just under the ribs and traveled up, up. He grabbed his assailant by the arms, clutching, his eyes bulging; and though he opened his mouth to speak, only a gurgle emerged. Hard fingers loosened his desperate grip and his knees gave out. He was dead before he had completely slumped to the floor.

His assailant stood a few feet away, looking dispassionately down at the still figure, its muscles contracting and twitching in the aftermath of death, blood flowing in a thin river along the varnished floor. It had been a peaceful death, all things considered; no noise to alert the watchman or anyone else who might be in the building. Rather a neat piece of work. With thumb and forefinger extended, the murderer reached down to remove the knife, wiping the blade carefully on a snowy-white handkerchief. Then, still dispassionate, almost casually, he turned away, flicking his knife along the edges of a painting chosen at random, cutting it from its frame. Many paintings were missing from the museum; this would be just one more.

With the canvas carefully folded within the pages of a newspaper and the knife returned to an inner pocket, the killer at last moved away, treading quietly through the gallery. The lighted offices that belonged to the museum staff posed one potential obstacle; the great south lobby on the first floor, another. Both were deserted. The museum doors opened quietly and closed with a soft snick, and all was peaceful again.

And as the carriage drove along Fifth Avenue, the killer, safely inside and now distant from the crime, had no idea of the one crucial mistake that he had made.

1

July 1896

Matt let his carpetbag drop to the parquet floor with a thud. "Good God."

"What is it?" Brooke looked up from pulling off her gloves, tinted gold to match her traveling ensemble of tan trimmed with gold braid, and drew in her breath. "Oh, my."

"Oh, my, indeed," Matt said, glaring about him with his hands on his hips. They were home, and about time, too, as far as Brooke was concerned. Their honeymoon in Europe had been eventful and wonderful, and very long. Much as Brooke had enjoyed being alone with Matt for three months, she had lately had the feeling that their real life together wouldn't begin until they were home, at the apartment in the Dakota, across from Central Park. The apartment that her aunt Winifred had so generously offered to decorate for them, even if she did disapprove of their living there.

"Dear heavens. I should have expected something like this," she said, gazing around. The entrance hall, where they stood, was a good-sized room in itself, but the decorations made it appear small, almost claustrophobic. In the one corner Aunt Winifred had put together an altogether astonishing array of furniture and decorations, starting with a red plush settee curving along the wall, scattered with cushions in every hue of the rainbow. Scarlet velvet curtains draped the settee like a tent, while a small table covered with a cloth of East Indian design held a Turkish lamp, some Japanese carvings in ivory, and a statue of the Buddha. Set at right angles to this Turkish nook was, incongruously, that staple of every home's hallway, a combination umbrella-and-hat stand in dark oak, with a large plate glass mirror set into it. More velvet draperies, these royal blue, cascaded to the sides. Brooke briefly closed her eyes. "It can't all be this bad, can it?"

"Knowing your aunt, it's worse," Matt said, and turned toward one of the doorways that opened off the anteroom. Ignoring the butler who held out his hand for Matt's bowler hat, as well as the maid in proper black and white who curtsied, they went into the parlor. The Oriental carpet was good, its jewel colors glowing even in the gloom, but otherwise the decorations were disastrous. A tufted sofa and club chairs of gold panne velvet competed for attention with a Steinway grand piano draped with a fringed paisley shawl and weighted down with silver picture frames, while the dark gold brocade draperies blocked any possibility of sunlight even entering the room. Any free wall space was taken up with paintings in heavy frames; Brooke was relieved to see that most of these were decent, though the standing electric lamp was so befrilled and furbelowed that it appeared to be wearing a very fussy hat. "Oh, dear," Brooke said inadequately, and turned, to see that Matt had stalked from the room. Bracing herself, she followed.

The library, down the hall from the parlor, wasn't quite so bad. Evidently this was meant to be a masculine room, for it was furnished with burgundy leather armchairs and a huge desk, and the drapery was minimal. The bookshelves lining the walls were actually handsome, filled with volumes bound in Morocco leather of red and blue and green. Almost passable, except for the huge bearskin rug. Matt took one look at that and turned on his heel, snorting; once again Brooke followed, her lips twitching.

The dining room, across the corridor, continued the pattern. The table and sideboard of dark, curved and curlicued mahogany were massive and ugly. The purple velvet upholstery of the chairs and the matching cloths covering everything only made matters worse, while the marble mantelpiece was obscured by yet another silk shawl. "The sideboard looks like an altar in Lent," Brooke murmured, and Matt, snorting again, stalked out. Her lips twitching even more, Brooke followed him. Surely the bedroom couldn't be any worse than what they'd already seen.

It was. Scattered across the fine Aubusson carpet were chairs and a vanity table in white and gold, the seats tufted in velvet of pale pink and blue. Upon a platform so high it required stairs to ascend, stood their bed, in solitary majesty under a canopy of white satin, which cascaded to either side from a crown molding above the head of the bed. Upon the molding was an insignia. Brooke frowned at it, and then bit her lips. "That's—Napoleon's seal," she said, her voice shaking as she pointed at the emblem.

Matt looked up. "What?"

"Napoleon's seal. Oh, Matt!" At last she gave way to the merriment that had been building within her through the tour of the apartment. She collapsed onto the bed in a fit of giggles and promptly slid off the slippery satin counterpane. "Royal blue, royal purple, and now this. Did you ever see yourself as an emperor?"

He glared at her. "It's not funny, Brooke."

"Of course it is." She sat up, wiping at her eyes. "It's so deliciously awful, it can't be anything but." And thank heavens her aunt wasn't here to witness their reactions to what she doubtless believed was a fashionable decorating scheme.

Matt stood, arms akimbo, a reluctant smile creeping onto his face. "At least she had the sense not to put twin beds in here."

"Matt." Brooke tilted her head toward the open doorway. They had servants to consider now, the butler, maid, and cook that her aunt deemed the very minimum of household staff. It meant that she and Matt would have to get used to a certain lack of privacy.

"I'll have nightmares in this room." Matt ambled over to a window and pulled back the mauve brocade drape, staring absently out at Central Park, across the street. "Makes me wish I'd stayed at Mulberry Street."

Brooke rose, removing her hat and then patting at her hair to make sure it was neat. "You could go back. It's still early in the day."

"You heard TR," Matt said, and this time he was the one to smile. " 'Enjoy yourself, my boy,' " he quoted. " 'Plenty of work for you tomorrow. Dee-lighted to have you back.' "

"I think he meant it, Matt."

Matt shrugged, reaching up to massage his neck muscles as he looked out again. "If so, he's the only one."

"That will change," she murmured, coming up behin
him to massage his neck for him. When their ship ha
docked, Matt's eagerness to find out what had happened a
police headquarters, particularly in the special squad t
which he was assigned in the detective bureau, was obviou
For he was every inch a policeman, like his father befor
him, and proud to be a member of the force recentl
dubbed "the Finest." Proud that he'd been hired b
Theodore Roosevelt, the president of the police commi
sioners, and more than a little concerned that his extende
absence would cause problems. And so Brooke had firml
told the driver of their hansom cab to stop first at polic
headquarters at 300 Mulberry Street before proceeding t
the Dakota. Matt had put up only a token argument.

The hansom cab pulled up before headquarters, locate
in the midst of tenements and saloons, and even a whor
house across the street, its stoop enclosed by a board fenc
It was a tall, drab marble-faced building, enlivened by ta
tered and faded awnings shading the windows from th
fierce July sun, and by the constant human cavalcade. A
Matt leaned forward to speak to the driver, Brooke looke
out at a scene that was new yet familiar: immigrant wome
shawls draped around their heads, scurrying toward th
shabby brick or rickety wooden tenements where they live
a peddler selling, of all things, toy police whistles and ce
luloid dentures; newly arrested miscreants descending fro
a paddy wagon and stumbling up the stairs of the buildin
prodded by the business end of a patrolman's club. On th
sidewalk a man with a notebook talked with a patrolma
who had pushed his bucket-shaped leather helmet back o
his head, while across the street more men lounged on th
steps of another, equally drab building, apparently at eas

ut their eyes sharp, alert. Police reporters, Brooke guessed,
vaiting for the next big story. New York City's police headquarters was different, and yet essentially the same, as the
maller Newport police station where Brooke had spent
ime growing up, the proud daughter of a cop.

Matt turned to her. "I just want a word with Captain
)'Neill," he said, referring to the head of the detective bu-
eau. "I'm not expected back until tomorrow, so this
houldn't take long—"

"But I'm coming with you," she said sweetly. "I don't feel
afe in this neighborhood."

The look Matt gave her was suspicious. "There are
nough cops around if you need help."

"And enough criminals." She glanced out again, and he
ollowed her gaze, to see a small, wizened-faced man with
humbs tucked into the pockets of his black-and-yellow
hecked vest, catching hold of one of the lampposts that
lanked the staircase and swinging himself to the sidewalk.
Apparently this time he had escaped the law. "Besides, I'd
ike to see inside," she said, and pushed past him to the
loor of the cab. "Would you help me down, please?"

Matt muttered something under his breath, but he
umped down to the cobbled street, turning to help her
lown. Instantly the aroma of New York in the summer as-
aulted her, a mixture of dust and horse droppings and the
lank, fetid smell that was unique to the tenements clustered
o close together. Raising her handkerchief to protect her
ace from the dust that likely as not contained powdery
lried manure, Brooke placed her hand on Matt's arm as he
ed her up the stairs. "This isn't necessary, you know," he
rumbled.

"Oh, come now, Matt. Aren't we partners?"

"If we should ever run up against a body on the Cli
Walk or an ocean passenger missing overboard again, ye
In my job, no. And I don't expect," he went on, openin
one side of the double door, "that we'll encounter tha
kind of crime again."

Brooke made a little face as she passed him. Partner
they were, equals in both their marriage and, when the op
portunity afforded itself, detecting, and yet Matt some
times seemed to forget that. And while it was true that sh
couldn't don a blue wool uniform and police the streets, sh
knew deep down that had she been born male, she, too
would be a cop.

Inside the headquarters the foyer was dim and stuffy, th
warmth enriched by the scents of overheated wool an
overheated, overfrightened civilians. To the right was
staircase; tucked in behind that was the metal cage of th
elevator shaft. The sergeant at the high desk to the le
glanced up incuriously at their entrance, and then looke
again. "Devlin," he said, his voice carefully neutral. "S
ye're back from yer honeymoon, are ye?"

Matt nodded crisply. "Yes, Sergeant. Is Captain O'Ne
in the detective bureau?"

"Himself's out. Workin'. If ye'll wait, I'll see if there
anyone else for ye to talk to—just a minute." This as th
telephone on his desk emitted a shrill ring. He raised th
cone-shaped receiver with the same bored, incurious loc
with which he'd greeted them, while beside her Brook
could feel Matt's muscles tight and bunched with strain. H
was, she guessed, very angry.

"Yes, sir," the sergeant said, suddenly sitting up straighte
his walrus mustache bobbing up and down as he nodde
"No, sir. Yes, sir, I'll tell him. Ye're to go up," he said

Matt, replacing the receiver. "Mr. Roosevelt wants a word with ye."

"Thank you. This is more like it," Matt muttered, taking Brooke's arm and leading her over to the stairs, for he still distrusted elevators.

"Well, of course," Brooke said serenely. "What did you expect?"

Matt raised his eyebrows, but said nothing. If she hadn't noticed the coolness of the reception, he had. Not that it was unexpected. Here he was, on the force for less than a year, and yet he'd gone on a three-month honeymoon. With all the efforts being made to reform the police, such a long leave didn't look good. Probably, he thought gloomily as they reached the second floor, Roosevelt was going to reprimand him. Even if he had approved Matt's request for leave.

Theodore Roosevelt's arrival at Mulberry Street the previous year had blown a wide, wild wind through the force. In the light of revelations of widespread corruption among the police, politicians and citizens alike had clamored for reform. Roosevelt, known to nearly everyone simply as "TR," had passed up the chance to be mayor of New York, but he gladly accepted the job as police commissioner. With the other three members of the board, he was a whirlwind of activity, holding hearings on officers accused of dereliction of duty or worse, and meting out suitable punishment; bringing in his own men to replace those gone either through forced resignations or retirement; and checking up on errant patrolmen himself in what he liked to call midnight rambles. He had met with some success. He had also made enemies, among them two of the other commissioners, with whom he was currently engaged in a struggle for

power. If TR were forced out of office, as Matt knew wa
possible from reading whatever New York newspaper h
could find in Europe, all his efforts would be for naught.

TR's secretary, Miss Kelly, smiled and told Matt an
Brooke to go into Roosevelt's office. Another innovation c
TR's, Matt thought, returning the smile, installing a your
woman as his secretary, and an attractive one at that. Doub
less she was a great deal easier to look at than the pair of me
who had served as assistants to the commissioners before

Brooke's fingers bit into his arm. "And will you be se
ing her very often?" she whispered.

"No," he answered, straight-faced, as he opened the o
fice door for her. "Maybe once a day."

The look Brooke gave him was expressive, but she ha
no opportunity to say anything more. Roosevelt was risir
from behind his desk to greet them, his large white teeth
so beloved by caricaturists, bared in a wide grin.

"Matt Devlin. Dee-lighted to have you back," h
boomed, reaching over to shake Matt's hand. "And Mr
Devlin. Dee-lightful to see you again. Saw you arrive, yo
know," he went on, indicating the window behind him wit
a jerk of his head as he sat, and they took chairs facing hin
"Eager to get started again?"

"Of course," Matt said, still straight-faced.

"Well, we could use you, my boy, we could use you." H
face turned serious. "Things aren't good around here, yo
know. Everything I've been trying to do is being blocked

"Yes, sir, so I've read. And I don't imagine having a d
tective go on a three-month honeymoon has helped."

Beside him he sensed Brooke giving him a sharp look, b
Roosevelt was speaking again. "No, I took some criticis
for that, but I approved your leave myself, my boy." H

rned his toothy grin on Brooke. "Besides"—he grinned,
s eyes behind his nose glasses glinting—"I heard you man-
ed to take care of some crime yourself while you were
ne."

"Yes, sir. But that was something we stumbled into."
att leaned forward in his chair. "I thought I'd check in
ith Captain O'Neill. See what he'll want me working on."

"There's plenty, my boy. Too much going on in this city.
urders are up this year, not to mention the rest of the vice
this city. But at least we've got the Bend cleared out," he
ent on, referring to Mulberry Bend, not far distant from
adquarters. It had once been one of the worst neighbor-
ods in the city, with dark, dirty tenements crowded with
wly arrived immigrants, all poor, all desperate. "It's a
rk now."

"But that's wonderful progress," Brooke said, smiling so
oadly at Roosevelt that Matt gave her a suspicious glance.
'erhaps now people will see the need to clean up the rest
the slums."

"I wish more people felt as you do, Mrs. Devlin." Roo-
velt gave her a toothy smile. "Then we wouldn't have the
oblems we do."

"I was wondering." Brooke's tone was artless, as if some-
ing had just occurred to her. After seven months of mar-
age, Matt already knew better. "When we left, Mr. Warren
the Manhattan Museum had just been found dead.
/hatever happened in that case?"

Roosevelt shot Matt a look. "You were working on that
se, weren't you, Devlin?"

Matt nodded. "Yes, sir." He was no longer surprised at
oosevelt's knowledge of such small details. "He was killed
ring a robbery at the museum."

"Yes." Roosevelt frowned. "Far as we know, that's all it is. Looks like Warren caught the thief in the act and paid for it. Hard to admit, my boy, but that case is still open."

Matt nodded again. He wasn't really surprised; nor did he imagine anyone was actively working the case. It was, after all, three months old, and, as Roosevelt himself had said, there was too much going on in the city. "Thank you, sir," he said, rising. "I'll call Captain O'Neill later to let him know I'm back."

"Do that, my boy. Dee-lighted to have you on the force," he said, and Matt and Brooke rose to leave the office.